newSGirL

newsGirl

Liza Ketchum

For young readers
in St. Paul —
Follow your dreams!

November 2014

Viking

VIKING

Published by Penguin Group

Penguin Group (USA) Inc., 345 Hudson Street, New York, New York 10014, U.S.A.

Penguin Group (Canada), 90 Eglinton Avenue East, Suite 700, Toronto, Ontario,
Canada M4P 2Y3 (a division of Pearson Penguin Canada Inc.)

Penguin Books Ltd, 80 Strand, London WC2R 0RL, England

Penguin Ireland, 25 St Stephen's Green, Dublin 2, Ireland (a division of Penguin Books Ltd)

Penguin Group (Australia), 250 Camberwell Road, Camberwell, Victoria 3124, Australia
(a division of Pearson Australia Group Pty Ltd)

Penguin Books India Pvt Ltd, 11 Community Centre, Panchsheel Park,
New Delhi – 110 017, India

Penguin Group (NZ), 67 Apollo Drive, Rosedale, North Shore 0632, New Zealand
(a division of Pearson New Zealand Ltd.)

Penguin Books (South Africa) (Pty) Ltd, 24 Sturdee Avenue, Rosebank,
Johannesburg 2196, South Africa

Penguin Books Ltd, Registered Offices: 80 Strand, London WC2R 0RL, England

First published in 2009 by Viking, a member of Penguin Group (USA) Inc.

3   5   7   9   10   8   6   4

LIBRARY OF CONGRESS CATALOGING-IN-PUBLICATION DATA IS AVAILABLE.
ISBN 978-0-670-01119-3

Printed in U.S.A.
Book design by Nancy Brennan
Set in Elysium

FOR THREE INSPIRING WOMEN:

My mother, Barbara Jane Bray Ketchum,
and my daughters-in-law,
Alison Kelly Macalady and Vita Weinstein Murrow

newSGirL

CHAPTER

1

California!

AMELIA WOKE with a start. The ship was strangely quiet,
the steady throb of her engine stilled. Amelia peered up at
the shadowy figure standing at her feet.

"Rise and shine, Miss Amelia."

Amelia rubbed her eyes. "Hello, Jim. Where are we?"

"Anchored in the bay. And the sun's about to come up."
Four-Fingered Jim reached out to her with his good hand.
"Hop to. The ship will be abuzz soon."

Amelia groaned as Jim helped her to her feet. Her back
ached from sleeping on the hard deck with nothing but her
crumpled cloak for padding. She stumbled to the railing.
"When did we come in?"

"Last night. Commander dropped anchor after you slept.
This passage is too treacherous in the dark." He squeezed
her elbow. "Go below; rouse your mother and Miss Duprey.
They'll need help with their luggage. The *Unicorn* is the mail
boat, so we'll have quite a stir when we come in."

Amelia waited until his back was turned. She *should* help
Mother and Estelle, but her stomach lurched at the thought

of the hold, with its smells of unwashed men, spoiled food, and rotten bilgewater. Instead, she slipped forward to the bow, picking her way through the familiar maze of casks, trunks, and coiled lines. She leaned out over the ship's rail. A single planet gleamed on the horizon, but the stars had faded. Amelia caught her breath. The pale light of the eastern sky fell across shadowy hills. Land!

"California!" Amelia clapped a hand over her mouth. She hadn't meant to shout.

"You're up early, Miss Amelia."

Amelia looked up into Commander Everett's washed-out blue eyes. "Good morning, Commander." Standing next to the captain, Amelia felt ashamed of her dirty calico, badly wrinkled from her night of sleeping on deck. Commander Everett's cap sat squarely on his high forehead. He had trimmed his shaggy beard and wore a pressed serge jacket buttoned from top to bottom.

"Have we reached San Francisco?" Amelia asked.

"Indeed. We passed through the Golden Gate last night—that's what they call this passage." Commander Everett pointed to the towering cliffs astern, rising above a narrow strait. "And we're lucky; the fog sits out at sea this morning. We'll weigh anchor soon and be ashore before you know it." He set a hand on her shoulder. "Raise your family. The long voyage is over."

At last! Amelia hugged herself tight with joy.

The bell rang for the change of watch and the First Mate

scrambled to the upper deck. "Kindle the engine fires!" he called. "Set the after sail!" The *Unicorn's* engine caught and rumbled. Sour-smelling black coal smoke poured from the chimney, and the paddle wheel sent spray flying. The deck vibrated beneath Amelia's feet. She licked her cracked lips, tasting salt as she had every day for weeks. Salt had stiffened her skirts, made her hair dry and brittle, and parched her hands until her skin was as chapped as her leather boots. Never mind. She was done with the sea—and the *Unicorn*—forever.

Passengers swarmed on deck as the sun came up. Amelia kept her place at the bow and pulled out the spyglass Uncle Paul had given her before they left Boston. "You'll see things we've never dreamed of," he'd said. "Be sure to write in your new journal so you can tell me all about it."

Amelia ran her hand over the smooth mahogany before she pulled the spyglass open. Her most prized possession was small enough to fit in her pocket, but nearly as long as her forearm when she opened it to its full length. She had already sent Uncle Paul a letter from Panama, to tell him about the whales and giant turtles she had spotted through the spyglass on their Atlantic passage. Now she could write to him from San Francisco.

Amelia twisted the lens to focus the spyglass as the *Unicorn* steamed past purple-green hills, rounded a peninsula, and headed for a tangle of masts, dense as a Massachusetts forest. How could their ship ever find a berth in that snarled mess? Beyond the ships a hodgepodge of houses, tents, and sheds perched on barren hills. The whole shabby town looked as if it might tumble into the harbor. Amelia set the spyglass on the railing. Could this be San Francisco? From the stories they had read in the newspapers, she had expected lofty buildings ablaze with golden light.

As the *Unicorn* steamed toward the harbor, Amelia noticed a tower on the crest of a hill, where two black boards moved like long arms. Below the tower, people waved bright-colored flags up, down, and sideways. Amelia raised her spyglass again. The flag wavers were boys, not men. They signaled as sailors did at sea, but their flags sported designs she'd never seen. Amelia collapsed the spyglass and put it away. What did it all mean? The *Unicorn* chugged on.

"Good morning, dear Amelia."

A gloved hand cupped her elbow. Amelia looked up into Mother's face. She was dressed as if for church, her hair pulled back under her bonnet. Her face was pale, but she smiled. "A new life, after an eternity at sea," Mother said. "A shop of our own, when our little house arrives."

Mother and Estelle had heard that women could make their own way in California, earn a good living; be independent; even buy property. They had big plans for their shop and the dresses they would make and sell. They had even shipped a tiny house on a clipper ship that sailed around Cape Horn, complete with Uncle Paul's instructions for how to reassemble it. On their few calm days on board the

Unicorn, Mother and Estelle had sat on deck, sketching dress designs on scraps of wrapping paper.

"If only Gran could see us now." Mother took Amelia's hand. "She thought we'd never make it here alive."

Amelia bit her lip. Gran hadn't wanted them to leave. She had called Mother a fool, and worse. Gran's tears had wet Amelia's shoulder when they said good-bye. "What if I never see you again?" Gran had asked.

"Perhaps you'll come and visit," Amelia said. But they both knew that wouldn't happen. Gran was too old for such a long journey.

Amelia stood on tiptoe at the railing, as if her future danced in the little waves slapping the bow. For Amelia, a new life also meant freedom—but in a different way. In California, no one would call her that terrible name. They wouldn't taunt her, whisper about her behind her back. She'd never told Mother what the boys said about her in school; it would upset her too much. And Mother would only say, "Hold your head high. You have nothing to be ashamed of."

If that was true, why had Mother dismissed Amelia's questions for so long?

Amelia gripped the rail. With the sun sparkling on the water, and the rolling hills beckoning from the shore, it was easy to believe in Mother's new life.

Or even, Amelia thought, *in my own.*

CHAPTER

No Job for a Lady

MOTHER WENT below to rouse Estelle and then reappeared on the ladder, where she hoisted two bags up to Amelia from the hold. "Can you get these to the gangway?" Mother asked. "I'll help Estelle finish packing."

Poor Estelle. On both the Atlantic and the Pacific crossings, every roll and lurch of the ship had tied Estelle's stomach in knots. Now she was so thin, a gust of wind might snatch her away. Never mind. They'd be on steady ground soon.

Amelia wrestled her carpetbag toward the railing, lifting it over the trunks, leather valises, and satchels that littered the decks, then returned for Mother's valise. The *Unicorn* passed a long wharf, bustling with activity, that jutted out into the bay. Ships of every shape and size shifted at anchor, and warehouses lined both sides of the dock. Somehow, the captain found a path through the maze.

Jim came up beside her, dragging a burlap sack. "Where will we dock?" Amelia asked. "And what did those flag signals mean?"

"Questions, questions. You're as nosy as a newspaper reporter."

Was that an insult? "I'm just curious," Amelia said.

"Don't fret; I'm only teasing." Jim set the sack down and picked up a coiled line. "That's Telegraph Hill. Mr. Abbott watches for ships from the tower. When he spies one sailing in, he signals with those long wooden arms—called the semaphore—to tell people what sort of ship we are, and where we're from. The *Unicorn* docks at Sacramento Street, the berth for the Pacific Mail Steamship Company. Could you make yourself useful?"

"Of course," Amelia said. A good excuse to avoid going below.

Jim pulled a penknife from his pocket and pointed to the burlap bag at her feet. "You'll find a stack of newspapers in that sack, and some twine. Tie the papers into bundles of ten. You can practice those knots I showed you. You safe with a penknife?"

Amelia nodded, though she could imagine Gran's voice scolding, *That's no job for a lady*. Never mind. Gran was home in Boston, thousands of miles away, and Amelia wasn't a lady. Yet. She opened the knife and sawed through the twine that tied the sack.

"Good girl," Jim said. "The boys will be along as soon as we dock."

"Boys?"

But the First Mate barked an order and Jim hurried off

with his rope, leaving Amelia's question dangling.

Amelia sliced off a piece of twine and pulled a stack of newspapers from the burlap sack. As she counted them into even piles, the paper's bold masthead jumped out at her: the *Boston Journal for California*. Amelia frowned at the date. *December 26, 1850*. December of last year? It was already March of 1851; the New Year had come and gone. The front page was covered with ads. She peeked inside. The paper wrote of a fire that had burned the post office in Cambridge. Who would read such sad old news?

The *Unicorn* inched toward the wharf, where an enormous crowd swelled, pushing toward the end of the dock. People cheered, waved handkerchiefs, hooted and hollered. Jim trotted back along the deck, ready to toss the line. "Jim, what's the fuss about?" Amelia called. "Do they think Jenny Lind is on board?"

"No. We've brought the mail. Folks here want news from home more than gold. Be a good girl and finish those bundles. My hands are full."

Amelia couldn't refuse. Hadn't Jim taught her to tie every knot a sailor needed? He'd also let her sleep on deck near the companionway, keeping an eye on her so Mother and Estelle wouldn't worry. Jim sometimes saved Estelle an extra bit of dry, salty hardtack, the only food she could stomach. Most important, when their first Pacific ship had run aground off Acapulco and the sailors on the *Unicorn* complained about taking them on board, it was Jim who'd stood up for them. "For shame," Jim had said. "You'd abandon two women and a child in a foreign land?" Amelia would do anything for her friend. So she knelt on the hard deck and tied her paper bundles like Christmas packages. Her fingers flew until her hands were smudged with newsprint.

Jim tossed a line to a sailor as the ship drew closer to the wharf. The sailor jumped onto the dock and cinched the line around a metal cleat. The *Unicorn* creaked and groaned, and men in street clothes ran along the dock to help the sailors secure the ship. The *Unicorn* nudged up against a piling, then settled herself a few feet from the dock.

The ship's passengers jostled one another until Amelia felt as if the men on board—all one hundred sixty of them—breathed down her neck. She pulled Jim's papers closer to the railing. Last night, Mother had whispered to Estelle, "It will be good to hear women's voices again." But Amelia didn't see a single skirt on the wharf. Was this a city of men? If so—who would buy dresses from Mother and Estelle?

"Move aside now, move aside!" the First Mate shouted. Two sailors set a gangplank in place, bridging the gap between the ship and the wharf. A boy in a broad-brimmed hat thumped across the narrow plank onto the ship and plunked himself in front of Amelia. He stood so close that his boots—which hadn't seen blacking in a long time—jammed up against her knees.

"Pardon *me*." Amelia scrambled to her feet and looked

the boy up and down. His unhemmed trousers needed Mother's quick needlework, and his eyes nearly matched the copper-colored curls escaping from under his hat.

"It's not polite to stare," the boy said. Amelia looked away, and the boy laughed. "What are you?" he asked. "A news*girl*?"

Amelia prickled all over, as if she'd stepped into stinging nettles. "Jim asked me to tie up his papers," she said.

"*Jim's* papers? Don't be daft. They're mine now." The boy swooped down, grabbed a loose newspaper, and scanned the inside page before he turned toward the wharf, brandishing the paper at the waiting crowd. "Pay-puz! The latest news from Boston! 'Fire in Cambridge Destroys the Post Office'!"

"Hey! You can't steal that!" Amelia reached for the paper, but the boy was taller. He danced out of her way, scooped up a bundle, and waved it in front of the crowd. "Pay-puz! Read all about it! Get the latest news!" he called again.

"*Latest news?*" Now it was Amelia's turn to laugh. "That fire happened months ago."

The boy shrugged. "It's news to them. Besides, do *you* know what's happened since you left? The people of San Francisco will pay me a pretty sum for this *old* news." He turned his back on her.

So the boys in California were as rude as the ones at home. Still, in eight weeks of travel, they'd had little news;

no letters from Gran or Uncle Paul. How could they? Letters from home had to follow the same long journey she had just made.

The boy standing beside her called out to a black-haired boy on the wharf, whose face was smudged with dirt. Amelia could hear Gran's scornful voice in her head: *Nothing but a ruffian.* The boy on the wharf held out his arms. "Jules— toss them here!"

Jewels? Amelia lunged for the bundle, but the boy jumped back, hoisting the papers high over his head. "Hey!" he shouted. "You trying to ruin me? These are worth their weight in gold."

"Jim!" Amelia cried. "He's stealing your papers."

As Jim hurried over, the boy tossed the bundle from the ship to his friend on the dock, then smiled and shook Jim's hand.

"Julius! It's been a while." Jim raised his voice above the tumult coming from the ship and the wharf. "Have you two met? Julius, may I present Miss Amelia Forrester, the *Unicorn*'s youngest passenger. You might thank her for tying up your papers." The boy grunted. "Amelia, meet Master Julius McKenzie," Jim went on. "Just fourteen but already one of San Francisco's youngest businessmen."

Amelia raised her chin. This Julius McKenzie was hardly a "master." Besides being rude, his trousers were missing a brace, and his white underdrawers showed through a hole at the knee. *Her* dress might be dirty, but at least it was carefully mended and her pantalettes stayed hidden. She met the boy's eyes, but he didn't even blink. Amelia turned away.

Jim's laugh startled Amelia. "Two of a kind," he said. "Each one of you too proud to say a word."

Proud? Was she? Amelia's face burned.

Julius scowled and rummaged in his pocket. He pulled out a mix of coins—including some Amelia had never seen before—and a rough quartz stone the size of her thumbnail. The boy poured the collection into Jim's good hand. Jim held the quartz between his thumb and middle finger and let out a low whistle. "The real thing."

"It looks like quartz," Amelia said.

"It is." Jim set it in her palm. "But study on it close," he said. "See that gold, embedded in the stone? It's a beauty."

Amelia held the stone to the light. Golden streaks wound through the quartz like veins.

"Be careful. You might catch gold fever yourself." Jim took the stone and smiled at Julius. "Don't tell me you've been to the diggings?"

Julius shook his head. "Don't need to. Plenty of gold selling papers here in Phoenix City." He pointed to the money in Jim's palm. "Seem fair?"

Jim counted the coins. "More than enough." He kissed the quartz, slipped it into his pocket, and pointed at the passengers pushing to get off the ship. "All this commotion for a few gold nuggets."

"Julius, let's go!" the boy on the dock called.

Julius tossed the bundles, one at a time, to the wharf, where a mob of boys surrounded the boy with black hair. They shouted in English, French, and Spanish. They were a ragtag bunch, some well-dressed, others in patched clothing. A few carried colorful flags rolled up under their arms. Were these the boys who had signaled from the hillside? Jim cupped Amelia's elbow. "Good work," he said. "Not a single bundle fell apart. Don't forget your knots when you go ashore."

"I won't." Amelia slid between Julius and the railing and held up her hand to block his next toss. "How much will people pay you for a paper?"

"Five or six times its worth. A single paper can fetch a dollar. Out of my way." Julius tossed the last bundle to his friend, then scrambled onto the railing and leaped across the water to the dock.

Amelia glanced at the price on the *Boston Journal*. Fifteen cents at home, a dollar here? Julius disappeared into the crush of boys, each grabbing for a bundle of papers. A much younger boy, who couldn't be more than eight, perched on a piling near the *Unicorn*. He was shivering, and his clothes were patched and worn—yet he surprised Amelia by pulling a man's gold pocket watch from his trousers. It winked in the sunlight. He studied the time, snapped it shut, and glanced up to find Amelia watching him. "Hey ho!" he called, and waved. His bright blue eyes were lively, and the splash of freckles across his nose made Amelia smile. She waved back. At least someone in this crowd of strangers was happy to see her.

CHAPTER

A Landlubber Again

THE SWEET, high whistle of the white-throated sparrow rose above the din: the song that Estelle and Amelia used to call one another in Boston. Amelia turned around. Mother beckoned to her from the companionway, where she stood with an arm around Estelle's waist.

Amelia wriggled through the crowd and caught hold of Estelle's outstretched hand. Estelle's collarbones poked up through the soft wool of her shawl, but she smiled for the first time in days.

"California," Estelle said. "I never thought I'd live to see it."

A swell lifted the ship, and Estelle's knees buckled. Mother steadied her, and they sat her down on the lid of their trunk, which a sailor had wrestled from the hold.

"Gracious," Estelle said. "I'm so weak." She pointed at the shore. "Maybe you can hijack that rig to carry me off the ship."

Amelia squinted at the sandy hill, where a strange machine dragged a string of hopper cars along the steep pitch. Steam belched from its smokestack. "What is that?"

"It's a steam paddy." Commander Everett stood before them, his shoulders squared. "They're reshaping this city by the day. Every time I arrive, they've filled in more of the bay." He held out his arm to Estelle. "Allow me to escort you to shore, Miss Duprey. You'll feel better on dry land. Fresh fruits and vegetables as soon as you can stomach them. You'll find plenty of produce on Long Wharf." He nodded to Mother. "It was a pleasure to meet you, Mrs. Forrester," he said. "You too, Miss Amelia."

"Thank you for a safe journey," Amelia said. So Mother would be *Mrs.* Forrester in this new city? That was the best news she'd heard yet.

"Ladies first!" Commander Everett bellowed. "Clear a path please!"

The crowd of men parted, and someone muttered, "Good riddance."

Amelia stiffened as she followed the commander onto the dock. Was it *their* fault that the *Unicorn* went short on food, or that the captain insisted on giving them their own stateroom?

The planked wharf shifted beneath Amelia as she stepped off the gangway, and her head suddenly felt light. "Help!" She grabbed for the nearest piling and held on for dear life. How could this be? The wharf lifted and fell, as if it had become the deck of another ship. Was the dock floating?

"Steady now." Four-Fingered Jim hurried across the

gangway and set both hands on her shoulders. "Happens to everyone. Soon you'll be a landlubber again. Look to the horizon, just as you did on board ship, to stop the spinning."

But Amelia had no interest in the horizon. She'd had enough of the sea to last her a hundred years. Instead, she braced her legs and focused on the land. Her eyes scanned the crowded wharf ahead of them, lined with a topsy-turvy collection of sheds, shops, and warehouses. Barrels, trunks, and wooden crates sat in disorderly piles on the rough planking. The newsboys had disappeared.

"All right now?" Jim let go and touched the brim of his cap. "Good-bye, Miss Amelia," he said. "Until next time."

"Next time?" Amelia met his kind gaze. "How?" she asked. "You'll be at sea—and we'll be on land."

"Yes, on land forever," Estelle cried, and her rippling laugh rang out for the first time in weeks.

"You never know," Jim said. "They say that all paths cross in California. Safe journeys to you all."

Amelia squeezed Jim's hand and felt the stub of his missing finger, but she didn't even cringe. "Thank you for everything."

"My pleasure." Jim's cheeks reddened above his beard. He nodded to Mother. "Your daughter is a right fine sailor, Mrs. Forrester. We're sorry to lose her."

Mother smiled. "We'll keep her on land, but I appreciate your kindness on the voyage."

Jim went back across the gangway into the melee of passengers pushing and shoving to get off the ship. Curses filled the air.

Estelle set a hand on Amelia's shoulder and pointed to the hill rising at the end of the wharf. Dust swirled above a jumble of tents and shacks. "Not a tree in sight," Estelle said. "The city doesn't look like much. What happened to those streets of gold?"

Two sailors staggered beneath the weight of Estelle's trunk. "Where shall we set this?" one asked.

Mother waved them to a cleared space near the gang-plank. The sailors dropped the trunk and went back for Amelia's carpetbag and Mother's valise. Estelle sat on her trunk. "Anything else, ma'am?" the first sailor asked.

Mother shook her head. "We have a crate in the hold, but Commander says we should come back for it tomorrow."

The sailor waited. Mother's face reddened from her lace collar to the wings of her hair, pressed flat against her cheeks. She pulled out her coin purse and handed him a two-bit coin. "I'm sorry," she said. "This is all I can give you."

The sailor took her coin and turned on his heel. The clamor of men grew louder as passengers wrestled their luggage off the ship, but Mother hardly seemed to notice.

"Is your purse empty?" Amelia asked.

"Almost." Mother twisted her hands as if she were wringing out wet washing and sank down onto the trunk beside

Estelle. "I had no idea that crossing the Isthmus would be so dear. We had to pay extra for passage on the *Unicorn,* and now we need to find a place to stay until our house arrives." She closed her eyes and rubbed her temples. "My head's in a swirl. I have to think."

Amelia's empty stomach growled. All through the long journey, from Boston to Panama by ship, across the Isthmus by mule and boat, and up the Pacific Coast, Mother had made the decisions and parceled out their money. "How will we eat?" Amelia asked now. "Or pay for a place to sleep?"

"I don't know yet. Give me a minute—my legs are like rubber." Two bright pink spots blossomed on Mother's cheeks. She and Estelle, sitting side by side, looked like little girls abandoned in the schoolyard. "We need someone with a cart to carry us up the hill." Mother dropped her chin to her chest, and Estelle rubbed her back, soothing her.

"I'll find something," Amelia said. They couldn't give up—not now. But the wharf was like a three-ring circus, busier than Boston on a parade day. Men rushed to and fro, hawkers yelled, mules brayed, sailors swore as they wrestled bags to shore, and a deep voice called, "Commander, where is the mail! Where are the mailbags?"

Next to a warehouse, a small group of men huddled around an open newspaper, reading eagerly. Had Julius made a sale so quickly? Amelia snapped open her carpetbag and rummaged among her clothes until she found her dress shoes, which she had wrapped in newspaper when they left Boston. She opened the parcel and set the shoes aside.

Estelle smiled, showing her dimples for the first time in days. "Amelia, what are you doing? You can't wear your Sunday best now. Speaking of that—where's your bonnet?"

"I don't know." Not really true, but Amelia hated the way her bonnet blocked her vision. "I need the newspaper. I'll explain later." Amelia smoothed out the wrinkles until the paper looked almost fresh, and admired her treasure. The *Boston Daily Advertiser* for January 1, 1851—six days later than the papers Jim had sold to Julius. She'd show those boys. She closed her bag and tucked the paper under her arm.

"Amelia, this is no time for reading," Mother asked.

Amelia ignored her. "Do you have any coins in case I find a wagon?"

"A few." Mother pulled another two-bit piece from her purse. "I hope this will be enough." She tried to stand but her face went white and Estelle grabbed her hand. "Goodness—I'm still light-headed," Mother said. "I need to sit for another moment. Don't leave the wharf. If you can't find a cart, come right back."

Amelia hurried away, pushing through the crowd. Her legs wobbled, then steadied. Men gaped at her as if she were some strange specimen caught in a butterfly net. Amelia dropped her eyes, lifted her skirts, and ran, her boots drum-ming on the planking. She took a deep breath. In among the smell of hides, brine, and sweaty men, she breathed a taste of smoke, of mint, of muddy earth.

California! They were homeless and nearly penniless—but they had arrived.

CHAPTER

❋ 4 ❋

Scarce as Trees

AMELIA SPIED a cart, a dray, and a Dearborn wagon as she tripped along the wharf, but all three creaked under heavy loads. Where the wharf met the shore she passed a saloon called the Apollo. The stench of stale beer drifted through the open doors, and men stood inside drinking, though it was still early in the morning. One man leered at her and said something in another language—was it German? She was glad she couldn't understand. When she glanced back over her shoulder, she saw that the saloon building was actually the stern end of a ship, set on pilings. What a strange city!

Amelia took a deep breath and stepped onto dry land. She was tempted to touch the earth, just to feel the thrill of firm ground again, but as the only girl in sight, she already stuck out like a black lamb in Uncle Paul's white flock. She looked up and down the busy street but didn't see a single stray cart or carriage. Mother had told her not to leave the dock—but unlike Boston, with its narrow, winding streets, the hill before her was wide open, the squat sheds and houses spaced far apart. It was easy to spot the *Unicorn*'s tall masts at the end of the wharf. Besides, she had her spyglass; surely she wouldn't get lost.

She started up the hill, struggling to find her way amid the constant bustle. Men in ragged pants, with beards hanging to their chests, stomped along carrying picks and shovels, pots and pans, parcels, baskets, and bulging sacks. Men prodded mules burdened with crates and barrels; boys badgered a team of oxen pulling a load of bricks on a stone boat. Men called out to each other in English, Spanish, and French—and in languages she'd never heard. The wide, dusty streets were all a-jumble: canvas tents set up next to brick houses and shops, next to sheds thrown together from scrap wood—and surely that wooden hulk, listing beside the road, was the bow end of a ship? Had the sea cast it up on the shore?

She passed a hotel, a livery stable, a ship's chandler, a tinsmith's shop—but no empty carts. Halfway up the hill, a group of men were constructing a house of corrugated iron panels, each side of the house fully finished, with square holes for windows and doors. She thought of the little wooden house that Uncle Paul had sent ahead in pieces. When would it come? Who would help them put it together? And how would Mother and Estelle buy land for the house to sit on if they had no money?

Amelia dodged a black rat—even bigger than the vermin on the *Unicorn*—and coughed when the wind swirled around her skirts, blowing dust into her eyes. She picked her way through garbage: empty bottles, gnawed bones, burlap sacks, a rotten cabbage, a dead bird missing a wing. When she stopped at the top of the hill to catch her breath, she realized she hadn't seen a single woman since she'd left the wharf.

Amelia's legs felt weak after so many days on board ship. She plunked herself down on an abandoned crate and gazed out at the bay. From this height, the tangle of ships seemed like a forest of winter trees. Hundreds of boats clustered close to the wharves; others knocked together in the bay. Their tall masts prickled like the backs of angry porcupines. Beyond the docks, ships at sail churned in every direction. Farther out, waves crashed onto a rocky island, where flocks of birds wheeled and shrieked above the spray. A tinge of green covered distant hills, and higher mountains rose in the mist. Amelia tingled all over. Wait until Mother and Estelle saw this view!

But they wouldn't see a thing unless she rescued them. Where should she go? Amelia stood up and headed for an intersection, where one street was covered with planking, and the other, deeply rutted, sported a wide timber for crossing. Was that a washboard, sticking up out of the dirt? And a shovel handle? So different from Boston's streets, paved in orderly cobblestone.

An empty cart sat on the other side of the rough road, next to a brick building, and the warm smell of fresh-baked bread drifted toward her. That settled it. Amelia lifted her skirts and stepped onto the timber. Suddenly, a deep bell rang out in the distance and a high-pitched bell clanged close by. "Watch out, miss!"

Someone clutched Amelia's arm and dragged her back onto the sidewalk just as two men, wearing red shirts and helmets, rushed by pulling a small fire engine. Its wheels rumbled on the planking and more men chased after it, shouting, "Fire! Fire!"

"Watch your step or they'll mow you right down."

Amelia turned to look at the plump, olive-skinned woman who had yanked her to safety. "Thank you," Amelia said. "I didn't see them."

"No trouble." The woman hoisted a basket and brushed dust from her skirt. "Looks like a false alarm—I don't smell smoke. But even a small fire is dangerous if the wind comes up. It roars through these canvas tents and wooden shacks. If you hear that deep bell, watch out. We had a fire last May that some said would be the end of us. But we fooled them. We rose again, like the phoenix from the ashes."

So *that's* what "Phoenix City" meant. Amelia smiled. She was learning something new every minute. "We just arrived on the *Unicorn*," she said.

"Then you're still green." The woman gave her a baleful look. "Not an orphan, are you?" Amelia shook her head, and the woman went right on talking in her clipped accent. "So many orphans in this city. Gold seekers come from all over the world. They start out full of promise, but many die. Their children wind up here on their own, tossed onto the shore like driftwood. It's a shame."

Amelia braced her shoulders. "I'm not an orphan," she said. "I'm with my mother and our friend Estelle."

"More gentlewomen! That's good news." The stout woman smiled. "Skirts are scarce as trees in these parts. Your father's not with you?"

"No." Amelia clenched her jaw, braced for the next question—*Where is he?*—but the woman only nodded. "We're all in the same boat," she said. "My husband went to the mines; left me to run things on my own. I'm doing well, if I do say so." She pointed to her empty basket. "I'm off to buy provisions for my restaurant. Tell your mother you're invited to my tent for dinner." She put out her hand. "Mrs. Liazos."

"Amelia Forrester." Amelia returned her handshake.

Mrs. Liazos nodded toward a side street. "See the tent with the table out front, and the awning? I serve dinner at noon sharp. I'll be expecting you." She hurried away, her skirts swaying, before Amelia could say good-bye. The crowd swallowed Mrs. Liazos like the whale gulping Jonah down for his supper.

Amelia tried to collect herself. Where was her newspaper? She must have dropped it when the firemen went past. She retraced her steps. The *Boston Daily Advertiser* lay crumpled in the dust. Passersby probably thought it was trash, like everything else in the street. Amelia put the paper back together and smoothed it out as best she could. The advertisements on the front page were dirty, but the news stories were legible inside. She still had news to sell.

Amelia glanced across the street. The cart had disappeared and Mother would be worrying. Still—Estelle could never climb that steep hill without help. There must be *someone* here with an empty wagon.

A team of mules passed, pulling a dray laden with lumber and bricks. The driver didn't even turn his head when she called out. Most people were hauling their goods themselves; one man struggled beneath a wooden yoke as if *he* were an ox, his buckets full of water that splashed as he stumbled along.

Amelia was about to give up when a slim man trotted past pulling a two-wheeled cart. A barrel bounced in the back, sloshing liquid. The man wore a blue tunic, almost like a dress, that fell to his knees. A black braid, even longer than her own, switched across his back.

"Wait!" she cried, and raced after him. "Stop, please!" She grabbed the sleeve of his tunic. The man cried out, twisted to the side, and his barrel tipped over. Amelia fell to her knees. The man shook his fist at her, rattling a stream of words in a strange language. He righted the barrel and pointed to its contents, which had spilled out into the dust. Amelia smelled pickling brine, but the bits of food on the ground were yellow and crinkled, not like any pickles she and Gran had made.

Amelia scrambled to her feet. "Excuse me, sir," she said. "I'm so sorry."

The man pushed back his wide-brimmed straw hat. His head was shaved in the front and his almond eyes flashed as he chattered in a scolding tone.

"Please." She held up her hand. "Do you speak English?"

The stream of words stopped. "Little," he said.

"Will you—help us?" When he didn't answer, Amelia pointed down the hill, to the harbor, then at the cart. "My mother—needs help. Two women." She pointed to herself and held up two fingers. The man raised his eyebrows, but said nothing. Amelia pretended to lift a heavy bag up from the ground, and set the imaginary weight in the cart with a groan.

The man grunted. "Carry bags," he said.

"Yes!" Amelia said. "Carry our bags—from the ship? It's called the *Unicorn*. A steamer." She made a puffing noise and waved toward the wharf at the foot of the hill.

The man shrugged and turned up his palms.

"You need money?" Amelia held up the two-bit piece. "This is all I have."

"Good." The man snatched the coin from her fingers, lifted the shafts of his cart, and trotted off down the hill, his barrel bouncing in the back.

"Wait!" Amelia cried, chasing after him. "How will you find them?"

But he was too fast for her. Amelia tripped and fell, and when she got up, he had disappeared. What a fool she was! The man had her money; he'd never even seen Mother; Estelle was weak with hunger; her own stomach growled—how could she help them now?

CHAPTER

✷ 5 ✷

I Need a Friend

AS AMELIA struggled to get her bearings, voices rose from a side street. "Newspay-puz!" voices cried. "Fresh news from home!"

Julius stood on a corner, brandishing a newspaper, while the black-haired boy shouted from the far side of the street. Julius's voice was low while the other boy's was high. "Paaay-puz!" they screamed in unison. "News! Read all about it!"

What a funny way to say "papers." Men gathered around the boys, pressing coins into their hands before snatching the papers away. One man stood stock still in the middle of the road, peering at a paper through round spectacles. A team of horses almost mowed him down.

Amelia hesitated. Should she? She crossed the street's rough planking and scrambled onto an overturned crate. "News!" Her voice squeaked. She glanced at the headline. "'Happy New Year, the Customary Wish of the Season'! Read the freshest news from Boston!" She raised the paper high above her head.

A young woman rushed over, her cheeks pink with excitement. "Is it true? You have the New Year's Day paper from Boston? I'm from Charlestown, right next door." She pulled a coin from her apron pocket. "Is a dollar enough?"

"Of course." Suddenly, Amelia's feet went out from under her and her head smacked the ground. Stars jiggled before her eyes. She gasped for air, but her lungs were empty. She choked and coughed and the woman helped her sit up, patting her back.

"Nasty boy," the woman said. "He stole your paper, knocked the breath right out of you."

Amelia gulped until, finally, precious air flooded her lungs. "Who hit me?" she asked, when she could speak again.

"A young hoodlum," the woman said. "Black hair, a face that needs washing, and strange eyes—I think one was brown, the other green. I won't repeat his rude oath."

Was it the boy from the dock? Amelia pulled her apron over her face. "I've done everything wrong. I've lost our money. Mother and Estelle are stranded on the wharf with nothing to eat. They don't know where I am—"

"Now, now. Don't fret." The woman helped Amelia to her feet. "The boy was fast, but I kept hold of my dollar. Did you just arrive?"

"Yes. And my paper is more recent than theirs."

The woman smiled. "Clever salesgirl. I bet they didn't like that. Feel better now?"

"I guess." Amelia touched the back of her head and

winced. "I'm getting a lump. Mother will be upset—"

"Not if you bring her a bakery treat. Let me see." The woman parted Amelia's hair. "No blood. You'll have a nasty egg but it won't show." The woman's gray eyes were kind beneath the hood of her bonnet. "My name is Rosanna Baker," she said, "but you must call me Rosanna. We must be nearly the same age. And you are—?"

"Amelia. I'm only twelve."

"I'm nineteen. But never mind." Rosanna tucked her arm through Amelia's as if they'd known each other forever. "Seven years doesn't matter, with so few women in town." She drew Amelia along the planked street. "A dollar should be enough to buy something for you and your—sister, was it?" Amelia was too tired to explain that she had no sister or brother—and no father, for that matter.

"How nice that I found you," Rosanna said. "I need a friend."

"So do I," Amelia said.

WITHIN A half hour, Amelia was headed to the harbor, feeling strong in spite of the lump swelling at the back of her head. Her throat was moist after a long drink of water, and the sack in her hands held soda crackers, three teacakes, and a pork jumble from Mr. Wilson's Biscuit Bakery. Amelia's stomach growled as the sack warmed her hands and sent lovely smells up to her nose. Rosanna had made Amelia promise that she'd come and find her when they were settled. "I live on an abandoned ship," she said. "It's safer while my husband is away. Listen for my nanny goats out near the Long Wharf."

Amelia laughed. Perhaps the news of fresh milk would temper Mother's anger—

But what was this? Amelia stopped short. The air was suddenly cold and the bay had disappeared. The fog bank, which had been sitting on the horizon this morning, had settled over the harbor, hiding the docks and warehouses. Only the tallest masts showed through its clammy blanket. Amelia squinted into the gloom. Was she on the right street? How would she find the *Unicorn*?

CHAPTER

✳ 6 ✳

A Printer's Devil

AMELIA STOOD still, trying to get her bearings. The mist softened the edges of buildings and muffled the sounds, so that a passing mule sounded as if it wore woolen boots, and nothing looked familiar. Amelia shivered in the damp air and pulled her cloak around her. Mother and Estelle would be freezing cold—and furious. How long had she been gone?

A dog's high-pitched yapping startled her, and a shaggy black terrier rushed out of the mist, wagging its tail. It leaped for her bakery sack.

"No!" She hoisted the sack just in time. "Go away!"

"Tip!" A man's voice bellowed from a brick building across the way. "Come back here." The terrier whirled and ran toward a man whose suspenders were stretched over his round belly. He stood beneath a bold sign that read, **ALTA CALIFORNIA**.

"Sorry," the man called. "Tip is our ratter—and sometimes he forgets his manners. Don't you, Tip?"

The terrier's ears drooped. Amelia laughed. "That's all right. He missed my sack." The man sounded friendly, so she crossed the street. "Could you help me? I'm lost."

"Easy to lose your way in this fog. Come on in." He waved her across the threshold. "Excuse our mess—I'm working on the next edition." He peered at her over his spectacles. "Where do you need to go? A girl your age shouldn't be wandering the city alone."

Amelia ignored his question and stood in the doorway, entranced. The man was right; the room *was* a mess—but a lovely one. A pile of newspapers listed to one side against the brick wall; the man's desk was buried under stacks of paper, pens, pencils, and books; and a big machine stood in the corner with a strange device on the side—like the spokes of a wheel without the rim. A table beneath the window held a wooden tray divided into many small squares. Metal letters in different sizes and shapes filled each square. A sharp smell tickled Amelia's nose.

"Cat got your tongue?"

Amelia startled. "Are you making a newspaper?"

The man's bushy mustache quivered when he smiled. "I guess you could put it that way." He waved one arm around the room. "Welcome to the offices of the *Alta California*, descended from San Francisco's earliest newspaper. We've come a long way from the gristmill where the first paper was born—but we're in a bit of a mess now. Like everyone else, our printer's devil has gone to the mines."

All this information left Amelia's head feeling as foggy as the city outside. "What's a printer's d—" She hesitated over the forbidden word.

"The boy who sets type for the paper. It takes a keen eye. I can hardly blame him for running off. Poor sap has to read my handwriting and set the letters backward, as if he's working with a mirror. Do you read?" When Amelia nodded, he handed her a folded newspaper. "Yesterday's paper. It's old news, but you're welcome to it."

"Thank you." The paper was enormous. She opened it to the front page with its many ads for vessels, and glanced at a bold advertisement beneath the masthead. "**BALLOOV LAUNCH!**" the advertisement cried in fancy letters. "**GET A BIRD'S EYE VIEW OF THE CITY—AND A QUICK TRIP TO THE MINES!**"

"You have a *V* instead of an *N*," Amelia said, pointing to the misspelled word.

The man picked up his spectacles and peered over her shoulder. "Right you are." He pulled out a drawer full of bigger letters and picked one from the middle. "Here's the culprit—a *V* in with the *N*s. Too bad you're a girl; I could offer you a job." He closed the drawer. "Where did you want to go?"

What was wrong with being a girl? Amelia didn't want to know. Instead, she turned the page and stared at a headline: A LETTER FROM CHAGRES. "We were in Chagres," she said. "We crossed the Isthmus, just like this man. Our ship crashed on the rocks near Acapulco but we all survived." She glanced at him. "If I wrote you a letter about it, would you print mine, too?"

The man gave her a look that made her feel as small as the terrier. "Dear child," he said, "I'm sure you had your own adventure, but we can't publish stories by little girls. And how would we know you were telling the truth?"

He said "little girls" as if she were like the vermin roaming the streets. "I don't lie," Amelia said.

The man waved her away. "If you're another orphan looking for a home, you won't find one here," he said. "Now vamoose; I've got a paper to put out."

"I am *not* an orphan." Amelia squared her shoulders and struggled to keep her voice steady. "My mother is waiting for me on the wharf, where the *Unicorn* docked—but I don't know how to find it."

"Easy enough. Follow this street to the Long Wharf. Turn right and it's the next dock on your left. But be careful. I wouldn't want *my* daughter wandering this town alone." He pulled his chair around and turned his back on her.

Amelia left without thanking him. Tip jumped up to greet her as she crossed the street. She gave his square head a quick scratch and combed the matted beard under his chin, careful to keep hold of her bakery sack. "Your owner doesn't like me," she whispered. "And he's *not* my father—thank goodness."

But who was? Never mind. She couldn't think about that now. The fog was still thick and clinging—with no sign of her family anywhere.

CHAPTER

Like a Freak

AMELIA GROPED her way along the street, clutching the bakery sack and the newspaper to her chest. "Can I help you, young lady?" a man called, but the editor's warnings rang in her head and she dashed to the next block, where she stopped to catch her breath. A small boy passed by, holding a wooden box. "Havana cee-gars, two bits!" he cried, with a French accent. Mexican men, such as she'd seen in Acapulco, swaggered by in the mist, their red sashes and silver trouser buttons gleaming against the drab colors of the shacks and tents. What should she do now?

As if her question had traveled thousands of miles, she imagined Uncle Paul's deep voice urging her to *Eat your breakfast; stay strong.* Very well. Amelia opened the bakery sack and sniffed the fresh bread. She took a small bite from a sweet tea cake, and before she knew it the cake was gone. She rolled the sack closed to keep from gobbling the rest.

Gulls shrieked overhead, their cries muffled in the fog. And then she heard another, more familiar sound: Estelle's rippling laugh.

"Estelle! Mother!" Amelia broke into a run, nearly colliding with an oxcart as she dashed across the street. She found the man with the pigtail at the next intersection, cooking something over a steaming brazier. Mother sat on the edge of his cart, holding a steaming tin cup, while Estelle perched on her trunk near the brazier, her mouth puckered around a slice of lemon.

When Mother saw Amelia she stood up fast, spilling her drink. "Amelia!" She set the cup down with trembling hands. "Look what you made me do." Her eyes narrowed. "Where on earth have you been?" She clutched Amelia's arm. "I told you not to leave the wharf—if you weren't so big, I'd throw you over my knees and paddle you."

"I'm sorry." Amelia's chin quivered. "I was lost in the fog." She held up her sack. "I sold a newspaper for a dollar and bought you some biscuits." That wasn't exactly what had happened, but she could explain later.

"We're lucky this nice Mr. Wong rescued us," Mother said. "I send you for help—and instead you disappear. You scared us half to death."

"But *I* found Mr. Wong—"

"Enough excuses," Mother said.

Estelle cleared her throat and raised her eyebrows. Amelia caught her warning: *Don't argue.* Instead, she nodded at Mr. Wong, who bowed and smiled in return. Then she reached into the sack for her treasures: a tea biscuit each for Mother and Estelle, soda crackers for herself, and the pork pie. It was too small to share, so she gave it to Mr. Wong. He took it in both hands, bowing and nodding again. Amelia bowed back.

"Bless you, Amelia," Estelle said, her voice croaky as a frog's. "I knew you'd find us." She held the biscuit to her nose, then smiled and took a delicate bite. "Even better than your grandmother's flapjacks. The world really *is* upside down. The streets are paved with dust, not gold, and the child goes scavenging for food. Did you find us a place to stay, too?"

"Not yet," Amelia said. She finished her soda cracker in two bites. "But we do have an invitation to noon dinner, if we can find the restaurant."

Estelle clapped her hands so loudly that Mr. Wong jumped and broke into a stream of unintelligible words. "You're an angel, *ma chérie*," Estelle said.

"I wouldn't go that far," Mother said, but her dry tone told Amelia that all was forgiven. For now.

WHEN THEY finished their tea, Mother asked, "So, Amelia—where is this eatery you promised us?"

"A few blocks higher and off to the left—I think." Amelia and Mr. Wong pushed and pulled the cart full of luggage uphill while Estelle and Mother trudged behind. Amelia squinted at each intersection, trying to see through the fog. Finally, she spotted a long tent beyond a row of rough frame houses. RESTAURANT! a sign announced in bold letters, painted on the canvas. A line of men stood outside, smoking and calling out to one another.

"This way." Amelia beckoned to Mother and Estelle. The men fell silent as they approached. A few tipped their hats; the rest just stared. Amelia's cheeks grew hot. "They make me feel like a freak," she whispered to Estelle.

Estelle nodded. "They're staring because you're a pretty girl," she said. But she was blushing, too.

One man sneered at Mr. Wong as he unloaded their bags. "What are you nice ladies doing with a Celestial?" he asked.

He said "Celestial" the way the newspaper editor had said "girl"—as if the word had a bad taste. "What does that mean?" she whispered.

"That's what they call the Chinese here," Mother said quietly.

"Why don't they like him?" Amelia asked, but Mother shushed her.

"Good-bye, Mr. Wong," Amelia said, and this time, *she* bowed first. Mr. Wong returned the bow and trotted away, his cart wheels creaking. "What a kind man," Mother said. "I wonder if we'll ever see him again."

Amelia lifted the canvas flap. Thick steam wafted over rows of empty tables, and a savory smell tickled her nose. "Mrs. Liazos?" she called.

"Welcome, welcome!" The heavy-set woman bustled through the steam, wiped her hands on her apron, and greeted them like long-lost kin. "If it isn't Miss Amelia—and you've brought your family with you! Women are a sight for sore eyes, in this city of men! I'm Mrs. Dorothea Liazos," she said, "but my friends call me Dot." She studied Mother, then Amelia. "The same hazel eyes—I see you're mother and daughter."

Amelia held her breath. Would Mother be *Miss* or *Mrs.* Forrester in this new town? Mother said simply, "I'm Sophie Forrester. And this is my dear friend, Miss Estelle Duprey."

"Pleased." Mrs. Liazos winked at Estelle and lowered her voice. "A single woman with blue eyes and golden hair? Miss Duprey, I predict you'll have your pick of men in this town."

Estelle smiled, but Amelia could tell she was only being polite. "We need a meal more than a man," Estelle said. "I was sick for much of our journey."

"Bless you—and excuse me for nattering on," Mrs. Liazos said. "I'm just that excited to see two gentlewomen. Some women live on the abandoned boats, for safety. I came by the Horn right after the gold discovery. It took us half a year. I'll be glad if I never see a ship again."

Estelle laughed. "I feel the same way."

Mrs. Liazos looked behind them. "Where is your luggage?"

"Outside," Mother said. "Should we bring it in?"

"Good idea," Mrs. Liazos said. "The town is full of

ruffians—but some men are kind. Watch." She lifted the flap and called, "Could someone help these ladies with their luggage?"

The men moved so fast, Amelia had to jump out of the way. In a few minutes, their baggage was stowed safely in a corner near the cookstove, and Mother and Amelia were sitting happily on packing crates pulled up to a long table made of planks set on sawhorses. Mrs. Liazos found an old cane chair for Estelle, who beamed as she sank into it.

Mother peeled off her gloves. "May I help you serve, in exchange for our dinners? Otherwise, I'm not sure how we'll pay you. We spent so much money on the crossing."

"I know how that is," Mrs. Liazos said. "Wait until you're on your feet. You won't have any trouble finding work. With women so scarce, these helpless men will shell out coins for the smallest household job."

"I don't like to take charity," Mother said.

"Don't worry. You can pay me back later. Today, you are my guests." She hurried toward the back of the tent, where kettles steamed on an iron stove.

Amelia stretched her aching legs out in front of her. Mrs. Liazos brought them tin bowls of corn fritters and hot lamb stew scented with rosemary, as well as a plate of mashed potatoes for Estelle. Amelia dug her spoon into the stew as soon as her bowl touched the table. Mother nudged her foot.

"Thank you, ma'am," Amelia said, her mouth full.

"Eat up while you can," Mrs. Liazos said. "The hordes are eager for my Greek cooking—I'll let them in now."

The crowd of men outside had grown rowdy, but when Mrs. Liazos lifted her tent flaps, the men took off their hats and filed in quietly, taking turns at the washbasin before they jostled past the table. There the line slowed, as each man raked his eyes over Mother and Estelle. One man winked at Amelia, and she nearly choked on her fritter. "I hate their staring," she whispered.

"Just ignore them." Mother studied her stew. "They'll get used to us, in time."

"If I were a boy, they wouldn't notice me," Amelia said.

"And if you wore your bonnet, as you should, you wouldn't attract attention," Mother snapped. Amelia felt stung. She pushed her food away as Mother leaned closer to Estelle, speaking softly. "We'll have to set ourselves up in a temporary spot soon," Mother said. "Commander Everett told me that storms have delayed many of the clippers. I wonder when our house will arrive."

Amelia thought of Gran's warning: *Two women in a strange country with a young girl—how will you survive?* Amelia wiped her damp palms on her skirt. Was Gran right? "Who will buy your ladies' dresses, with so few women here?" she asked.

"I don't know." Mother tossed Estelle an uneasy glance. "My throat is parched. I'll fetch us more water." She left the table.

Amelia had an idea. She jumped up, catching her bowl before it tipped over. "Estelle—when you packed the goods for your shop—did you wrap them in newspaper?"

"I did," Estelle said. "Look in the upper tray of my trunk." She winked at Amelia. "Are you up to no good?"

"No—I promise!"

Estelle lifted the key on its chain from around her neck and handed it to Amelia. "Don't lose it now. And keep those bolts of fabric clean."

"I will." How wonderful to see Estelle's dimples again! Amelia gave her a quick hug and hurried toward their luggage, her stew and corn fritters forgotten.

CHAPTER

✳ 8 ✳

A Muss!

AMELIA OPENED the trunk with her back to the slow-moving line of men. Estelle had used newspaper to wrap up three bolts of cloth: a fine wool delaine, a maroon calico embroidered with tiny pink flowers, and a small roll of checked gingham.

Amelia smoothed the newspapers out on her knees. She had the *Boston Semi-Weekly Advertiser*, as well as the *Boston Evening Transcript*, Gran's usual paper. The *Transcript* was old—from December 18—but Amelia nearly whooped with delight when she saw the *Advertiser*'s date: January 8, nearly two weeks later than the papers Jim had sold to Julius, and she had two copies. The dates stood out in bold type. Wait until the restaurant customers saw this.

She replaced the cloth, locked the trunk, and edged her way back to their table, where she scanned the headlines. "Mother, look—'Destruction of the Eastern Railroad Ferry-boat by Fire'!"

"Since when do you read the news out loud?" Mother asked.

Amelia opened the paper and raised her voice. "They print California news, too."

An older man with a thatch of white hair looked up from his meal. "Have you got eastern papers, miss?"

"Yes. Look at this *Semi-Weekly Advertiser,* from Boston." She jabbed the headline and squinted at the story's fine print. "Two fires on the same day."

The older man dug into his breeches pocket. "Would you sell it for two bits?" he said.

"I'll double that." A big bear of a man, with a beard falling below his chin, pushed back from the table. "I'm from New Hampshire, myself." He held out a dollar.

"And I'm from Lexington. Even closer." The older man reached across the table, dropped three coins next to Amelia's bowl, and snatched the paper away. "Six bits. First come, first served," he said.

The burly man raised his fists. "You've no right—"

"A muss! A muss!" someone shouted.

Amelia clutched the papers to her chest. She hadn't meant to start a fight! Both men looked ready to exchange blows when Estelle stood up. "Excuse me!" Estelle sounded like a baby bird chirping, but the crowd stilled. "We have more papers in our luggage. Once we're settled, I'm sure Amelia would be glad to sell them. In the meantime, please share with one another."

"Sorry, miss." The angry man from Lexington stared at his feet like a scolded schoolboy.

"I have three papers," Amelia said. "A dollar apiece." She held up the *Transcript*. "'Six Thousand Boys in Baltimore Hear Jenny Lind Sing.'"

Amelia took in a mix of coins for the remaining papers, while Mother helped Estelle back into her chair. "Your days as a teacher serve you well," Mother said quietly.

Amelia smiled to herself. How many weeks since Mother and Estelle had teased each other in the old way? Perhaps things in California would be all right after all.

But this dream vanished too soon. As Amelia returned to her dinner, a familiar face appeared in front of her. It was the dark-haired boy who had knocked her to the ground— and stolen her paper. As he stared at her she saw that Rosanna Baker was right—his eyes were mismatched: one dark as coffee, the other a dull green. He yelled at Mrs. Liazos, who was ladling stew in the back.

"Mother!" he cried. "What is *she* doing here?"

The steady clink-clank of spoons on metal stopped and the tent fell silent.

"Nico!" Mrs. Liazos said. "Where are your manners?"

Nico. So that was his name. Amelia held her ground, her heart knocking, as he jabbed his thumb at the older man reading the *Advertiser*. "I assume this is *your* doing?"

Mother set down her fork. "Amelia—do you know this boy?"

"Not exactly." Amelia wasn't about to tell Mother about her own "muss," as the men called it. "He was on the wharf this morning, when the *Unicorn* docked."

"That's right," Nico said. "We came to collect our papers, rightfully ours. And now you're horning in on our business. I warned you—keep your hands off."

Amelia touched the lump at the back of her head. "If that was your idea of a warning—"

"Don't meddle where you don't belong."

"I can't sell a newspaper to buy food for my family?" Amelia asked.

"Hear, hear!" The older man clapped his hands. "Her news is more recent than yours, Nico! You'd better watch out; she's got an edge on you."

Mocking laughter rippled through the tent. Nico's face darkened but he held his ground. "Just stay out of it," he said, nearly spitting. "It's a rough life. Not proper for a *young lady* like yourself."

"Nico!" Mrs. Liazos called at last. "Come here and make yourself useful."

But Nico ducked his head and slipped out from under the tent. *Young lady.* Amelia heard the scorn in his voice. She picked up her tin cup to take a sip of water, but her hands were shaking and she spilled some on her skirt.

Mrs. Liazos hurried over. "I apologize," she said. "Nico has gone stone deaf on me since his father took off for the diggings."

"Has your husband had any success out there?" Estelle asked.

Mrs. Liazos's mouth drew into a straight line. "Not so's I've heard." She lowered her voice. "Truth be told, we've no idea if he's dead or alive, or if he's coming back at all. He's in some godforsaken place called Jackass Hill." She glanced at Amelia. "Nico is a big help to me. You wouldn't interfere with our business now, would you?"

Amelia was speechless until Mother's boot pressed hard on her toes. "No, ma'am," Amelia said.

Mrs. Liazos turned her back and Mother gave Amelia a worried look. "Goodness," she said. "Only a few hours in San Francisco, and already you've made an enemy? What on earth was that about?"

"Nico thinks girls shouldn't sell newspapers," Amelia said.

"He's right," Mother said. "And you'll be too busy helping in the shop and going to school to bother with newspapers."

Was there a school here? Amelia didn't want to know. She cupped her chin in her hands. Her head weighed at least a hundred pounds. Although it was only a few hours since the *Unicorn* had steamed into the harbor, this was surely the longest day of her life.

CHAPTER

✳ 9 ✳

A Paper Treasure

AMELIA WOKE the next morning to the sound of a whistling wind, mingled with the pealing of a bell and a boy's voice calling, "Clean your boots! *Bottes à cirer!*"

Where was she? Amelia rolled onto her back. Dim light filtered through a canvas ceiling that flapped and rattled in the wind. Then she remembered: she was in a borrowed tent. In San Francisco.

She lay still, listening to the sounds of the city waking up. Wagon wheels creaked past, and the steady thump of boots on wooden planking seemed so close that Amelia pulled the blanket over her shift. Could people see in?

She wiggled her toes. Her feet ached from hiking all over the city yesterday, and her arms were sore from cranking the windlass on a well to fill the restaurant buckets, as well as the one in their tent. Although Mrs. Liazos was cool toward Amelia after the newspaper incident, she had taken pity on them at the end of the day, suggesting this tent near the restaurant as a temporary shelter.

"The man who owns the tent is in the diggings with my

husband," Mrs. Liazos had said. "He asked me to look after it for him. Can't think of a better way than to let you ladies rest there. If he comes back, though, you'll have to bunk somewhere else."

Mother and Estelle had accepted in an instant, even though Amelia noticed pinpricks in the canvas overhead that would surely let in the rain. "We'll have a real roof over our heads when the little house arrives," Mother had said.

When she finally unpacked and slipped under her blankets, Amelia had pretended to sleep while Mother mended a man's shirt by candlelight.

"Our funds are low," Mother had whispered. "That man who bought Amelia's paper begged me to mend this flannel shirt, but mending won't feed us. Prices are very dear; you saw those signs on the wharf—a dollar and a half for a barrel of water! I'm afraid we'll lose the money I set aside to buy our plot of land. And Amelia is right; women are scarce. Who will buy our dresses?"

Estelle squeezed Mother's knee. "Perhaps the men will," Estelle said, "though they might object to shirts of lace and silk." They both laughed softly, and Amelia had snuggled under the blanket, relieved. "We'll make out all right," Estelle said. "I'll be stronger in a few days, and Amelia will help us. Come to bed, Sophie."

Now that morning had come, along with hunger that pinched her belly, Estelle's words rang in her head: *Amelia will help us.* How? She needed a plan. Amelia sat up. Estelle was alone, sleeping soundly on the pallet she shared with Mother. Her yellow curls poked out from under the blanket. Amelia reached for her dress, pulling it on over her shift. It smelled musty and rank after so many weeks at sea.

Her stomach growled as she tiptoed around the tent. No sign of food anywhere, not even a crust of bread. She dipped a tin cup into the bucket of water and drank fast, hoping to fool her stomach for a while. How could she earn more money?

Amelia thought of the *Alta California*, and the letter from a traveler that the editor had printed. He said he'd never accept a letter from a girl. Could she fool him somehow?

Amelia opened her carpetbag, pulled out her leather diary, and found the page where she had scribbled a letter to Uncle Paul from Panama. Estelle had found many mistakes and she'd made Amelia copy the letter over on another piece of paper before they sent it. Amelia read her messy first copy now.

March 1, 1851
Dear Uncle Paul,

We are in Panama. It is a city with thick stone walls and crummbling churches. It took us four days to cross from the Atlantic Ocean to the Pacific. First we rode up the Chagres River in a steemer. Then two men paddled us upstream in a boat called a bungo. After that we rode on mules through the jungle. Im glad you taught me to ride, because the mules carried us over a very steep track. We climbed up and up through the jungle. I hardly dared to look down. We saw colorful birds and flowers. Monkeys chattered in the trees and our guide killed a snake 8 feet long! The mule had a bony back and I wished we had brought Skipper with us. I hitched up my skirts and rode like a man so I wouldn't fall off.

From your devoted niece,
Amelia

Amelia sighed. Thinking about Skipper, Uncle Paul's pony, made her homesick for her uncle and their morning rides through the woods. Would she ever see him again?

She frowned at her sloppy writing. She'd written this letter before the shipwreck, so the editor might think it was boring. And Estelle's corrections, in blue pen, were all over the page. "We need to get you back in school soon," Estelle had said. But Amelia had no interest in school right now. Not while Mother and Estelle needed money. She loved learning—but she hated what happened outside, away from Teacher's ears, when the older boys called her that terrible name. . . .

She closed her eyes. Long ago, she'd taught herself a trick to block the sound of that name from her head: if she hummed a tune, or mouthed the words quietly, she could banish the oath. "Oh! Susannah," she sang now, as she searched for her pen and ink. "Do not cry for me—I come from Alabama with my banjo on my knee . . ."

She carefully tore a clean page from her diary and set to work copying the letter, correcting the spelling as she went along. When she reached the end, she wrote about the shipwreck, how they were cast up on the rocks in a storm. *Everyone survived,* she wrote. *But a sailor on our ship said the captain was asleep when we hit the rocks.*

She waved the paper to dry it, folded the letter, and slipped it into the pocket of her skirt. She opened the tent flap and peered outside. Bright sunshine sparkled on the bay and the wind felt warm on her face. "I had a dream the other night . . ." Amelia sang.

"When everything was still," Estelle crooned from her pallet.

Amelia turned around. "I'm sorry. Was I too loud?"

"Don't worry—those gongs and bells are noisier than you are." Estelle sat with her knees pulled up and her blond hair loose all over her shoulders. She looked like a young girl.

"Where's Mother?" Amelia asked.

"She went to the wharf, to see when the clipper might come in, and to find a plot of land for the house."

"I hope she buys some food."

"I do too. But everything is so dear." Estelle looked worried. "Bring me my comb, and I'll straighten us up a bit." Amelia sat on the edge of the pallet while Estelle loosened her braid and worked her way through the tangles.

"Ouch!" Amelia yelped when the comb scraped the swollen lump on her head—her "gift" from Nico.

Estelle gently probed Amelia's scalp. "You have an egg here. What happened?"

"I fell when I was lost in the fog," Amelia said. Truthful enough.

"Poor thing. I'll be careful." But the next minute, the comb stuck in a tangle and Amelia protested again. "Sorry," Estelle said. "Your hair is like mine: too long."

"Let's cut it off," Amelia said.

Estelle's laugh was infectious. "Silly girl. Short hair would save us trouble—but everyone envies your chestnut curls." She parted Amelia's hair and braided it quickly, fastening it with ribbon. "Now your turn to do me—and then I have a surprise for you."

"Breakfast?" Amelia asked.

Estelle winked. "Not exactly—but it could lead you in that direction."

"Tell me!" Amelia loved it when Estelle teased her. But Estelle stayed quiet while Amelia combed out her hair. "Why is my hair so dark and curly? Mother's is the opposite, sandy and straight," Amelia said.

Estelle tensed beneath Amelia's hands. "Perhaps your gran had dark hair, before she went gray." She took the comb from Amelia and pointed at the tent's corner, where the trunk's lid sat open. "There's your surprise." Heavy bolts of calico, gingham, and white cambric sat in neat piles next to a stack of folded newspapers, their creases as smooth as if Estelle had pressed them with a hot iron.

"Oh!" Amelia jumped up and scooped the papers into her arms. "Five copies—a treasure!"

"I hope so. One is old, but perhaps people won't mind."

"Five papers means five dollars!" Amelia kissed Estelle.

"I read a few stories, while I was folding them." Estelle took a copy of the *Transcript* from the top of Amelia's pile. "Here's one about women wanting the right to vote—and about ladies who wear breeches, or pantaloons, as I did in Panama."

"Where are your pantaloons?" Amelia asked.

"My Turkish trousers, as your mother calls them?" Estelle winked. "They're packed away in the bottom of my trunk. And don't tell your gran that I left my stays behind in Panama."

Amelia laughed. "I won't. Mother's not wearing them either—is she?"

"Not anymore. With so much hard work ahead of us, we can't cinch ourselves into corsets every day. Who knows, perhaps we'll be like the famous Mrs. Weber in England, who always wears pantaloons beneath her skirts."

Estelle was giving her ideas, but Amelia kept them to herself. Estelle added the *Transcript* to the pile of papers and set them in a cloth bag. "You sell the papers nearby and I'll watch our things, in the tent. You'd best wear your bonnet."

Amelia drew back. "Why? If you have given up your stays—"

"No man would dare bother a girl in a bonnet," Estelle said.

Amelia wasn't so sure, but she stood still while Estelle set the bonnet on her head and tied the ribbons under her chin. She was almost dizzy with hunger.

"Don't go far," Estelle said. "From the sounds of people passing by, you should find plenty of buyers right on this street. Be careful."

"I will." Amelia tried to cinch the bag closed, but the papers were too big. "If I sell these, what shall I buy for you?"

"I'd give anything for fresh fruit." Estelle frowned. "Stay clear of that boy, Nico. He's an angry young man."

"I'll do my best," Amelia said. She slipped out of the tent into the sunshine.

CHAPTER

✳ 10 ✳

Think of Him as Dead

AMELIA RAN along the planked street, her boots tapping out an uneven rhythm. Estelle's bag knocked against her knees. Five papers! Where could she sell them? The men bustling past looked far too busy to read. She couldn't go to the restaurant where Mrs. Liazos had warned her not to "interfere." What about the Biscuit Bakery? It was a busy place—if she could find it again. Amelia's bonnet made her feel like Uncle Paul's Belgians with their blinders on. She stepped aside to avoid a team of oxen and turned down a street that reminded her of Boston. Brick buildings rose above smaller, wooden frame structures. All the build-ings boasted signs swinging over their doorways. They advertised CARPENTERS; WHALE OIL; ROOMS TO LET; even WARM AND COLD BATHS. One sign promised books in English, French, Spanish, and in a language she'd never seen.

Books in French would please Estelle. If the city had a bookstore, it must have readers. And readers might buy newspapers.

The street ended in a plaza, so wide and barren that

Amelia drew back under a shop's awning, hugging her bag to her chest. Part of the square was fenced, but no animals grazed on the hard-packed ground. A few empty wagons sat next to a tall flagpole where an American flag snapped in the breeze. A long adobe building with a sloping roof stood on the far side of the plaza. In the distance, groups of men huddled together, so closely packed that they looked like a mob about to erupt. Amelia shivered. Was it safe to sell her papers there?

A miner passed her, laden with tools, knives, and pots and pans. He might have been a store on foot. "Excuse me, sir," she said, reaching for her bag. "Would you like a news-paper?"

The man barked a laugh. "Don't mock me, miss. One more ounce and I'd be flat on my back."

"I'm sorry." She edged around him, headed for a store called *El Dorado*, when a door opened and a man tumbled out, followed by shouts and the stench of whiskey. Amelia turned on her heel and ran, but stopped short at the next corner. Was *this* the way she had come yesterday? Although the streets were wide compared to Boston's twisting cow paths, she couldn't tell one from the next. The bakery was nowhere in sight, and every man who passed gawked at her.

She wiped her face on the hem of her cloak and squared her shoulders. The newspapers were heavy. If she quit now, she'd have to carry them back to the tent—and she'd still be hungry.

Amelia peered at a poster tacked up on the side of a small frame house, announcing the same balloon launch that the *Alta* had advertised: "Get a bird's-eye view of the city and the bay, aboard the Star of the West!"

This poster showed a picture of the balloon: a round globe decorated with stars and covered with netting. Ascension at North Point, weather permitting, April 1st (no fooling!) Come one, come all!

What was the date today? Amelia had lost track of time. Wouldn't Uncle Paul be impressed if she saw a balloon take off?

"Lost, are you?"

Amelia looked down into the freckled face of a boy who seemed familiar. "I guess so. Who are you?"

"Patrick," he said. "I saw you on the *Unicorn* yesterday, talking to Julius."

"Oh!" Amelia said. "You're the boy with the fancy watch, who waved to me."

Patrick beamed, reached into his pocket, and pulled out the timepiece. Although it was a rich, elegant gold, the watch was attached to the boy's trousers by a frayed cord. "It belonged to me da. He give it to me before he died." Patrick's face was solemn. "See"—he turned it over—"there's his initials. PWF. Patrick William Flannigan, same as mine. And *his* da give it to him before he left Ireland." Patrick flipped the watch open to show her the face with its Roman numerals.

"You're going to lose it," Amelia said. "Let me fix that cord." She set her papers down, loosened the knot, and fixed the watch to his trousers with a clean bowline. "There. You'll keep it now."

"Thanks. Your da teach you to tie knots?"

"No. I learned from Jim, on the ship." Before she could stop herself, she said, "I don't have a father."

Patrick frowned. "'Course you do. Everyone has a da. Else you wouldn't be here."

"True." Amelia hoisted the bag of papers. She'd said enough.

"Julius give you those?" Patrick asked.

"They're mine. We brought them from Boston." Amelia glanced at the barren square. "What is this place? Could I sell papers here?"

"They call it the Plaza. Usually, it's all a-bustle. But everyone's at the post office today, waiting for the mail." He pointed to the distant corner of the square where small structures sat on either side of a tall building. "Lookit all those men."

"I thought they were a mob."

"Not a bit," Patrick said. "They're waiting in line for letters to be sorted, patient as can be. Come on."

She followed him across the square, skirting one saloon, then another, holding her breath against the rank smells. As they drew closer, she could see why the streets and the square were empty. Long lines of men stood in front of a metal-clad building. Some sat in chairs, reading books; others held leather bags to their chests; some smoked pipes as if they had all the time in the world.

Amelia tugged at Patrick's sleeve. "Surely men reading books want a paper!" When he shrugged, she asked, "Do you sell papers with Julius?"

"No. He says I'm too small. But sometimes I'm their lookout, on Telegraph Hill. I watch to see which boats are coming in. It's hard to make out the difference between steamers and clippers, till they get close. I wish the lookout man would let me use his telescope. You can see all the way to China with that thing."

"Really?" Amelia stifled a laugh. A little machine in her mind began to turn, a machine with greased cogs that fit neatly into spinning wheels. "Why does Julius need to know which boats are coming?"

Patrick shook his head as if she were incredibly stupid. "So he can spot the mailboat, a course. And beat the other gangs to the newspapers."

Amelia grinned. Patrick had just given her another idea for earning some money. Now, if she could only persuade the editor to print her letter . . .

"Ta," Patrick said, giving her a quick wave.

"Wait," Amelia said. "Do you know how to find that paper called the *Alta*?"

He laughed and pointed to the other end of the Plaza.

"You were looking at her. The brick building on the other side of that fence."

Amelia rubbed her eyes. "Really? So I was right on this square yesterday and didn't know it. You can get lost in that fog."

"Not if you know your way." Patrick squinted at her. "What's the *Alta* got for you?"

"Nothing." At least, not yet. Amelia wasn't ready to share her plan. "I like Tip," she said. It was a lame excuse, but Patrick nodded.

"He's a good dog, that one," he said. "Follows me sometimes. See you."

"Thanks for the *tips*," Amelia said.

Patrick wrinkled his nose. "Bad joke." He hurried away, keeping to the edge of the Plaza. Amelia watched him go. Was he on his own? He said his father had died. From the looks of him—with his cap too big, his jacket so short, his clothes mended many times—perhaps he'd lost his mother, too? How horrible. But still—he had known his father. He even owned something that belonged to him. She had nothing. Not even a name.

Just think of him as dead, Mother always said, as if that settled it. But, of course, it didn't.

CHAPTER

✳ 11 ✳

No Girls in Our Gang

AMELIA APPROACHED the long lines at the post office with slow steps. The sight of so many men—all strangers—made her heart race. Estelle had given her a job to do, but she'd also warned her to stay close. She was about to turn back when a gust of wind snaked down the street and a flash of maroon cloth billowed up ahead. She'd seen that skirt before! Amelia hurried along the line and set a hand on the woman's arm. "Mrs. Baker—I mean, Rosanna?"

Rosanna turned and squinted at her. "Oh, the newspaper girl! I didn't recognize you in a bonnet. How's that egg on your head?"

"Excuse me," said the man behind them. "You can't just barge into the line. We've been in this string for hours."

"She's with me." Rosanna Baker slipped her arm through Amelia's.

Amelia smiled up at her rescuer. Rosanna's eyes twinkled with mischief and she seemed young to be married. Where was Mr. Baker? Amelia was too shy to ask.

"When will they open the doors?"

"Soon, I hope," Rosanna said. "Some men have been waiting since dawn; a few even came yesterday evening. The mail was on yesterday's steamer."

"That was our ship, the *Unicorn*. How do you find your mail?"

"My name starts with *B*," Rosanna said, "so I'm in the *A* to *E* string. When you reach the counter, you call out your name, and the man looks in his box to see if you have a letter."

"My surname starts with an *F*, so I belong in the next string." Amelia thought of something. "I wonder if we carried letters to us on our own boat?"

"How could that be?" Rosanna asked.

"Our first ship ran aground in Acapulco. We lost almost a week, waiting for another vessel. If Gran wrote as soon as we left, maybe her letters caught up to us."

"Your ship ran aground? How scary. Did you lose passengers?"

"Not one. But we had to abandon the ship." She shifted the strap of Estelle's bag to her other shoulder. Her papers were getting heavy. Amelia spoke softly. "I want to sell these papers—but I'm scared they'll mob me. Some men got into a muss over my papers last night."

Rosanna raised her eyebrows. "I'll protect you. Let's try something." She pointed to Amelia's bag and said, in a bright, clear voice, "Newspapers from Boston? How wonderful! I haven't heard news from home in months."

Sure enough, the man behind them lowered his book. "Eastern papers?" he asked.

Amelia bent to untie Estelle's bag. "I have the *Semi-Weekly Advertiser*. Look, they had a fire in Cambridgeport."

The man shut his book and reached for the paper. "How much?"

"A dollar," Amelia said. The man dug out a mix of coins, and she stowed them in her bag.

"Save one for me," a man demanded from the next line. The papers disappeared as fast as she could hand them out. Amelia's heart raced. How silly, to pay dearly for old news and advertisements for things they could never buy in California! Within minutes, she'd sold all five papers, including the *Daily Advertiser*. In spite of its date—December 11—the man who bought it paid two dollars. "Listen to this!" he called out, pointing to an inside story. "'A new mail route from Mexico to California will save thousands of miles.' Think of that. No more standing in line all night." Men shoved close to read over his shoulder.

Amelia grinned and slipped back in line next to Rosanna Baker. The money had come in so fast, she couldn't keep track—but she must have earned at least six dollars.

"Aren't you a clever saleswoman?" Rosanna said. "Why don't you work for me? You could help me sell my goat's-milk cheese."

"I love goats," Amelia said. "But I have to help my mother and Estelle with their store."

"So you'll have a shop, too? What will you sell?"

"Things for sewing: cloth and notions. Mother and Es-telle will design and stitch women's dresses, too."

"Too bad they don't stitch *men's* clothing. Men are des-perate for clean shirts and trousers." Rosanna lowered her voice so the men in line wouldn't hear her. "Believe it or not, some men will buy a new shirt rather than fuss with sending it to Washerwoman's Bay. And the few women here want the latest fashions—though I can't imagine why. Who wants to drag a silk dress through the mud? Still, I'd order a pretty dress if my husband came home with his pockets full of gold. Where will you have your shop?"

"We don't know yet. My uncle made us a little house and Mother shipped it on a clipper a while ago. It was supposed to come soon, but we heard there are bad storms around Cape Horn. We're staying in a tent until it arrives. Then we need land to set it on."

Rosanna's gray eyes grew bright. "Perhaps you could live on the ship with me and my noisy goats—at least, until Mr. Baker comes back from the mines. We're near the Long Wharf; people pass by all day long. We could have a food *and* clothing shop—but look! The line is finally moving."

Sure enough, their line surged forward, carrying them along as if they were in a school of fish. "I'm going to slip into the next string," Amelia said, and wiggled her way into the F to J line. She could hardly breathe in the crush but it was worth it, if they had a letter from Gran or Uncle Paul.

Shouts came from inside the building. Amelia craned her neck. A bearded man hobbled down the steps, brandishing a letter, while another stomped away empty-handed. Rosanna gave her a tiny wave as they bobbed along. No one moved out of her way, even though Rosanna was a lady—and a very pretty one, too, Amelia thought, with her tiny waist, wide smile, and long eyelashes. Manners were different out here.

Amelia was standing on tiptoe to see how close she was to the door, when a boy appeared on the steps, a clutch of letters in his hand. Amelia didn't recognize him at first, until he spotted her and frowned. It was Julius, dressed in a new shirt, with a kerchief tied in a single knot. Julius strode toward her and pointed at a man whose face was hidden behind a Boston paper. "I see you're at it again, *Miss* Forrester," he said.

Amelia ignored him. "You have a lot of mail."

"They're not my letters," Julius said. "Men pay me to take their place in line. I've been here all night, but it pays well."

"Move along, miss," a rough voice urged from behind. Amelia was happy to oblige, but Julius inched along beside her.

"Nico and I don't like you moving into our territory," Julius said.

Having Rosanna Baker nearby made Amelia bold. "Who put you in charge of the city?" she asked.

"No one." He cleared his throat, looking embarrassed. "That's how our gang works. And we're successful." He touched his tie. "I bought this with my earnings yesterday. So find something else to do. No girls in our gang."

"What if a new boy came to town?" Amelia asked. "Would you take him in?"

"It depends. Why, do you know someone?"

"I might." Amelia watched him hurry away with his letters. A scheme was cooking like a slow stew in her head—but she had no intention of sharing it with Julius.

CHAPTER

✳ 12 ✳

A Sign of Death

"MOVE ALONG!" The same man shoved her from behind and nearly knocked her down. "First you cut into the line—now you hold us up with your flirting! That skirt don't give you privileges."

Flirting? Amelia inched forward, too embarrassed to turn around. She was only twelve, too young for such foolishness. She clenched her jaw. Much to her surprise, she had discovered she liked selling newspapers. Julius couldn't stop her, could he? Of course, her supply had run out. She'd have to find another source of papers soon.

After a long wait, Amelia reached a noisy, narrow room where a team of men stood behind a counter. Boxes heaped with letters waited in front of them, and the men in line shouted out their last names when they reached the counter. Voices rang out in other languages at the far end of the room. Amelia scanned the last string. Was that Mr. Wong? His face was half hidden under the brim of his straw hat. He wore a clean, pressed tunic that made Amelia feel ashamed of her dirty dress. "Mr. Wong!" she called.

He turned, gave her a shy smile, and bowed low.

Amelia smiled and bowed back. Perhaps San Francisco wasn't a city of strangers after all.

"You'd best avoid his kind. Those Celestials are nothing but trouble."

Amelia glanced over her shoulder. The man who had shoved her was insulting Mr. Wong—but he looked like trouble himself. His belly was so distended, she was surprised the buttons didn't pop right off his plaid vest, and his scraggly beard and beady eyes matched his mean voice. "Mr. Wong is our friend," she told him.

"Elias Howard!" called the burly man in front of her. The sorter went through the box, his fingers ticking off the letters one by one. No wonder this took forever. But she'd no right to feel impatient. After all, she'd cut into the line. And Mother would be so pleased if she brought home a letter—

But she'd completely forgotten about Estelle, whose last name started with a *D*. Could Rosanna ask for Estelle's letters? Amelia scanned the room, but her friend had disappeared in the crowd.

The fat man jostled her again. "Stop dallying!"

The mail sorter looked up and scowled. "Behave yourself, sir," he said, "or we'll send you to the end of the line." A few men jeered with approval. To Amelia's surprise, her tormenter turned on his heel and stomped out the door without waiting for his mail. Good riddance.

The two men ahead of her came up empty-handed. It was her turn at last. "Forrester," she said.

The mail sorter squinted at her over wire-rimmed glasses. His eyes were kind. "Spell it, please."

She did. As he looked through the letters, he asked, "Are you here alone, miss? It's a rough crowd for a young girl."

"I'm with my friend," Amelia said, although Rosanna was nowhere in sight.

The sorter pulled a cream-colored envelope from the stack. "Here's one for a Mrs. S. Forrester," he said.

"That's my mother!" Amelia recognized Uncle Paul's firm handwriting, marching in its upright way across the paper. Her hands shook as she reached for the envelope.

"Hold on, miss." The sorter held the letter up to the light. "You're in luck—the sender prepaid the postage."

Dear Uncle Paul. He would do that. "Nothing else?" she asked, hoping for a letter from Gran.

"Not today. Off you go—and be careful, miss." The clerk's voice was kind but firm.

Amelia swallowed her disappointment and moved out of the way. She sniffed the envelope, hoping that Uncle Paul's comforting smell of fresh hay, lanolin, and horsehair would cling to the envelope—but the letter smelled dank and musty, like the hold of the *Unicorn*. Should she open it? She was tempted, but the letter was addressed to Mother alone.

Then she noticed something else: Uncle Paul had addressed Mother as *Mrs.* Forrester. Had everyone decided that Mother would be a missus out here? If so, that would make Amelia's life easier. No one would know that she, Mother, and Gran all shared the same surname. She could say her father was dead and be done with it.

She slipped the letter into Estelle's bag, cinched the strings tight, and stood on the top step, scanning the crowd. No sign of Rosanna. Perhaps she'd gone home empty-handed. Why hadn't she said good-bye?

Never mind. Time to visit the *Alta*, then the bakery. Mother and Estelle would be pleased if she brought home fresh biscuits again. Amelia was wiggling through the lines when a woman's shrill scream came from inside the post office. Amelia gasped and pushed her way back through the crowd, ignoring the oaths and protests of the men in line.

"Step aside! Give her room!"

The crowd parted. Rosanna Baker lay crumpled on the floor, her face as white as her lace collar. The hand on her chest clutched a square envelope, edged with black. "Mrs. Baker!" Amelia cried, and sank to her knees beside her new friend. She patted her cheeks. "Rosanna, wake up."

"She's had a shock, miss." The clerk from Amelia's line suddenly appeared beside her. He pointed to the letter in Rosanna's hand. "That black rim is a sign of death. Loosen her collar, will you? Better you should do it than me."

Amelia untied the narrow ribbon at Rosanna's throat and fanned her face with her apron. "Rosanna. Mrs. Baker?" she said softly.

Her friend's eyes fluttered open and she looked around, dazed. "What happened?"

"You fainted," Amelia said.

"Let us help you up, ma'am," said the clerk. He took one arm, Amelia held the other, and they lifted Rosanna to her feet. She leaned on them and steadied herself. "I'm all right now," she said, but her voice shook, and Amelia kept a tight hold on her arm. Rosanna shoved the letter into her apron pocket.

"I'll walk you home," Amelia said.

The crowd pulled back as they headed for the door—*as if we carry Panama fever*, Amelia thought. Once they were outside, Rosanna pulled away. "I'd best open this on my own. Come see me tomorrow." She started down the hill, her back ramrod straight, without saying another word.

"But wait!" Amelia cried. "I don't know where you live."

"Go past the Long Wharf and listen for the goats," Rosanna called over her shoulder.

Amelia watched until Rosanna disappeared below the brow of the hill. Had she become a widow, or had someone died back in Charlestown? Thank goodness Uncle Paul's letter had no black rim.

CHAPTER

✳ 13 ✳

Little Pitchers

AMELIA CROSSED the square to the *Alta California* and found the editor picking letters from the trays and placing them inside a metal frame. Amelia waited until he looked up. He squinted at her and sighed. "The girl who wants to write," he said. "Not today. I'm a busy man."

Amelia pulled the letter from her pocket and set it on the window ledge in front of him. The editor groaned. "Didn't I tell you, we don't take stories written by little girls?"

"Please, sir. It's about our shipwreck," Amelia said.

The editor scanned her letter quickly. "Not a bad description of the Isthmus crossing," he said. "But the wreck is old news. We posted a news item about that accident days ago." He waved his hand to dismiss her.

She pointed to her last sentence. "Did *your* story tell about the captain falling asleep at the wheel?" she asked.

He tossed the letter aside. "Why would I believe slander from a child? Run along before I throw you out." He waved her away and slammed the door shut behind her.

Amelia's eyes smarted as she hurried to the bakery. What

did *slander* mean? She'd wasted all that time, copying her messy letter. Now her dream was nothing but a wild goose chase. Even worse, as she stood in line to buy her biscuits, she realized she'd left her letter to Uncle Paul behind.

Amelia was out of breath when she finally reached the tent, and bright sunshine lit the canvas with a soft, buttery glow.

"Amelia!" Mother's eyes flashed and she gripped Amelia's arm when she ducked inside. "Where have you been? You *must* not wander off alone. Mrs. Liazos says the city is no place for a young girl."

"That's because she doesn't want me to sell papers!" Amelia cried.

Estelle put her arm around Mother. "Sophie, don't be angry. It's my fault. I sent her out to sell the papers from my trunk." But her face was pinched with worry. "Amelia, I thought you'd stay close."

"I didn't go far. And no one bothered me." Well, almost no one. There was that annoying man in line. And Julius. Never mind. Amelia handed her a sack full of tea biscuits. "Here's some breakfast—or lunch. And I have another surprise." She rummaged in Estelle's bag for the letter. "I stood in line at the post office while they gave out the mail. This letter might have been on our very own ship, or on a boat from a few days ago." She set the envelope on the trunk.

"But how—" Mother picked it up with trembling hands.

"Amelia, you're going to turn my hair white overnight." She slid a fingernail beneath Uncle Paul's seal.

"I'm sorry, Estelle," Amelia said. "I couldn't stand in the line for your name—but I brought you something else." She dug into the bag.

"Fresh fruit?" Estelle asked with a smile.

"Not this time." Amelia's fingers felt about in the bag and came up with a silver dollar. "From your newspapers," she said, "and there's more." She set the coin on the quilt and was about to dump out the bag for the rest of the money when Mother sucked in her breath.

"Sophie, what's wrong?" Estelle stood up quickly and leaned over Mother's shoulder. "Is someone ill?"

Amelia's mouth felt dry. "What does Uncle Paul say?"

Mother didn't answer. She kept reading, her lips moving slightly as she turned the page. The tent was silent. Amelia thought of the dark warning on Rosanna's envelope.

Mother folded the letter and slipped it back into the envelope. Her lips pursed into a straight line. "It's nothing," she said. "Uncle Paul—" She cleared her throat. "He and Gran hear about shipwrecks and storms. They wonder if we made it safely, and if our little house has arrived." Mother glanced at Amelia. "He sends you his love and hopes you'll tell him what you see with your spyglass."

"I wrote him from Panama. And he can send me his love himself." Amelia reached for the letter but Mother shook her head. What was she hiding? Amelia's brain buzzed with scrambled thoughts. "Did someone die?"

"Of course not. Why do you ask?"

"My friend Rosanna Baker's letter had a black border." Amelia shivered as she remembered the terrible scream. "She fainted."

"How terrible—that's the sign of death." Mother frowned. "Your *friend*? Who is she?"

"Rosanna—Baker. She helped me—" Amelia stopped. She didn't want Mother to know about Nico's attack. "She showed me where to buy the teacakes yesterday. I met her again this morning at the post office. I helped her after she fainted, but she went home alone."

Estelle touched Amelia's hand. "Only twenty-four hours in a strange town, and you've already made a friend."

"I hope so," Amelia said. "And Rosanna—Mrs. Baker— said you should make clothes for men as well as women. She has her own shop. She said we could sell our goods there until our house comes. "

Estelle clapped her hands. "Amelia, you're a genius!"

"Not really. Anyway, there is one thing you might *not* like. She lives on a ship."

Estelle groaned. "Never again."

"Her ship must be close to shore," Amelia said, "because she has goats and fresh milk."

"That sounds promising." Mother pulled Amelia into a

quick hug. "I'm sorry I was angry," she said. "But please, no more frights." She bent over their bolts of fabric. "Most of our cloth is for women's dresses. Still, making shirts for men is a good idea. We talked about that last night." She picked up her bonnet, tied it under her chin, and opened the tent flap. Sunshine poured into their dingy quarters. "It's like a summer day—so warm for March! Let's eat our biscuits and walk to this woman's shop. Could you find it?"

"Maybe. She said it's near Long Wharf—and that her goats are noisy."

Mother hesitated. "She may not want company after a loss." She glanced at Estelle. "What do you think—is it wrong to intrude?"

Amelia thought of Rosanna's stricken face. "We should help her," Amelia said. "Her husband is away. She said she needed a friend."

"I'll watch our things." Estelle set the silver dollar in Amelia's palm. "Keep this with you in case you do see any fruit. My appetite has finally returned."

Amelia dropped the coin into the bag and peered outside. On this clear day, the Long Wharf would be easy to find. She turned around in time to see Mother tuck Uncle Paul's letter into Estelle's hand.

"Read this while we're gone," Mother told Estelle softly. "Don't let it worry you."

"Is something wrong with Gran?" Amelia asked.

"They're both fine, just lonesome for us. Little pitchers have big ears," Mother said.

Amelia hoisted Estelle's bag, grabbed a biscuit, and ducked outside to eat it, her cheeks burning. It wasn't fair. She wasn't "little"! Hadn't she made them six dollars this morning, while Mother and Estelle had nothing but empty pockets?

CHAPTER

✳ 14 ✳

Telegraph Hill

MOTHER EMERGED from the tent, took Amelia's arm and pulled her over on the rickety sidewalk. "Look," she said. "Isn't it beautiful?"

Sunshine dimpled the bay and a stiff breeze sent clouds skimming above the hills on the far side of the harbor. Small boats heeled before the wind, and the flocks of gulls were as thick as clouds overhead. Mother cupped her hand under Amelia's chin. "I know you're used to running loose, especially at Uncle Paul's, but we have to be careful here." She pointed to the next hill, where the strange signal tower stood. "There must be a nice view from the top."

Amelia remembered her idea. She patted the spyglass in her deep apron pocket. "Let's climb it and see."

To her surprise, Mother's face lit up. "Yes, let's. Estelle will be fine for a while. Perhaps I can show you something."

"What?" Amelia asked.

"You're not the only one with surprises up her sleeve." Mother took Amelia's hand and they hurried down a planked street like schoolgirls, dipping into the col between the two hills before they started up again, lifting their skirts. "Down one hill and up the next," Mother sang out. Men tipped their hats as they passed, and Mother gave them polite nods in return. The path wound its way through scrubby bushes. Mourning doves beat their wings, startled, as they rushed by. The earth smelled of crushed mint under their boots.

They were both panting when they reached the summit, where the wind tugged at their skirts and hummed through the tall grass. Amelia led the way to the wooden tower, which looked like a windmill with its long arms. The man who appeared from the small shack was well dressed in a suit and waistcoat. His cheeks were ruddy, with lacy veins showing through. "Two gentlewomen! What a surprise." He swept off his cap, revealing a balding forehead, and bowed. "Welcome to Telegraph Hill," he said. "I'm Mr. Abbott."

"What a wonderful view," Mother said.

Amelia gazed out over her new world. To the north, green hills glowed through the mist. The high bluffs that Commander Everett called "the Golden Gate" were visible in the west. The city itself was laid out below, its shacks, tents, and brick buildings climbing up and down the lumpy hills. The air up here was fresh and moist. Amelia turned. Mr. Abbott was showing Mother his telescope, set up inside the small shed.

"I watch for the ships as they come in." He pointed to the flagpole. "When I see a ship's colors, I run up the flag for that country, so everyone knows where she hails from."

Amelia drew closer. "When our ship arrived, we saw boys waving flags."

"Ah, the newsboys." The man tugged his mustache. "You must have been on the mail boat. The boys use their flags to tell the city they'll have newspapers soon. Julius and his gang have learned to read my signals."

So she was right: if she wanted to sell papers, she'd have to keep track of the ships herself and then run to the docks. But Mother had said *no more frights*. She needed a plan— especially since the editor had turned her down.

Amelia pulled out her spyglass. At first, the bay was fuzzy, like a dream you can't remember when you wake, but slowly, as she twisted the lens, a small circle sharpened in front of her. Ships of all shapes and sizes plied the narrows between the harbor and the rocky shoreline to the east.

The bay seemed so close, through the spyglass, that she felt she could touch each wave smashing on the cliffs of the Golden Gate. She could see the foam shining on the rocks when the waves receded, and the twin masts of a small ship, headed toward the Pacific. She could even make out a sailor hoisting the sails and a gentleman in the stern, waving his cap at the city he was leaving behind.

The man leaned over her shoulder. "May I see your tele-scope?" he asked.

Amelia set the spyglass in his hand, though she hated to give it up. He rolled it on his palm, pressed it to his eye for a moment, then carefully closed it. "A beauty," he said, giving it back. "It's an English model; quite a treasure for a young girl."

"My uncle gave it to me," Amelia said.

Mother stepped up to the big telescope. "Can you see Happy Valley from here?" she asked.

"Of course—let me focus for you." Mr. Abbott spun his telescope so that it pointed away from the harbor. "Lots of New England folk have settled there."

"So I hear." Mother peered through the lens. "Amelia, look; it's spring! There are flowers on the hillsides."

Amelia stood on tiptoe, but she wasn't quite tall enough to reach the eyepiece. The man pulled over a block of wood and Amelia stepped up. She tried to find the flowers, but the lens only showed her rows of tents and makeshift houses, with a pair of carpenters balanced on a roof. "What is Happy Valley?" she asked.

"The place where I might buy a plot of land for our little house—if we can afford it. Land prices are so dear," Mother said. "What do you think, Amelia? It seems like a lucky name."

"I guess," Amelia said. But really, the valley looked like the rest of the city: disorganized and half-built. She swiveled the scope around and aimed it at the warehouses and shops lining the long wharf until she found what she was looking for: two animals on a grassy hillside next to an oddly shaped building. Were they goats—or just big dogs?

Suddenly, one of the animals leaped up onto a big rock.

"I see the goats!" Amelia said, keeping her eye trained on the wharf. She pointed. "Mrs. Baker's ship is right . . . down . . . there."

Mother smiled at Mr. Abbott. "Thank you for your kindness."

He tipped his hat. "Anytime." He pointed to the back side of the hill. "Stay away from the Barbary Coast—full of unsavory folks. Not safe for ladies like yourselves." He smiled at Amelia. "Come see me again. Children are as scarce as a day without wind."

They waved and lifted their skirts above the tall grass as they descended the hill. "What a friendly man," Mother said. "We've had nothing but kindness since we arrived."

Amelia nodded, though the lump on the back of her head, still smarting beneath her bonnet, told a different story.

CHAPTER

✳ 15 ✳

Goats in the Chaparral

AS THEY neared the street where Amelia had spotted the goats, two men staggered past, smelling of liquor. Mother shuddered and pulled Amelia close. "I don't like the looks of this place," she said. Just up the street stood the stern hull of a ship, its rudder facing them. A tall building sat on the ship's deck, and an American flag flew above a sign that read, NIANTIC HOTEL. The next shop, Boggs Liquor Store, was tucked up against a saloon. "I can't believe a woman would live here by herself," Mother said. "And what brought these ships onto dry land?"

At that moment, two sad bleats sounded nearby. Amelia laughed. "There they are!" They followed the blatting noises down the street to the hull of another ship. The holes that had once held the ship's anchor lines looked like droopy eyes on a sad face. A tall ladder rose from the street—where the ship's keel sat—to the deck high above. Amelia stepped back from the hull and craned her neck. She'd never realized how much of a ship was underwater. She was seeing it as a fish might, from deep within the sea.

She walked around the side and peered up again. White bed linens, pinned to what was once the ship's rigging, flapped in the breeze, and a small sign read, FRESH GOAT'S MILK AND SUNDRIES.

"This must be it. What are sundries?" Amelia asked.

"Various bits of things." Mother beckoned to Amelia from the foot of the ladder. "You first."

Amelia started up but stopped on the third rung. The street was full of men—as usual. "They'll see right up my skirt."

"Pretend you're at Uncle Paul's, climbing into the hay-loft. I'll be right behind you."

Amelia gritted her teeth. If only she could wear Estelle's Turkish trousers! She climbed as fast as she could, but her boots caught her hem on every rung. How did Rosanna Baker manage? Mother also glanced down as she climbed, and shook her head when she stepped out onto the deck. "I hope this isn't a wild-goose chase. What now?"

A little house sat on the ship's deck, leaning against the mast. The house had a low door, painted bright blue, which opened before they could knock. Rosanna Baker stepped out, carrying a pail. She had changed into a dark dress, and her head was uncovered, showing her tangled hair. She stared at them, dazed, her face streaked with tears. "The shop is closed," she said, and then dropped the empty pail with a clatter. "Oh, Amelia. I didn't recognize you." Her chin quivered.

Mother's skirts swished as she hurried across the deck. She clasped Mrs. Baker's hands in her own. "Excuse us for dropping in without warning. I'm Sophie Forrester, Amelia's mother. She told me that you fainted at the post office. May we help you?"

"I'm not sure." Rosanna Baker sank onto a crude bench and twisted her hands in her apron. Mother sat down beside her. "I've had quite a shock," Rosanna said. "My brother—" She swallowed hard. "My younger brother Stanley has died in the diggings." Rosanna tucked her head against Mother's shoulder and burst into loud, angry sobs. Amelia turned away. She'd been sad when they'd left Gran and Uncle Paul, but Rosanna's sorrow was different.

When her crying softened, Mother asked, "What happened?"

"Otis, my husband, said in his letter that Stanley had— an accident. Otis doesn't think he can manage their claim alone." Rosanna wiped her face with the hem of her skirt. "I'm making a scene, and you don't even know me," she said.

Mother stroked Rosanna's hand. "It's all right," she said. "Go on."

"Otis and Stanley went to the diggings first, after we arrived. I wanted to go with them, but Otis sent word that the mines are too rough for women." Rosanna wiped her eyes and nose with her apron. "The city isn't much better. That's why I bought the goats—they're my friends and watchdogs."

As if they could hear her, the goats began to bleat from the hillside behind them. Rosanna tried to smile. "My girls want attention."

"May I see them?" Amelia asked.

"Of course." Rosanna wiped her eyes. "Come, I'll show you." She led Amelia to the stern, where a narrow gang-plank bridged the gap between the ship's deck and the hill behind it. Two goats—one white, the other charcoal gray—perched on a rock in the brush. Each was tethered to an iron post. When they spotted Rosanna, they set up a chorus of bleats and lunged to the end of their ropes, nearly choking themselves. They looked so foolish and pathetic that Amelia didn't know whether to laugh or cry. "Are they hungry?" she asked.

"Yes," Rosanna said. "We've had a dry winter, so there's not much for them to eat in the chaparral. Imagine, I've had to buy hay shipped all the way from New York State. They make such a racket, no one would dare steal them." Rosanna turned to Mother, her face drawn. "I don't know what to do now."

Mother wrapped one arm around her shoulders. "What does your husband say?"

"He'll try to sell their claim, but he needs my help in the diggings, to settle things. I can't leave the store untended.

And my poor goats . . ." Rosanna turned to Amelia. "Remember this morning, I said we should join forces? Could you stay here while I'm gone?"

Amelia and Mother shared a quick look. "I'll feed the goats," Amelia said, "if Mother can milk them."

"So you know how?" Rosanna asked.

"I had plenty of practice, growing up on a farm," Mother said.

Rosanna wiped her eyes. "We've only just met—perhaps you have other plans. I might be gone a few weeks."

"We're living in a leaky tent right now," Mother said. "To tell the truth, I'm not sure how we'll buy the land for our house if we have to pay rent until it arrives." She glanced at Rosanna's cottage. "There are three of us, with all our goods—"

"Don't worry," Rosanna said. "*You* need a place to stay, and *I* need to join my husband. It's a perfect fit. The store isn't much, but it's dry and safe. I'll show you."

The goats bleated in unison. Mother laughed. "Amelia, go talk to those poor creatures," she said. "See if you can cheer them up."

"Yes, do. The white goat is Daisy," Rosanna said. "The gray one is Charcoal—Charrie, for short."

Amelia took a step out onto the plank. It was high above the street, and she didn't dare look down. When the goats saw her, the white one lunged and wrapped its rope around the feet of the gray one. Amelia forgot her fear and tripped across the plank to untangle them. "Silly beasts."

The goats pulled and pranced as she freed Charrie and retied her to the stake with some half hitches. The goats butted her chest, snuffling and rubbing their noses against her cloak. Amelia stroked one, then the other, scratching them behind their ears. Their fur was bristly yet smooth. The goats nibbled her hands, looking for food. Amelia knelt on the ground and pulled them close, peering into their golden, almond-shaped eyes. She traced the white stripe on Charrie's nose. "Hello, Charrie. Hello, Daisy," she said. "You'll be my friends, won't you?"

They answered with soft bleats and then leaped onto the rock, their hooves slipping and sliding as they pushed and butted each other, each one wanting the top spot on the boulder. It was rude to laugh while Rosanna was so sad— but Amelia couldn't help it. "You goats are just too foolish," she said. Three new friends in one day!

CHAPTER

✦ 16 ✦

Robbed!

AMELIA FOUND Mother and Rosanna sitting at a table inside, chatting in low voices. Rosanna waved her hand around the room. "Welcome," she said. "It's not much, as you can see. Your mother and I were just planning how we'd set things up."

Rosanna's home and shop were in one long room that was bigger than Amelia had imagined. Sunlight shone through the windows onto a scrubbed planked floor. The shelves on one side of the room were nearly empty, except for a bowl of apples, a basket of brown eggs, and some tins labeled "Wedding Cake." Rosanna's bed was tucked in the corner.

"As you can see, I have plenty of room for your goods," Rosanna said.

The white envelope, with its menacing black rim, lay on a bare table. Amelia's stomach growled. Her tea biscuit had disappeared ages ago, and Estelle longed for fresh fruit. Would it be rude to ask the price of the apples?

Mother was telling Mrs. Baker about their plans. "My friend Estelle and I brought bolts of cloth, needles, and thread, and we've designed the dresses we plan to make—but I've seen hardly any women."

"They're here; some live on the abandoned ships in the harbor," Rosanna said. "Men would come in droves if you could stitch some shirts and trousers. Are you a good seamstress?"

Mother smoothed her wrinkled calico. "You'd never know it from the way we're dressed, but in Boston, I made some fairly nice gowns—we have a few in our crate, in the *Unicorn*'s hold."

"Their dresses are beautiful," Amelia said. "Estelle makes the patterns and Mother stitches them."

Mother raised her eyebrows. "Rare praise from my daughter."

Rosanna went to the corner, moving as if she were half-asleep, and held up a pair of trousers. "These are too small. More—" Her voice shook. "More my brother's size than that of most men. Stanley was only seventeen; he hadn't reached his full height. Perhaps you could use them as a pattern. We thought the Celestials might want them, as they tend to be short—but they're clever; they make their own things. Of course, you'd need some sturdy cloth."

Rosanna set the pants on the counter. Amelia scooped up the trousers and held them to her waist. "They'd fit me," she said. "What do they cost?"

Rosanna forced a smile. "Don't tell me you're thinking of wearing trousers!"

"Amelia, be sensible," Mother said. "You can't dress like a boy."

Amelia opened her cape and raised her arms. "My dress is too small. Look how short the sleeves are—and my hem is torn. Estelle wore pantaloons under her skirt in Panama. Remember?"

"How could I forget?" Mother winked at Rosanna. "My friend Estelle gets carried away sometimes. Of course, we both want things to be different for women; that's why we're here." She lowered her voice, as if sharing a secret. "In Boston, we heard women speak about our right to vote."

"I went to those meetings myself." Rosanna clasped Mother's hands. "I knew we would be friends. And it *is* wretched, keeping our skirts out of the mud. Look at me; I've cut off my dress above the ankle. But Amelia—I saw a woman in blowzy pants the other day, and a crowd of men hooted at her. You don't want to draw attention to yourself."

Amelia wanted to say that just being a *girl* drew attention, but she held her tongue. "I'd still like to buy the trousers, and some apples for Estelle. I can pay you." She rummaged in Estelle's bag.

"Amelia, stop this nonsense," Mother said. "We need every penny you earn until the shop is set up. I'll stitch you a new dress as soon as we get our crate from the *Unicorn*."

"But I could sell more papers if I wore trousers." Amelia was too worried to explain. She shook the bag and listened for the *chink-chink* of coins. Nothing. Her heart raced. Estelle had returned one silver dollar so she could buy her some fruit; where was the rest? Amelia dumped the contents of the bag onto the counter. The lonely dollar fell out, along with a crumpled handkerchief and some hairpins. *Why* hadn't she put her money in her hidden apron pocket? She stared at Rosanna. "I sold five newspapers for six dollars—remember?"

"Of course," Rosanna said. "But how—"

"I've been robbed!" Amelia cried. "Julius."

"Who's Julius? Amelia, what's come over you?" Mother asked.

Amelia clutched Mother's sleeve. "I'll be back at the tent in an hour. I promise." Before Mother could stop her, she dashed out the door, clambered down the ladder, and forced herself up the hill, ignoring Mother's calls from the ship's deck. Those boys couldn't get away with this.

CHAPTER

17

Captain's Quarters

WHERE COULD Julius be? Amelia had rushed along the street and was halfway to the Plaza before she stopped dead. What was she thinking? Julius could live anywhere. The hills of the city marched away in every direction, each a warren of houses, shops, tents, sheds, and shacks. She'd never find him, even with her spyglass.

One of Uncle Paul's sayings rang in her head: *Think first, act later.*

She'd done the opposite. Now what?

Amelia waited until she caught her breath. Nico would know how to find Julius. She hated to ask him for anything, but what choice did she have? She headed for the restaurant tent, half hoping he wouldn't be there.

But when she lifted the tent flap, she found Nico curled up in a chair, asleep with his mouth open. His black hair fell over his eyes and he looked like a young boy—until she cleared her throat to wake him. He sat up quickly, and his mouth took on its familiar sneer. "Well, if it isn't *Miss*

Forrester." He stood and pulled on his cap, facing her with a swagger. "Ma's not here. No handouts today."

It was hard not to stare at his mismatched eyes, now that she was up close. Amelia spoke through gritted teeth, determined to be polite. "I'm not looking for your mother. And I'm not a beggar. I need to talk to Julius."

"Do you now? Haven't seen him. Taken a shine to him?"

"Don't be foolish." Amelia was tempted to leave, until she remembered her missing money. "He has—" She hesitated. Nico wouldn't like it if she called Julius a thief. "He has something I need."

Nico's right eyebrow lifted. "And what might that be?"

"None of your business." Amelia turned on her heel, ducked under the flap, and glanced at the sun. The shadows seemed longer. Had she been gone an hour yet? If only she had a watch like Patrick's. She sighed and headed for their tent, feeling stupid. If Julius *had* stolen her money, he must have spent it by now.

Heavy boots thumped on the wooden planking and Nico caught up to her. "Julius lives in the other direction. I'll take you there, for a price."

Amelia held out her bag. "I haven't a cent. Look inside, if you don't believe me."

"I'll take one of your Boston newspapers."

"I sold them all." She pushed past him. "Never mind—I don't care about Julius."

Nico's laugh sounded more like a bark. "You could have fooled me. But I'll show you his quarters. Nothing better to do." Nico took off down a rutted street.

Amelia hesitated. Should she trust him? After all, he'd nearly knocked her senseless yesterday. Still, her missing money could buy eggs for their supper, or tinned peaches for Estelle; even hay for the goats. So she lifted her skirts and hurried after him.

Two blocks down, Nico turned right and led her into an alley. Angry shouts sounded from an open doorway. Amelia almost turned around, when she realized they were behind the post office. At least she knew her way to the tent from here. The hem of her skirt caught on something, and she heard the rip of fabric as she hoisted it higher. All the more reason to find her money.

When she caught up to Nico, he pointed to a row of brick and frame houses across the street. "Someday, when my pa comes back from Jackass Hill, we'll be rich as Croesus. Ma says we'll buy a brick house that will never burn down."

Even Nico had a father. As if he'd read her mind, he raised an eyebrow and asked, "Where's *your* pa, then?"

"Dead," Amelia told him, because that was the easiest thing to say. "He died before I was born." Not exactly the truth, but Mother always said, "He's gone, so he's dead to me." Which wasn't the same thing. And it didn't answer the question of who he was, or why he'd left. But that was none of Nico's business. "So, where is Julius?" she asked.

"Right here." He waved at the stern end of a ship's deck. "How do you like it?"

Amelia stared. The building in front of her looked exactly like the poop deck on the *Unicorn*, where Commander Everett had slept, complete with the little cabin, the wheel, a railing, and a flagpole. A light glowed from inside, and a blue flag with a bear walking across it snapped from the railing. "Julius lives *here*?"

Nico didn't answer. He tapped out a complicated rhythm on the round porthole. The window swung open and Julius peered out. His head was bare and his red-brown curls fell across his forehead. He frowned at Amelia.

"What are *you* doing here?" he demanded.

"I need to talk to you," Amelia said.

"I'm listening," said Julius.

"Could I come in?" Amelia asked. She couldn't accuse him of thievery here on the street. Besides, she was dying to see his "quarters," as Nico called them.

"All right." Julius glanced up and down the street. "But make it quick—and don't let anyone see you."

Amelia swallowed a laugh. Was she *that* dangerous? She followed Nico inside.

CHAPTER

✳ 18 ✳

The Bargain

JULIUS'S HOME was so intriguing that Amelia almost forgot about her missing money. She'd been in Commander Everett's quarters once, on board the *Unicorn*, and the room Julius led them through was almost an exact replica of the captain's stateroom. The narrow bunk, with low sides to keep you from falling out in rough seas, was fitted with a red wool blanket, its corners tucked in so tight that even Gran would approve. A round metal looking glass hung on the wall above a china washbasin, and a compass on a chain dangled over the bed. Best of all, three books sat on the tiny shelf nearby.

Books. How long since she'd read a story? The few books they had brought were sitting in their crate, in the hold of the *Unicorn*. Amelia stepped closer to read the titles on their spines. "Shakespeare," she whispered, in awe. She drew back when she noticed the pocketknife lying open on the shelf. The blade gleamed as if it had just been sharpened, and the round wooden handle was the same color as her spyglass.

"Leave that alone." Julius beckoned her into another

spotless chamber that must have been the officer's mess. The low table had a lip around its sides, and narrow partitions to keep the plates from sliding. Pewter mugs sat on the shelf, kept in place by a thin railing. A camphene lantern, hanging on a chain, sent a warm glow around the room. A *home*, Amelia thought. Would their little house ever come? When it did—would it feel this cozy?

"Well?" Julius said. "Don't gape. I haven't got all night."

Amelia startled. She'd forgotten her errand. She glanced from one boy to the other. Nico sat astride a bench, giving her an odd look—almost as if his brown eye laughed at her, while the green one regarded her with scorn. Julius stood waiting, his arms crossed. If she accused Julius of stealing, then Nico would know she'd been selling papers again. But if not—

She took a deep breath. "Remember this morning, when I saw you at the post office?"

"Of course. You were selling papers."

"Didn't I warn you!" Nico said.

Julius sent him a sharp look. "Let her finish."

"I sold five papers for six dollars." She held up Estelle's bag. "Someone must have slipped the knot. I have just one dollar left."

"You probably didn't tie it tight," Nico said.

"But I did. I learned my knots on the *Unicorn*."

Julius's copper eyes narrowed. "Are you saying I'm a thief?" he asked.

"You were right next to me," Amelia said, her heart at a gallop. "You knew I'd sold the papers."

"I do *not* steal," Julius said. His words were ice. "I might borrow things that aren't mine—" He waved his arms around the small chamber. "A captain's quarters, for instance, sitting empty beside the street—but if the owner comes back, I'll be gone in a trice, the place so clean he'll never know I was here. But I am not a thief. My parents taught me well." His voice caught. "May they rest in peace."

Amelia flinched. "I'm sorry," she said. "I didn't know—"

"You don't know anything about me," Julius said. A muscle twitched along his jaw. "You've got a family; you have no idea what it's like to live on your own. And don't go blabbing this around. You think I want to end up at the Orphan Asylum?"

"Of course not." Wherever it was, Amelia knew the Asylum must be terrible. Even though she didn't have a father, she had Mother and Estelle. She couldn't imagine surviving here without them. Julius suddenly seemed much older than fourteen.

Nico's fingers drummed an uneven rhythm on the table. "Find what you wanted?" he asked her.

Amelia pulled her cloak tight around her. "I'd better go."

"Wait." Julius held up his hand. "I can guess who took your money. Remember the fat man behind you?"

"With the plaid vest? He kept shoving me."

"That's the one. Fancies himself a fine dresser, but it's all stolen goods, or money won playing faro in the gambling saloons. He's got quick fingers. He'd pick your bag or your apron pocket and you'd never notice. He's probably spent it on liquor by now."

Amelia felt like a fool. "What if we make a bargain," she said, before she'd even thought it through.

Julius's mouth twitched. "What would you have in mind?"

"Don't laugh. I think we should work together."

Nico jumped to his feet, nearly knocking over the bench. "You'd sell papers with *us*? What are you going on about? Are you daft?"

Julius placed his palm on Nico's chest, as if he were a horse that needed soothing. "Hold on. She sold five papers in as many minutes," he said. "Maybe we could use her."

"She had fresh papers, more recent than ours. Besides, she's a *girl*," Nico said, pulling away. "In case you hadn't noticed."

"Oh, I have," Julius said in a dry voice. "Don't worry."

"But Jules—think about it," Nico said. "How does someone in a dress climb over railings onto the deck? How can she run to the ship when we send the signal? She walks like a girl, talks like a girl—she *is* a girl! It makes no sense. Our gang will never accept her."

"Good point," Julius said.

Amelia cleared her throat. "Excuse me!" They talked about her as if she weren't even there. "I have something that you need."

"Do you now?" Nico asked.

Amelia reached into the deep pocket of her apron and pulled out the spyglass. "I could watch for ships from Telegraph Hill."

Julius nodded. "That might work."

"Mr. Abbott does that already!" Nico was sounding desperate.

"When he shows up." Julius raised an eyebrow at Amelia. "Mr. Abbott has been known to stay too late at the card tables—and then he misses the early boats. If the mailboat arrives at dawn and Mr. Abbott's not at his post, we don't know a ship is in port until she's at the dock."

"So I could wait on the hill with my spyglass—"

"Jules!" Nico interrupted, nearly sputtering. "You can't mean to let a girl into our gang—they'll laugh us out of town."

"What's funny about being a girl?" Amelia demanded.

Nico socked the table. The cups and plates danced. "You really *are* daft, aren't you?"

Julius whispered to Nico, who shook his head. "It won't work! If she's in, I'm out."

Amelia held her breath. Julius didn't speak and Nico's neck reddened above his tight collar. "Suit yourself." Nico spat on the polished floor at Amelia's feet and pushed past her. "Find your own way home." He ducked under the low doorframe and disappeared.

"I'm sorry," Amelia said. When Julius didn't answer, she asked, "What if I didn't look like a girl?"

"And how would you do that?"

"I'll show you." Amelia ducked into the stateroom, pulled off her bonnet and snatched the pocketknife from the shelf. "Wait!" Julius cried, but too late. She clutched her braid and drew the knife once, twice, three times across her hair, as if she were sawing through a thick rope. The knife was sharp and quick. Hanks of thick chestnut hair clung to her cloak and slid to the floor.

"Nico's right—you *are* mad!" Julius stood in the doorway, staring. Amelia waved the knife at him. "Don't move!" She laughed; Julius almost looked afraid. She stepped in front of the mirror. Her hair was a shaggy mess: half the braid was gone while the rest dangled from her head. She raised the knife, sliced through the plait close to her scalp, and just missed cutting her neck. Her hair slipped to the floor and, for a moment, it almost seemed alive. She dropped the knife with a clatter.

"Well?" Amelia cleared her throat. "Do I look like a boy now?"

Julius rolled his eyes. "Not exactly."

Amelia stood on tiptoe. Her reflection rippled in the metal. She might not pass for a boy—but the person in the mirror was *not* Amelia. Her eyes were huge in her white face, her hair poked out every which way, and her neck was scrawny as a chicken's. What had she done?

CHAPTER

✳ 19 ✳

A Visit from Mr. Y

"YOU'RE IN a sorry mess," Julius said.

"I know." What would Mother say? Surely she'd be punished. Amelia tried to scoop up her hair with her hands—as if she could put it back and start over—but it was slippery as fresh-cut hay. "Do you have a broom?"

Julius opened a cupboard under the bed and handed her a tiny whiskbroom and a dustpan. She swept the hair into a pile while Julius swabbed Nico's spit.

"Toss it here," Julius said. He held out a rumpled sheet of newspaper.

Amelia dumped her hair onto the paper and wrapped it up quickly. Too late for regrets. "You're not selling this newspaper?" Amelia asked.

"No. It's an *Alta* from last month." He laughed. "News from the city must be fresh, while news from the east can be stale as old bread." He cocked his head to the side, squinting at her. "If you want to work with us, you'll have to dress like a boy—and behave like one, too."

Amelia held her breath as Julius opened a cupboard under the table and pulled out a checked wool cap. Had he decided to let her join his gang? "Try this," Julius said. "My California slouch suits me better and I can roll it up for a pillow at night."

Amelia settled the cap over her spiked curls and returned to the looking glass. "Now I'm a boy from the neck up." She turned to look at him. "I was about to buy some trousers—that's when I discovered my money was missing."

Julius shrugged. "What you wear is your trouble, not mine. The shipping schedule is scrambled due to storms, so another mailboat is due day after tomorrow. If you find the right clothes, meet us on the signal hill before dawn, with your spyglass."

"Will Nico recognize me?"

"He may. I won't tell the others, but don't expect me to protect you against him."

"How could I?" Amelia pocketed his cap and put on her bonnet. "You watched him knock me down yesterday. I've still got a lump on my head."

Julius flushed. "I'm not responsible for Nico."

"Still, you left me lying in the dirt."

"Boys in our gang don't expect coddling," Julius said.

That stung. Amelia glanced at the porthole. The shadows were long and she'd been gone for more than an hour. "I'd better go." She drew the hood of her cloak up to cover her neck. It was only later, as she picked her way down the dusty alley, that she realized she'd never said good-bye—or apologized to Julius for calling him a thief.

AMELIA DODGED miners with their tools and made a wide circle around a noisy crowd outside the saloon. It was hard to picture cheerful Mr. Abbott in one of those dark, smoky places. Worries ricocheted in her head as she hurried along their street. What would she say to Mother and Estelle? How would she explain herself? And Mother had said she couldn't dress like a boy. Julius was right: she *was* in a terrible mess.

She slowed down as she neared their tent and paid closer attention to the men who passed her. Did men really move differently from women? She'd never thought about it before. One man swaggered; another strode past with a loping walk, almost like a horse; another trudged under the weight of a load of bricks. A fourth man caught her staring and winked. She stumbled and dashed away, ashamed.

Their tent was quiet and the flaps hung limp. "Mother? Estelle?" No answer. Amelia whistled the white-throated sparrow's song, their private signal that sounded like, "Old Peabody, Peabody, Peabody!" She listened for Estelle's reply. Nothing.

Amelia ducked inside. When her eyes adjusted to the dim light she lit a candle—and gasped. The tent was all

a-jumble—their belongings scattered, a bolt of calico un-
furled in the dirt, Estelle's clothes flung every which way.
Amelia tiptoed through the mess, holding the candle high.
Her pallet was upended and a nasty smell oozed from the
earthen floor. She clapped a hand over her nose and mouth,
set the candle on a crate, and lifted Mother's fine wool cloak
from the dirt.

Uncle Paul's letter, still in its gray envelope, fluttered to
the ground. Amelia held still. The street sounds were the
same as this morning: bursts of talk, a few shouts, the creak
of wagon wheels—but no laughter from Estelle, no quick
steps announcing Mother's return. Amelia pulled out the
letter and held the pages up to the wavering light. Uncle
Paul's hand was like his voice, steady and firm:

Concord, Massachusetts
January 1851
   Dear Sister,
   It is only six days since you left, and it may be many
weeks before we receive a letter from you—although
perhaps you will send one from the isthmus. Mother and I
read stories in the papers of ships run aground, of a steamer
whose load of coal caught fire. Of course, we remember
the sad shipwreck that took the life of our neighbor
Margaret Fuller and her family; that makes us worry for
your safety.

As promised, Mother has moved to the farm with me, but she prefers to let out her house in Boston, in case you come home. I didn't try to dissuade her—although I know that you don't change your mind once you've made it up. We saw that with Amelia.

I have news that may disturb you: Two days after we returned from seeing you off, I was surprised by a visit from Mr. Y. He was passing through Concord for the first time since we met him so many years ago. He was cordial and well dressed and asked for you. I told him that you were traveling, but he wasn't satisfied. He pressed me with questions. Of course I kept my own counsel about you. He wouldn't say where he lived or what business he is in now. I wonder what he has learned about Amelia from the neighbors, who know her well.

Mother wasn't home when he came by, and I haven't told her—

Wheels creaked outside and Mother called out, "Estelle, look—there's a light in the tent!" Her voice rose. "Amelia? Are you here?"

Amelia's hands shook as she folded the letter, stuffed it back into its envelope, and tucked it under Mother's cloak. She snuffed out the candle and opened the tent flap. An orange sunset, like a bar painted with a wide brush, lay on the horizon over the sea. Mother and Estelle stood outside with Mr. Wong and his cart. He bowed to Amelia, but she was too upset to remember her manners.

"Mother," she said, and burst into tears.

"What's wrong? You *promised* me—" Mother rushed over, but Amelia stepped back and pointed, holding the tent flap open with one hand.

Mother peered in. "Estelle—we've been robbed!"

Amelia stayed outside. Let them think she wept for the mess of their belongings. In fact, she cried for Uncle Paul, for the secrets in the letter, and for the twisted feeling in her belly, pointing to a truth as slick and dark as the rats in the *Unicorn's* hold.

Amelia turned her back on everyone and was sick, right there in the street.

CHAPTER

20

Only Hair

MOTHER AND Estelle rolled up one side of the canvas to let in the last of the daylight. "What a relief," Mother said. "I can't find a thing missing."

"Nor can I," Estelle said. "Look." She held up her oval brooch. "They might have taken this daguerreotype of my mother—it was sitting in the top tray of my steamer trunk."

Amelia plunked down on her pallet and pulled her hood up over her bare neck. Her stomach had stopped heaving, but she didn't dare move. Once she had longed to wear a brooch like Estelle's. Now she was half a boy—who must put on a flannel shirt and a silly pointed tie and canvas trousers—things she didn't own and could never buy. She rested her forehead on her knees.

While Mother and Estelle gathered their clothes and folded their bedding, Mr. Wong tiptoed across the dirt floor. His singsong voice rang out and he plucked Estelle's sleeve, pointing at the ground. Estelle bent over and then burst out laughing. "Sophie, look. Pig tracks! And watch out; they've left their mess in the dirt. No wonder we're not missing anything."

Mother covered her nose. "Thank goodness for Mrs. Baker's offer. I told Mrs. Liazos we're moving to the ship tonight—and none too soon. Amelia, I'm too tired to even scold you. Why are you sitting there under your cloak? Pack up your things and help us. We need to get down the hill before dark."

"I was sick outside. Didn't you see?" And then, because it was true, Amelia wrapped her cloak tighter and said, "I have a chill."

She hoped for sympathy, but Mother threw up her hands. "What on earth! Perhaps my mother was right: you're too young for this journey."

Amelia was too shocked to cry. She pulled up her knees and hid her face in her skirts. Estelle rushed over and rubbed her back. "Don't worry. We would never have left you behind. And you can't help it that you're sick." Estelle glanced at Mother. "She needs food. We all do."

"I know that," Mother snapped, rolling up their blankets. Mr. Wong backed out of the tent. Who could blame him? It was more than the bad smell that made the tent seem close and cramped.

Amelia took a deep breath, then another. Her stomach cramped, but nothing else came up. She got to her feet, waited for her legs to stop wobbling, and hurriedly packed her things. Did Mother wish she and Estelle had come alone? Or had Uncle Paul's letter caused her anger? She held back tears, remembering what Julius had said—that *his* boys wouldn't be coddled.

Uncle Paul's words hummed like bees as she stowed her extra dress in her carpetbag. If only she'd had time to read the whole letter! Something about "keeping his own counsel"—what did that mean? And what had Mother decided about Amelia, so long ago, that made Uncle Paul say that she didn't change her mind about things? Even more important—who was Mr. Y? She couldn't ask Mother, because then she'd know that Amelia had snooped. How could she ever learn the truth?

MOTHER MOVED briskly, holding a borrowed lantern aloft, and even Estelle managed to hurry along beside the cart. A few streetlights flickered on a single street up near the Plaza, but the city grew darker as they approached the bay. Amelia stumped behind the loaded cart, her hand on Estelle's trunk to keep it from tipping out. A fierce wind tugged at her skirts. She tied the hood of her cloak tight around her neck. Soon—too soon—Mother would see her shorn head. And then: More trouble.

Bars of yellow light fell across the road from the saloon's open doors and welcoming lanterns swung from the railing of Rosanna's ship, casting jerky shadows on the ground. Amelia helped Mr. Wong hoist their luggage to the deck, using a pulley that Rosanna had rigged up for hauling her store goods. Amelia fastened Estelle's trunk to the pulley with strong knots, holding her breath as the trunk swung and spun, rising from the street to the ship's deck high above them. A small crowd gathered to watch and two men from the nearby saloon scrambled up the ladder to pull the trunk onto the deck. The goats bleated and pulled at their tethers while Mother, Estelle, and Rosanna rushed about, showing the men where to set their baggage.

It was pitch-dark by the time they were finished. Amelia stood on tiptoe and leaned out over the railing. What would Gran think of their new home? She wouldn't want Amelia living next to a saloon—yet the men who helped them had been friendly. And would Gran believe that people lived in tents in a city? The row of tents above the ship looked cozy now, each one with its warm light glowing inside the canvas.

Rosanna thanked the men who had come to help, and they touched their hat brims. One man stared for a long moment at Estelle and blushed before turning toward the ladder. But when Mr. Wong bowed to thank him, the man curled his lip and looked ready to spit. "Dirty Celestial," he muttered. Amelia gasped. Had Mr. Wong heard him?

Luckily, their Chinese friend was busy with Mother, who pressed a bolt of linen into his hands. "Thank you for helping us," she said.

Mr. Wong left with a smile and a bow. Amelia thought of the fat man behind her at the post office, who had warned her against talking to Mr. Wong. "Mother, why are people nasty to Mr. Wong?" she asked.

"It's not just Mr. Wong," Rosanna said. "Many people are cruel to the Chinese. Perhaps they're jealous. My husband says the Chinese are the best miners in the diggings." As she spoke of the mines, Rosanna's face sagged, and Mother took her hand.

"It's a clear evening," Mother said. "We could sleep on the deck until you leave."

"Don't be silly." Rosanna wiped her eyes with the corner of her apron. "We'll squeeze. And I could use the company." She poured grain from a burlap sack into a bucket and gave Amelia a lantern. "You can light our way across the plank."

Amelia lifted the lantern high and balanced carefully as they crossed to the pasture, happy to postpone her reckoning. Rosanna freed the goats and they scampered across the plank in the dark, butting each other playfully when they reached the deck. Rosanna picked up some short lengths of clothesline. "I keep them hitched at night, so they won't jump overboard."

"I'll tie them." Amelia secured their lines with half hitches, helped Rosanna pour oats into a small tub, and scratched each goat between the ears. "What's your ship's name?" She couldn't help stalling.

"I don't know," Rosanna said. "You'll have to think of

one." She buttoned her jacket. "The wind burrows right into your bones."

But it wasn't the wind that made Amelia shiver.

Inside, it was crowded but cozy. Candles sputtered on the table and a whale oil lamp sent a circle of light across the stove, where a fire crackled and the smell of cabbage wafted from a big pot. Mother and Estelle were setting their things on shelves. Amelia's hands shook as she untied the ribbons beneath her chin. Estelle perched on the edge of Rosanna's bed, her yellow curls freed from her own bonnet. Mother unpinned her sandy braid, letting it fall over her shoulder. When Mother turned her back, Amelia tossed her bonnet aside.

Rosanna fed the stove. The oil lamp didn't reach the dark shadows in the corners. Maybe no one would notice. Amelia untied her cloak and stood up tall, waiting.

"Amelia, help me make up the pallets." Mother gave Amelia a blanket, stared at her, and gasped. She groped at the back of Amelia's neck, as if she expected to find the braid tucked into her collar. "What on earth—"

"Sophie, what's wrong?" Estelle said. "You look as if you've seen a ghost."

Mother made a small noise that was almost a laugh. "Perhaps I have." She pointed at Amelia. "Look what's she done!"

"What happened?" Rosanna asked.

When no one answered, Amelia said, "I cut off my hair."

"But *why*?" Mother's chin trembled and she cupped her hand over Amelia's head. "Your hair was so beautiful. And what's this?" Her fingers touched the lump at the back of Amelia's head.

Amelia pulled away. "I—I fell yesterday, when I was looking for a cart. It's all right." But nothing was all right. Why had she been so stupid?

"It's as short as a boy's." Estelle put her hands on Amelia's shoulders and tipped her head to the side, considering her from all angles. "But your natural curl will come out. How did you cut it?"

"With a knife," Amelia said.

Mother dropped into a chair.

Rosanna stepped close, flicking Amelia's hair with her fingertips. "I could trim it for you, shape it a bit. I do that for Mr. Baker."

Amelia felt like a prize squash at a county fair, being poked and prodded by the judges. If only she could disappear!

The room was silent, except for the ticking of the stove as the fire warmed the metal. Finally, Mother cleared her throat. "Mrs. Baker, perhaps you're sorry we came."

"Not at all! Whether Amelia has a braid or not is nothing to me. After all, she's just a girl." Rosanna smiled, though her eyes stayed sad. "It's a good distraction, having you here. And please call me Rosanna, as Amelia does. Now, how about some cabbage soup? My ingredients are paltry, but at least it's hot."

While Rosanna filled four tin bowls, Mother and Estelle found their blankets and made up two pallets in the corner. They had left Estelle's trunk outside, under a length of old sailcloth, but the little house still felt crowded. "Isn't this wonderful?" Estelle asked. "Here we are, on board a ship, safe and sound—but no waves to make us queasy!"

Mother nodded, but her eyes strayed toward Amelia, and she pursed her lips in disapproval. Finally, Amelia couldn't stand it. "Mother, it's only *hair*," she said. "It will grow back."

"But why?" Mother asked again.

Amelia screwed up her courage. "Because . . . I need to look like a boy so I can sell newspapers. Then we'll have enough to eat."

Mother's eyes filled and she stroked Amelia's head. "I should never have pressed you for money. Estelle and I will start sewing tomorrow. People will buy our clothes as they did in Boston, and soon we'll have enough for a plot of land. I'm proud you are my *daughter*, Amelia."

Hurting Mother's feelings was even worse than making her angry. Amelia sank onto her pallet and pulled her cloak over her head, too queasy and exhausted to eat.

SHE MUST have slept, because she woke under her blankets with an empty belly. Where was she?

Whispers came from the corner, where a single candle sent shadows rippling along the rough walls. Mother sat on their pallet in her nightdress while Estelle loosened Mother's braid, untwisting the strands. They slid over her shoulders like a waterfall. Estelle ran the comb through the tangles, and Mother tucked her chin like an obedient child. "What was she thinking?" Mother said softly. "I should have guessed when she tried to buy trousers from Rosanna. And I found a boy's cap in her apron pocket. Where did she get this idea, to sell newspapers?"

"From those boys on the dock, I think." Estelle set her comb aside. "Perhaps it's a good thing for her to be disguised, at least until we're settled. The city doesn't seem safe for girls."

"Maybe California gives Amelia too *much* freedom," Mother whispered. "She's so willful, since we left home. Look what's happened in just a few days."

"Hush." Estelle pressed a finger to Mother's mouth. "Sophie, Amelia is still a girl. She doesn't understand our dreams for women. And she's had nothing but a biscuit since yesterday's noon dinner. It's time to dip into the money you set aside for the land."

"I already have," Mother said. "More times than you know. I'm afraid."

Estelle made soothing noises and held Mother tight.

Afraid of what? Amelia wondered. Had Mother spent all the money for their little house? Or was she worried about what Uncle Paul had said?

She swallowed a sigh. Mother and Estelle seemed to have a secret language sometimes, as if each knew what the other was thinking. She hated being the odd one out. She held still, fists clenched, waiting. Would they speak of Uncle Paul's letter? But neither Mother nor Estelle said another word. Estelle blew out the candle. The room was dark and still. Wind muttered at the corners of the house and sang in the ship's torn rigging. The sound carried Amelia away.

CHAPTER

✳ 21 ✳

Persistent

MIRACLE OF miracles: Rosanna kept a washtub underneath her bed. Even better, she had a curtain that could be pulled across a corner of the room for privacy. A bath! After a breakfast of hot milk and porridge that warmed her from the inside out, Amelia was happy to carry water to heat on the stove. The well was in the scrubby brush, which Amelia was learning to call the "chaparral," beyond the goats' little pasture. She trotted through the fog, turned the windlass, and hauled bucket after bucket to the ship, feeling more confident each time she crossed the plank. The goats tripped toward her as she went past, nibbling her skirts. Amelia laughed and whispered into Daisy's floppy ear. "*You don't care how I look, do you?*" she asked.

First Mother disappeared behind the curtain to have her bath, then Estelle. When it was Amelia's turn, Rosanna added more hot water to the tub. Amelia pulled off her clothes, wrinkling her nose at her own acid smell, and lowered herself into the water.

Bliss. Steam curled around her ears as she slid down,

pulling her knees up until she was nearly submerged. She scoured herself from head to toe with the rough cake of lye soap, then dunked her head, rubbed the soap through her curls, and rinsed it out—just like that. Mother and Estelle would be combing through their tangles for hours.

Amelia toweled herself off and looked down at her chest. She could still pass as a boy, if she could find some boy's clothing—a big *if.*

As she had promised, Rosanna trimmed Amelia's hair to even it up. "Now you're not so shaggy," Rosanna said, and turned to help Estelle stack bolts of cloth on the shelves.

When Amelia emerged from the house, wearing her old, but clean, calico, Mother was stitching something in black lace; she didn't look up. Amelia perched on a crate, pulled out her journal, and wrote a letter to Uncle Paul on a fresh page. She pressed hard on her pencil.

March of 1851
Dear Uncle Paul,

  We arrived in San Francisco a few days ago. We are staying in a ship that sits on land. It belongs to our new friend Rosanna Baker. Rosanna says that when sailors abanndoned their ships and went to the mines, people from Chile made bridges from the ships to the shore. Then they filled in the water under the bridge with sand and mud. We climb a ladder from the street to our ships deck. We will stay here until your little house arrives.

The city has many pretty horses but they work hard.
The sand is so deep in some streets that the horses sink
all the way to their hocks. I saw one horse with a silver
harrness. I miss my pony. Has she had her foal?

> *With love from your devoted niece,*
> *Amelia*

She presented the letter to Estelle, who read it over quickly. "A few spelling mistakes," she said. "Watch your commas and apostrophes."

Amelia took her journal to a far corner of the deck and added a postscript when she was sure no one was looking:

P.S. Mother receeved your letter yesterday. She told
me that a stranger stopped by the farm. Who was it?

Amelia tore the letter from her journal, folded it, and slipped it into her apron pocket. Of course, Mother hadn't "told" her anything. She had never lied to Uncle Paul, but he was so far away, and the letter would take forever to reach him—perhaps Mother would never know.

When Amelia went inside for an envelope, she found Mother fitting a black lace collar to Rosanna's dress. "Thank you," Rosanna said. "It's beautifully stitched. Now the world knows I'm in mourning." She wiped her eyes and beckoned to Amelia. "I've written a letter to my mother, to share my sad news. Come with me to the post office. And I need to buy a steamer ticket to the diggings."

Mother glanced up at Amelia and frowned. "Put on your bonnet," she said. "And don't leave Rosanna's side."

Amelia nodded and covered her head, then pulled her hood up over her neck so that no one could tell that her hair was gone. As Rosanna started down the ladder, Mother took Amelia aside and gave her two silver dollars. "This is the money from my mending yesterday. Buy us some meat, if it's not too dear, or maybe some eggs. Don't waste it." The worry in Mother's eyes clung to Amelia as she scrambled down the ladder to the street.

The post office was quiet. They mailed their letters, leaving Uncle Paul and Rosanna's mother to pay the postage on the other end, and skirted the Plaza. The saloons were already noisy, though it wasn't even noon. Still, two rough-looking miners stopped in front of them, doffed their hats, and bowed to Rosanna. "Sorry for your loss," one said.

Rosanna nodded to the man and took Amelia's arm. "It was kind of your mother to stitch this collar for me. Now I don't have to explain my sad face. I'll try to be a better friend when I come back from the mines."

"You *are* a good friend." Amelia meant it.

A furry black ball rushed at them through the fog, and Amelia jumped aside. "Tip!" she cried. The little Scottie whirled, jumped up like a circus dog, and pasted his muddy paws on her skirt. His rough tongue lapped her hands.

Rosanna laughed. "You know this dog?"

"He lives at the *Alta California*—the newspaper office nearby." Amelia thought of her visit the day before. "I need to stop there for a minute."

The smile had already faded from Rosanna's eyes. "I must book my passage—so be quick."

"I promise." Amelia snapped her fingers at the terrier. "Come, Tip." She knocked on the door. The editor sat at his desk with his back to them, writing. "We shouldn't interrupt," Rosanna said, but Amelia went in.

The editor glanced at her and frowned, but when he saw Rosanna, he stood up. "Persistent, aren't you?" he said to Amelia. "How can I help you ladies?"

"I forgot my letter," she said.

The editor laughed and pointed to the table heaped high with newspapers, blue-lined tablets of paper, chipped cups, and broken pencils. "If you've got a few hours, I'm sure you could unearth it in that pile." He nodded at Rosanna. "Pardon me, ma'am, but I have a paper to get out." He returned to his desk.

Rosanna nudged Amelia. "Time to go," she said.

Amelia held her ground. "What does 'slander' mean?" she asked the editor.

He answered without looking up. "That's when you say something about a person that's not true—something that hurts their character. The way you spoke about your captain."

"What if it *is* true?" Amelia asked.

"Facts," the editor said. "That's what we want. Facts. Not rumors."

Amelia followed Rosanna down the street. "He doesn't like me," she said.

"He's busy," Rosanna said. "And he's right; you are persistent."

"What does that mean?"

"That you don't give up."

Amelia followed her friend to the wharf and waited for her outside the ticket office, where another poster for the balloon caught her eye. "BALLOON LAUNCH BY AERONAUT BEALE!" it said. Amelia squinted at the small print. *"Come to North Point at dawn on April 1st· No fooling! Weather permitting."* What sort of weather did you need for a launch? And what was today's date, anyway?

"What's the sign say?" A hand plucked at her sleeve and Amelia looked down into a small boy's eager face.

"Patrick!" She smiled and read the poster out loud.

"What's an aeronaut?"

"The man who flies the balloon, I guess," Amelia said.

"Would he let us climb on board? That would be grand!"

"Us?" Amelia's laugh turned into a frown when she saw his puzzled stare. "Why are you looking at me that way?"

"You look different." He pulled out his pocket watch and Amelia was glad to see that her knots still held. "I have to go. Promised to see Julius and Nico."

"Why?"

"Another mail boat might come in tomorrow. Their schedules are all messed up by that storm, and the ship-wreck."

"That was *our* ship that ran aground." Amelia grabbed his shoulder. "Will you meet the boat?"

"'Course. Now let go. You're pinching."

"Sorry." Amelia released him. "Take me with you tomor-row. We're living on a ship now, near the Niantic."

Patrick smirked. "You live in the *saloon?*"

"No, silly. On the ship with the goats."

"I know that place."

"Good. So, come to the ship before dawn and whistle at the bottom of the ladder. I'll bring you a surprise." She took a deep breath. "Two surprises. One of them is something to eat."

His face brightened at her mention of food, and Amelia nearly gave him one of her silver dollars—but then Rosanna emerged with her ticket. *"Promise* you'll find me in the morning?" Amelia demanded.

"I'll try." Patrick touched the brim of his cap—like a little man, Amelia thought—and took off. Amelia watched. Pat-rick didn't walk with short, quick steps, as a woman might. Instead, his body swayed from side to side—and he kept his hands in his pockets. Could she ever walk that way?

"Another friend?" Rosanna asked. "First the dog, then the editor, now this boy?"

"The editor is not my friend," Amelia said. "The boy's name is Patrick." She followed Rosanna to the wharf, hardly noticing where she put her feet. She'd made a pact with Patrick. She could probably come up with the food she'd promised, but what about the other surprise?

Uncle Paul's words thrummed in her head, like a song she couldn't stop singing: *Think first, act later.* Once again, she'd ignored his advice.

CHAPTER

✳ 22 ✳

As Strong-Willed as You Are

WHEN ROSANNA led her out on the wharf to see the food stalls, Amelia couldn't help staring. One man was selling grizzly-bear meat, elk steaks, a bird called a "black-tailed dove," and antelope haunches. "Antelope!" she exclaimed. Under a nearby tent, a mountain of oysters sat on a table beside a stack of fish with gleaming eyes and shiny scales. In another stall, a vegetable seller arranged beets as big as pumpkins next to enormous onions. Rosanna peeked at Amelia's face under her bonnet. "Your eyes are as big as her vegetables."

"What should I buy?" Amelia held up her two coins. "Mother told me not to waste her money."

"Two dollars won't go far. My steamer ticket was dear: eight dollars! I only have a few coins left. We'll put our money together."

The food cost more than even Mother had imagined. Their coins bought them a handful of potatoes, an onion, a half-dozen oysters, and two carrots. Their purchases barely covered the bottom of the basket, but Rosanna seemed pleased. "Oyster stew cooked in goat's milk. That will keep us warm until I leave in the morning."

If only Rosanna could stay—but of course, she couldn't. She had a husband, and a brother who had died. Rosanna was a woman and Amelia was only a girl—a girl who had to look like a boy by tomorrow. But how?

Amelia was so lost in thought that she nearly bumped into Rosanna at the foot of the ship's ladder. "It looks as if they've been busy." Rosanna pointed to a paper sign that fluttered from a nail on the ship's hull.

DUPREY AND FORRESTER, SEAMSTRESSES, the sign said. MEN'S FLANNEL SHIRTS. WOMEN'S CLOTHING OF PARIS AND NEW YORK FASHIONS.

"Goodness!" Rosanna said. "How do they know what women wear in Paris and New York?"

"I don't know." Amelia scrambled up the ladder, forgetting to worry about men looking up her skirts, and found the ship transformed. Their crate, which had sailed in the hold of the *Unicorn*, stood open on the deck. Inside the house, Estelle was sketching patterns on scraps of paper, while Mother knelt on the floor, surrounded by bolts of colorful fabric and skeins of creamy white and coffee-colored yarn from Uncle Paul's sheep.

Mother's hair still hung wet on her shoulders. She sat back on her heels when she saw them. "A successful morning!" Mother announced. "The men who helped me bring the crate from the ship turned into customers and ordered shirts." She held up a bolt of striped cloth and chuckled. "I'll use a woman's apron fabric for a man's shirt. Who will know the difference?"

Amelia laughed. Mother hadn't sounded so happy since that day, many months ago, when she'd announced they were moving to California. Amelia peered into the crate. "Any more newspapers?" she asked.

Estelle shook her head. "I'm afraid not. We wrapped it all in butcher paper."

Mother put an arm around Amelia's knees. "Give up this silliness about being a newsboy," she said. "We'll be all right."

Amelia pulled away. "I can't," she said. "I made a promise. Besides, look how little food we bought with our money." She pointed at the basket. "Mother, please—I want to help with the store. And you said you needed more money for the land. Let me dress like a boy—just for tomorrow." Mother's mouth drew into a straight line—never a good sign. Amelia thought of the bundles she'd tied up on the *Unicorn's* deck—was it only a few days ago? And weren't there ten in each bundle? "I'll bring you ten dollars. I promise." Of course, she'd have to pay something for the papers—or would she?

Mother threw up her hands. "Amelia, what am I going to do with you?"

Estelle laughed. "She's as strong-willed as you are, Sophie. You might as well give up."

Was that a compliment, or an insult? No matter, because Mother said quickly, "I won't have you going off alone."

"I won't," Amelia said. "I'll be with Patrick."

"Patrick?"

"I met Patrick today," Rosanna said quickly. "He looked like a sweet boy." Luckily, Rosanna didn't mention that Patrick was only eight years old and bony as a stick. Rosanna winked at Amelia when Mother's back was turned, and for a moment, Amelia felt as if they were the same age.

She spent the afternoon helping Estelle and Rosanna arrange the store while Mother cut, basted, and stitched. By nightfall, Mother had finished a fresh striped hickory shirt for Amelia. "It feels strange, with no collar," Amelia said, as she buttoned it up.

"That's the reason for the kerchief." Estelle tied one around her neck. Rosanna gave her the trousers from the shelf, but they slipped down over Amelia's hips, revealing her pantalettes, so Rosanna pulled a pair of braces from a box. "I bought them for my brother," she said, and stopped Amelia's protests by adding, "they shouldn't go to waste."

The three women turned Amelia to and fro as they shortened the braces to fit, set Julius's cap on her head one way, tipped it another, tied the necktie so that one end was longer than the other. "A foolish fashion," Mother said, and shook her head as if she'd given up on Amelia completely. Amelia felt like a doll they had purchased in a shop—if boy dolls even existed. "What about a jacket?" Mother asked.

"She can use her cloak," Estelle said. "Men wear them here. But perhaps we should cut off the hood?"

While they fussed with her clothing, Amelia undressed and slipped under her blankets. Mother knelt beside her on the pallet and rubbed her hair. "So short and curly. I can't get used to it." She pursed her lips. "Amelia, you *must* sell your papers, hide the money in your pockets, and come straight back. No fooling around."

"I promise. And thank you for making the shirt." Amelia kissed Mother's hand. She curled up under her blanket but her heart raced as if she were already dashing up Telegraph Hill. As Julius had said, it was all very well to *look* like a boy, but could she *behave* like one, as he had demanded? She'd soon find out.

CHAPTER

✦ **23** ✦

California Newsgirl

THE ROOM was pitch-black when Amelia woke to someone shaking her shoulder. Estelle touched a finger to Amelia's lips before she could make a sound. "There's a boy whistling at the foot of the ladder," she whispered.

Amelia sat up. "It's Patrick. Tell him I'll be right there."

Estelle gave Amelia the bundle of clothes and slipped outside. A sliver of gray light slid through the open door. Amelia stifled a groan. Her back ached from sleeping on the thin pallet. She used the chamber pot and dressed as silently as she could. Except for her underclothes and worn boots, nothing was her own. She fumbled with the unfamiliar buttons at her waist. Estelle returned and helped her fasten the suspenders before knotting the kerchief around Amelia's neck. "You'll fool them now," she whispered.

Amelia pulled on her cloak, laced her boots, and set Julius's cap over her cropped curls. Her spyglass just fit in one pocket, an apple in the other. But now she couldn't shove her hands in her pockets, as she'd seen Julius do. How did boys manage, without deep apron pockets? She gobbled a biscuit from last night's supper and tied another one up in a napkin for Patrick, hooking it over her wrist. Finally, she was ready.

Estelle followed her to the ladder. Fog lay out at sea and the air was raw and damp. Amelia shivered. The harbor was already waking up. A mule trotted past on the street below, hauling an empty wagon, and two men rolled barrels toward the nearest wharf. Estelle kissed Amelia's forehead, her touch as gentle as the flutter of a moth's wings. "You're a California newsgirl now. Be careful. Sell your papers and come right back."

"I will. Say good-bye to Rosanna for me." A low whistle sounded from the bottom of the ladder. Amelia set a foot on the top rung and looked down. The street seemed far away this morning. Was she as daft as the boys had said?

A shadowy form waved from below and she heard a shrill whistle.

She took a deep breath. Now or never.

Amelia took one step down, then another—and suddenly, she was free! No need to worry about catching her skirt on each rung. She slid to the ground and bumped into Patrick, who stumbled backward. "Who—wha—where's Amelia?" he asked, stammering.

"She's gone!" Amelia laughed. "I turned into a boy." She stepped closer so he could see her in the thin light. "What do you think?"

He squinted. "Why'd you do that, anyway?"

"Julius said no girls in his gang. So I'm a boy now."

Patrick snorted. "So you say. Where's my surprise?"

"*I'm* the first surprise." Amelia slipped the cloth from her wrist, untied it, and passed him the biscuit. "Here's another one. And listen—don't tell anyone I'm a girl. Promise?"

"All right. But they'll figure it out." Patrick gobbled the biscuit and pointed across the bay. "Sun will be up soon."

"Let's go then." Amelia took a few steps and broke into a run, like a horse let loose from its pasture. Her arms pumped, her stride lengthened, her boots drummed on the planking. No skirts twisting around her shins, no hems dragging in the mud, no bulky petticoats. Her trouser legs rubbed against each other like soft sandpaper. Though her breath rose in puffs of smoke, running warmed her from the inside out. Patrick scampered to keep up as she dodged barrels and crates, jumped to avoid a man galloping by on a horse, and dashed toward the signal hill. She passed many men in the street, but no one gave her so much as a passing glance. That, Amelia decided, was the most freeing thing of all.

Footsteps sounded behind them. "Patrick, hold up!" someone called.

Amelia recognized Nico's surly voice. Now what? She ran faster but Patrick snatched at her sleeve, nearly tripping her up. "What's your name?" he hissed.

Good question. Amelia sucked in her breath. She couldn't be "Amelia." Her mind made jackrabbit leaps along with her feet as she scrambled for boys' names starting with A. Arthur? August? No; she'd never answer to a name so unlike her own. Emile? Yes, that was a good one. It sounded French. She could be Emile Duprey, Estelle's younger brother. She drew up at the foot of Telegraph Hill and leaned close to Patrick. "I'm Emile," she whispered. "Tell him we just met."

"You there—wait!" Nico grabbed for her but Amelia ducked out of his way. "Who are you?" Nico demanded.

Amelia cleared her throat and tried to make her voice sound lower. "Emile Duprey." She tossed the name over her shoulder, as if it were as comfortable and worn as her boots.

Nico scowled at Patrick. "She's *Miss* Forrester, isn't she?" he demanded. Patrick didn't answer. "You can't fool me," Nico called. "That's Julius's cap."

"Never heard of 'Miss Forrester,'" Amelia said. "Sorry."

To her surprise, Nico turned away. "Suit yourself. But don't expect me to look out for you."

"As if you would. Come on, Patrick; let's find Julius." Amelia trotted through the chaparral. Perhaps it was her new clothing, or the full bowl of soup she'd had last night, but her legs felt stronger today. She stopped to look down on the harbor. Gray light filtered over the warehouses, sheds, and tangled ships. The arms on the semaphore atop Telegraph Hill stood motionless. Was Mr. Abbott there? The building looked deserted. She pulled her spyglass from her pocket and scanned the hill.

"Hey," Patrick said. "May I try that?"

"In a minute."

He nudged her. "Let me see, or I'll give you away."

Amelia sighed and set the glass in his hands. "Be careful." Patrick held it to his eye and gasped, then put out his hand. "It's all so close," he said.

She snatched it back and pressed the lens to her eye in time to see four small figures appear from different directions. They converged on the grassy slope like birds homing in on a dovecote. Amelia recognized Julius handing out flags as the boys ran past. She sauntered toward him with a swagger that she hoped made her look like a boy and cleared her throat to deepen her voice. "Good morning," she said.

Julius started to hand her a flag—then blinked and stared. He didn't recognize her! Amelia swallowed her triumph and put out her hand. "I'm Emile," she said. "Emile Duprey. Remember me? You said I could join your gang if I brought my spyglass."

Julius studied her outstretched hand as if he didn't know why it was there, and finally shook it. Now the other boys were watching—and listening, too. "Right. Pleased to see you again, *Emile*." His copper eyes met her own. Was that the flicker of a smile?

He withdrew the flag. "You don't know our signals, do you?"

"Not yet," Amelia said. "Though I learned the SOS code, when our ship ran aground in Acapulco."

"You were on *that* ship?" one boy asked.

Before Amelia could answer, Nico appeared. "Sun's coming up. No time for stories," he said.

He was right: the sky glowed a pale pink over the mountains.

"Meet our new boy," Julius said, nodding at Amelia. "Nico, Emile."

Nico's face was a frozen mask. Julius pointed to her spyglass. "Eh-meele," Julius said, exaggerating the syllables in her new name. "It looks like Abbott had another long night with the cards. Climb to the brow of the hill and stand below the semaphore with the glass." He glanced at Patrick. "You go with—uh, Emile. When the steamer sails through the Golden Gate, wave your arms like this." He demonstrated, pinwheeling his arms in a circle.

"I know that signal." Patrick beckoned to Amelia. "Let's go."

"Hold on." Nico stepped so close to Julius their chests nearly bumped. "Since when do we add another newsboy? Should I reduce *my* share of the take because a complete stranger decides to join our gang?"

"That's right." The tallest boy in the gang glared down at her. "And what kind of name is *Emile*, anyway? Don't you belong with the foreign boys?"

"We're from Boston," Amelia said. "My sister and I speak English like the rest of you." She took a risk and jabbed her thumb at Nico. "His mother is Greek. If *I'm* foreign, then so is he."

Nico sputtered but Julius drew himself up. "We can use an extra hand while Roland's ankle heals. When he comes back, we'll see how things are."

Amelia slowly let out her breath. She'd passed one test. She raced Patrick to the top of the hill and nearly beat him. So far, being a newsboy was an adventure.

CHAPTER

* 24 *

Shanghaied in Your Sleep

AMELIA STOOD on tiptoe, the spyglass pressed tight to her eye, waiting. When the first ship poked through the narrows, Amelia started to wave her arms but Patrick stuck his elbow into her ribs. "She's a clipper. I can tell, even without the glass."

He was right: the clipper, with three masts, was fully rigged. Could it be the ship that carried their little house? The clipper sailed around the point, a queen proceeding to her throne. Her square sails, gleaming in the sunlight, billowed like filled hoopskirts. In the harbor, men pushed off toward the clipper ship in small dories and lighters while teams of horses hauled wagons out to the wharf.

"Hey," Patrick said. "Don't forget your job."

Amelia swung the spyglass around in time to see another ship come through the narrows, but it was a smaller sailboat with a single mast, followed by a bigger sailing vessel. Finally, when Amelia's arms were beginning to ache, a thin plume of smoke appeared in the distance. She held her breath. In a moment, its side paddlewheel and black smokestack steamed into view. "Here she comes!"

"A steamer? Let me see." Patrick whistled to the boys and grabbed the spyglass while Amelia circled her arms like a windmill gone mad.

The line of boys raised their flags; bright colors and symbols danced and swooped in the wind. Amelia laughed. Without the spyglass, the steamer was just a speck in the blue distance. Now her shouts had set the boys in motion. She felt like a general directing his troops in the Mexican War.

The ship chugged along, finally rounding the end of the peninsula, where it headed toward the docks. "What do we do now?" Amelia asked.

"Run to the wharf," Patrick said. "I need to find Henry."

"Who's Henry?" Amelia asked, but Patrick was already gone. Amelia dashed after him, holding herself back on the steep pitch. Whoops and catcalls sounded as a small band of boys hurtled past her, arms flailing, boots slipping and sliding in the wet grass. Two dark-eyed boys called out to each other in Spanish; the boy shouting in French was the one who sold cigars on the street. This must be the "foreign gang."

Amelia chased them down the hill. She nearly knocked into a man who stumbled past, carrying a crate. "Out of the way, lad," he said.

The crate clipped her side, but Amelia hardly noticed. *Lad!* She'd fooled him. And a "lad" wouldn't wait on the sidelines, avoiding a crowd of men; he'd push his way right through.

So she did.

Amelia found the other newsboys out on the dock. The wharf was full, with ships jostling against one another for position, so the steamer had anchored out in the harbor. Julius and Nico bobbed in a rowboat beneath the dock, Nico wrestling with the oars while Julius pushed off. Patrick had attached himself to the tall boy who had challenged Amelia. Was that Henry? He looked tough, in spite of his patched clothing. She didn't want another fight, so she stood apart, watching.

The boys from the news gang kept their hands in their pockets, and some rocked from their heels to their toes. They fidgeted and elbowed each other. One boy tweaked his braces until Amelia thought he might break them and lose his trousers. The tall boy spit into the water and the others leaned over to watch his spittle hit the sea. Were all boys so foolish? Must she behave this way, too?

Nico and Julius untangled themselves from the other boats and rowed toward the steamer. Amelia raised her spyglass. Each had an oar, and they were moving quickly. Patrick wriggled through the crowd and stood on tiptoe. "Can you see Julius?"

"Yes, he's just reached the ship. They're trying to tie up." If *she* were with them now, she'd hitch the boat tight with a bowline.

"Let me look." Patrick reached for the spyglass and she let him hold it, though she was afraid he might drop it in the water. His face, splashed with freckles, looked small, almost helpless, behind the long lens.

"Is Henry the tall boy?" Amelia asked.

"Right. We're mates," Patrick said. "Look, they're coming back. They'll want help. Follow me." He handed her the glass and wriggled through the crowd. Amelia tagged along. Without her skirts, she could push and shove like the others. She stood beside Patrick at the end of the wharf as a flotilla of small boats returned to shore, laden with passengers and luggage. A beefy man rowed a well-dressed passenger toward the dock. His dory was bow-heavy beneath his valise. The men's voices carried easily over the water.

"Hope there are more women in this town than there were on board ship," said a man sitting in the stern.

"Don't count on it," said the rower. "And women are different here. They go their own way."

Amelia almost laughed out loud. Mother and Estelle certainly fit that description. Could she say it about herself, too?

The dory knocked into a piling and the beefy man tossed a line onto the dock. "Here, boy; hold us steady, will you?"

Boy? Amelia tucked her chin to hide a smile as she caught the rope, found a wooden cleat, and cinched the line tight with two half-hitches.

The oarsman helped his passenger onto the dock. "Where'd you learn those knots?" he asked.

"On board ship," Amelia said.

"Interested in being a cabin boy? The clipper needs one."

"No, thank you." Amelia touched the brim of her cap, as she'd seen the other boys do.

"Careful." Patrick appeared at her side. "They'll shanghai you in your sleep. You wake up at sea, headed for China. That happened to a boy we know. Let's help Julius unload." Patrick slipped away, the soles of his worn boots slapping against the dock, and Amelia followed. Time to show Julius she was ready to work.

CHAPTER

✳ 25 ✳

Read All About It!

JULIUS, NICO, and Henry lugged the heavy bundles of papers along the wharf and Amelia followed, threading her way through the crowds. She hoped Patrick wouldn't give her secret away. She could probably trust him—but would Nico tell the others she was a boy? Perhaps he'd wait and use her secret against her if she did anything wrong, or if he needed something. Then what?

She couldn't worry about that now. Julius set his bundles on a flat boulder uphill from the wharf. "We've got more papers than usual," he said. "You'll each get fifteen." Julius and Henry counted them out and Amelia stumbled backward when Julius set a pile in her arms. Could she carry that weight up these hills? She set her stack on a barrel and lifted a paper from the top of the pile. "Look—the *Boston Courier* for January sixteenth. Right after we left home—" Amelia swallowed her girlish voice. She'd forgotten who she was. She ducked her chin and scanned the headlines, her eyes gobbling the words as if they were fresh peaches. "Listen to this! 'A Railroad to San Francisco'!" Amelia rocked back on her heels. Could Gran and Uncle Paul come to visit?

Patrick wiggled through the line of boys and crouched beside her. "What else does it say?"

Amelia squinted. Such a long first sentence—she puzzled over the small print and the big words. "It talks about 'the importance of the railroad to the Pacific,'" she read, and looked up into a circle of expectant faces. Nico was bent over, tying up his own stack, but she guessed he might be listening, too. "Do we all have the same papers?" she asked.

"Yes," Julius said. "Time to go."

"Where should I sell them?"

"Wherever you can." Julius gave Henry the last stack, which looked even bigger than hers. Did some boys get special favors? Amelia tried to settle her bundle on her hip as the other boys did, but she lost her grip and her papers slid to the ground. She scrambled to catch them before the wind snatched them away. Nico sneered as he jogged past. "Customers won't buy dirty papers," he said.

"At least I can read the headlines," Amelia muttered. She folded the papers carefully and tucked them under her arm.

"Meet at my place at noon," Julius told her. "We'll settle up then. And be sure you earn a dollar for every paper you sell. You share your earnings with me." Julius hoisted his own bundle and followed Nico up the hill.

"How much do we give you?" Amelia asked, but Julius was already out of earshot. She glanced at Patrick. "How do they sell papers if they can't read the headlines?"

Patrick shrugged. "Julius tells us. Or they just shout, 'News! Fresh off the boat! Read all about it!'"

So Julius could read. That explained the books on his shelf. She glanced at Patrick. "Where's your pile?"

"Don't have one. Julius says I'm too small to sell them. But look." Patrick pulled his shoulders back and stood on tiptoe. "I'm near as tall as you."

"What do you do while they're selling?"

"Not much. Sometimes I help Henry call out the headlines—but he doesn't want me today."

"So how will you earn money?"

Patrick shrugged and traced a circle in the dirt with his boot.

"How long have you been here?" Amelia asked.

"In California? Since my birthday in October." Patrick squinched up his face, figuring. "I'm half a year past eight now."

"Where do you live?"

He wouldn't meet her eyes. "Depends. In different digs."

Was he one of the homeless orphans Mrs. Liazos had complained about? Amelia wanted to wrap him in her cloak and take him back to Rosanna's, but she guessed he might hate that. Instead she said, "You know the city and I don't. If you show me around and help me carry my papers, I'll share my earnings with you."

"You still have to give Julius his cut."

"That's all right. Besides, you have a watch. You can tell me when it's getting on to noon." She counted out five papers for Patrick and set the rest of the bundle on her hip. The other boys were way ahead of her, striding up the hill as if their papers weighed nothing. Could she haul her bundle that far? She didn't have a choice.

CHAPTER

Dos Reales!

AS THEY left the harbor behind, they passed men who were already reading the *Courier*. The other boys had a jump on her. "We should pick a place where no one else will go," Amelia said. "Where does Julius sell his papers?"

"The Custom House," Patrick said.

Amelia didn't know where that was. Her stomach growled. "It's time for breakfast. What about one of the restaurants? Won't they have crowds?"

"Nico sells papers at his mother's tent," Patrick said. "They didn't give you a spot, then?"

"No." Of course they hadn't told her where to go—they wanted her to fail. Amelia shifted her bundle to the other hip. It felt heavier with each step.

"We could try the Plaza, where men get their boots blacked," Patrick said. "If we go the back way, we might beat the others."

"Good idea. I'll follow you."

Patrick darted down an alley, ducked past a row of tents, and led Amelia through a maze of crooked streets where

each building was more makeshift than the next. A shirt-
less man waved as she hurried past. "Boy, are those papers
off the boat?"

"Yes, sir." She was embarrassed that he was half-dressed,
but a boy wouldn't be shy, would he? "It's the *Boston Courier*,"
she said. "One dollar."

Before she could even recite the headline, the man said,
"I'll buy one."

Amelia kept her eyes on her boots while he fished in
his pocket for coins. "Three bits," the man said. "Take it or
leave it."

"Fine," Amelia said, although three bits left her one
bit short of a dollar. She pocketed the coins and hurried
after Patrick. Being a boy was more complicated than she'd
thought.

THEY ENTERED the Plaza at the corner near the long
adobe building, where about a dozen men were getting their
boots blacked. Each man stood with one foot on the ground,
the other on an overturned box. The boot blackers—boys
about Amelia's age—knelt in the dirt in front of their customers. They spread blacking on the boots, polished them
with soft cloths, and chattered with one another in French.
A small crowd of men stood in line behind them, smoking
while they waited.

"We're here first," Patrick said, breathing hard. "Ready?"

Amelia cleared her throat, about to call out her head-lines, when a man on a pony trotted past and the crowd broke into cheers. The pony's black coat gleamed in the sun and his socks were as white as Gran's collars after washday. Silver ornaments glittered on the pony's saddle and bridle. He pranced in a tight circle and his rider drew him up in front of Amelia.

"Dos reales, dos reales!" the crowd chanted.

The pony nudged Amelia's chest and she grinned, rub-bing the knob between its ears. "Hello, boy," she said softly. The pony whickered and nudged her again. She reached for the apple in her pocket but his rider pulled back on his reins and barked something in Spanish. Amelia glanced at Patrick. "What do they want?"

Patrick laughed. "You have to give the pony two bits."

"But I only have a few coins. Can I feed him an apple?"

"Dos reales, dos reales!" the men roared. Finally, Amelia dug out a two-bit coin and set it on her palm. The men hooted with laughter as the pony wrinkled his lips, took the coin between his yellowed teeth, and dropped it into the waiting hand of a shoeshine boy. The pony set one hoof on a box and waited while the shoeshine boy smeared the hoof with blacking and polished the hoof until it gleamed, as if the pony wore a fine leather boot. All the men ap-plauded when the pony presented his second foreleg and Amelia cheered him on too. Could Skipper ever learn that

trick? Suddenly Patrick nudged her. "Papers," he said.

Amelia startled. She'd forgotten why they were there. "News!" she called. Her voice squeaked. She took a deep breath and tried again. "News from the *Boston Courier*! Railroad to San Francisco!"

"Paay-puz! Read them while you wait!" Patrick cried.

The men circled them like crows flocking to carrion, and the papers flew from their hands as fast as Amelia and Patrick could hand them out. "Papers, one dollar!" Coins of all shapes and sizes dropped into her palm. Some were foreign. "How do I know if they've given me a dollar?" she called out, but Patrick was too busy to reply.

Within minutes, their supplies had dwindled to two copies. Amelia drew back from the crowd to catch her breath. Patrick was right; the men were happy to read while the boys blacked their dirty boots. Men stood in small groups, reading over each other's shoulders, calling out bits of news to one another as they waited.

Amelia stood on tiptoe, looking for more customers, when a chorus of shrill taunts and hoots sounded from the far side of the Plaza. "A muss!" Patrick cried, and darted off.

"Wait!" Amelia rushed after him, clutching her papers. A gang of boys scuffled with someone on the ground. "Dirty Chinaman!" one boy shouted. He brandished a knife in one hand and a long black braid in the other. The mob jeered. A man's legs, sheathed in blue pantaloons, thrashed in the dirt, and a soft slipper flew into the air.

"Mr. Wong!" Amelia gasped, dropped her papers, and edged toward the crowd. "Stop!" she cried. "Don't hurt him!" But the boys kept after him; one boy even kicked him in the ribs. "Help him!" Amelia screamed. Someone pushed her from behind and suddenly Amelia was caught in the twisted mess of arms and legs. She ducked her head to avoid the rain of blows.

"Leave Emile alone!" Patrick beat his way toward Amelia, jabbing and punching. Amelia's cap disappeared, and a sharp elbow caught her in the ribs. She dropped to her hands and knees and wriggled toward Mr. Wong, who was curled up on his side, his arms and hands protecting his head. Amelia crouched over him and turned to face the boys. "Stop, you cowards! Stop!"

"Oooh," one of the boys cried, taunting her. "Lookee this! A boy loves the Chinaman. Guess you don't care how Chinamen steal and cheat."

"But they don't. Mr. Wong is a good man." Amelia struggled to keep from crying.

"Watch out!" Patrick ducked his head like a ram and slammed into the belly of the boy holding the braid. The boy's knife flew, and he doubled over, dropping to his knees. Patrick tripped another boy with his boot and slipped away from a third as if he were greased. Mr. Wong coughed and vomited into the dirt.

The boys recoiled and jumped aside. The boy with the braid scrambled to his feet but Amelia whirled on him and lunged for the black pigtail. "Give it back," she said.

He lifted it over his head, sneering at her. "What's it worth to you?" he asked.

"A dollar." She dug into her pocket and pulled out the coin.

"Don't!" Patrick's face shone bright red under his freckles. "Our earnings—"

"You'll get your share." Amelia paid the boy and snatched the braid from his hands. She planted her feet wide, though he could beat her up in an instant if he wanted to. "He's done nothing to you. You're the one who steals," she said, lifting Mr. Wong's braid. If only her voice were deeper. "Go away." Her heart hammered in her throat. For a moment, the Plaza was silent except for the wind, swirling dust around her boots.

Finally the boy wiped his hands on his pants. "Smells rotten here. We'll leave this Chinee lover to clean up." He spat at Amelia's boots. She flinched but didn't move. When the boys moved off, she squared her shoulders and handed Mr. Wong the braid. Would he recognize her?

"My queue," he said softly. He cradled it in his cupped hands and coiled it like a piece of thick ribbon. "Like they cut off my arm. No good now."

His words made her skin prickle. Amelia helped Mr.

Wong to his feet. He blinked fast, staring at her with a puzzled expression. She put a finger to her lips, but too late. "Miss Amelia," he said. "Why?"

Amelia couldn't explain. She returned Mr. Wong's bow of thanks and stood watching while he limped away, his shoulders hunched as if he expected another attack. Why did so many people hate the Chinese? She didn't understand this city at all.

CHAPTER

✳ 27 ✳

Jingling Coins

AMELIA AND Patrick picked up the newspapers that had blown apart in the wind and tried to reassemble them, but the pages were torn and crumpled. "Why'd you go to all that trouble for a Chinaman?" Patrick demanded.

Amelia couldn't answer. She stumbled to the edge of the Plaza and plopped down next to the fence where she took stock of things, like a dog licking its wounds. Her heart pounded, a bruised muscle pulsed in the small of her back, and her fingernails were chipped and dirty. "Mr. Wong is our friend," she said at last. "He helped my family. Those boys were nasty." Nothing made sense. She had cut off her braid on purpose, but Mr. Wong's shorn braid was like a missing limb to him. She put a hand to her head and gasped. Julius's cap was gone.

"Missing something?" Patrick pulled the cap from his coat pocket.

"Thank you. And thanks for standing up for me." Amelia brushed off the dust. The cap was slightly crumpled, but it still fit easily over her curls. She touched a bruise on Pat-

rick's forehead. "You've got quite a lump, and we're two papers short." She sighed and emptied her pockets, staring at
the odd collection of coins. "Will Julius take all this foreign
money?"

"Of course," Patrick said. "It's as good as American."

They sorted the pile. In addition to American coins,
they had an English Crown ("The same as a dollar," Patrick
said), Mexican *reales* ("*Dos reales* is two bits," he reminded
her), some French francs, and a few English shillings. "We
have almost eleven dollars. We'd have more if you hadn't
paid off the bully," Patrick said.

"*And* if you hadn't made me pay for the pony. If only
they all paid us in American coins." Eleven dollars was
more money than Amelia had seen in a long time, but she'd
started with fifteen papers. What would Julius say?

As they left the Plaza, they passed the pony, tied to
the fence outside a gambling hall. The pony whickered
and pricked his ears when he saw them. Shouts sounded
from inside, but there was no sign of the pony's owner.
Amelia reached into her pocket and pulled out the apple,
now slightly crushed, and offered it to the pony on her
flat palm. He curled his lips and took the fruit gently. Juice
trickled from his mouth as he crunched it in a few bites.
Amelia untangled his mane from his bridle and whispered
in his ear, "Tastes better than money, doesn't it?" She ran
to catch up with Patrick.

* * *

A HALF hour later, Amelia stood at the end of the line out-side Julius's borrowed home, waiting while he settled the accounts. As she shuffled forward, a familiar voice broke into her thoughts. "How'd you do, *Eh-meele*?"

"Leave me alone, Nico."

"Heard you got roughed up." He bounced from one foot to the other, as if he enjoyed the idea, and his brown eye wandered while the green one stayed fixed.

"You heard wrong," Amelia said, and turned away. She hoped his face wouldn't give her nightmares.

When it was her turn to meet Julius, she groped first for her apron pocket, forgetting, once again, that she wore trousers. "Almost eleven dollars," she said, and poured the coins into his outstretched hand. "I sold thirteen papers and lost two."

"*Almost* eleven?" Julius glanced at her from under the brim of his hat. "I get twenty-five percent, no matter how many papers you sell."

Amelia shrugged, though her stomach complained, re-minding her that every penny meant something more to eat. Her share was seven dollars, plus a two-bit coin. At least she understood percentages; she could thank Estelle for that. "I'll do better next time."

"'Next time' might be ten or eleven days off," Julius said.

"So what do you do until then?"

"Sell local papers," Julius said. "The *Alta*, the *Pacific News*, a few others. But you have to make your own arrangements." And with that, he was gone.

Amelia wanted to scream. She'd gone to all this trouble to sell papers twice a month? She already knew what the *Alta* editor would say to her. Or did she?

She stood frozen a moment, thinking. The editor had turned her away when she was a *girl*. What would he say if she came to him as Emile, with a fresh story?

"Wake up." Patrick stood in front of her, tapping his toe.

"Sorry." She gave Patrick four dollars, plus a French franc.

Patrick frowned. "That's more than half."

"It's my fault we lost those papers," Amelia said.

"I'd better go," Patrick said.

"Wait." An idea was prickling in her mind, though she couldn't name it yet. "Remember where we saw that poster about the balloon?"

Patrick nodded. "Up on the Plaza."

Amelia smiled. "Right. And wasn't Wilson's bakery nearby? Can you show me the way?"

"Sure. But why?"

"I'm hungry—aren't you?"

A LITTLE after one o'clock, according to Patrick's watch, Amelia was finally headed to Rosanna's with a warm graham loaf under one arm. Coins jingled in her right pocket, and the balloon poster, which she had torn from the building when no one was looking, was carefully folded up in the other. Patrick had left to join Henry, but Amelia stopped in at the *Alta*'s office. She leaned against the doorframe with one foot crossed in front of the other, the way Julius did in his captain's quarters, and watched the editor scribbling furiously in his notepad.

"Need help delivering papers?" she asked, her voice as gruff as possible.

He didn't even turn his head. "Not today. Check with Julius."

So Julius was the boss all over town. Amelia was about to leave when she noticed the paper's masthead set out in big, fancy type on a flat table beside the door. She puzzled out the words, set backward: **DAILY ALTA CALIFORNIA**, the masthead announced. And underneath, in smaller, blocky type, it read: SAN FRANCISCO, TUESDAY MORNING, MARCH 25, 1851. "Is that today's date?" she asked.

The editor finally turned around. "We're setting tomorrow's paper," he said. "Today is Monday." He glared at her. "Do I know you?"

"No sir." She touched her cap and hurried away before he could get a closer look. So the balloon launch was eight days away. Would her plan work?

She raised the bread to her nose. The aroma was too

enticing. She broke a small piece off the end and gobbled it down, then another. The warm bread soothed her stomach and quickened her steps. Mother had been expecting her for hours. But surely this bread—along with her stack of coins—would make Mother happy.

CHAPTER

✳ 28 ✳

Young Woman of Business

THE GOATS greeted Amelia with happy bleats as she approached the ship. "Hello, Daisy! Hello, Charrie!" Amelia wrapped the graham loaf in her cloak like a package and slung it over her shoulder as she climbed to the deck.

She rested on the top rung of the ladder and took in the scene in front of her. Mother perched next to a makeshift table, a board set across two barrels, stitching something from red flannel, while Estelle stood on tiptoe at the foot of the mast, slashing at the torn sailcloth with a knife. A small jug of wildflowers sat on an upturned crate between them. Amelia smiled. Almost like home.

"Hello," Amelia said, and scrambled onto the deck. Mother's sewing fell to her lap and she gave a little start as she looked her up and down. "Amelia!" she said. "For a moment, I thought you *were* a boy, come to call on us. Your disguise is convincing." She frowned. "But we agreed that you'd sell your papers and come right back."

"I did. It takes a while. Look." Amelia set down her cloak, then dug into her pockets for the coins and poured them out onto the cloth. The silver and copper coins gleamed against the flannel. "It's not as much as I hoped. I lost two papers—and I had to share my earnings."

Mother pursed her lips as she counted the coins. She touched the belt of her apron. "I'll put this in my secret pocket. Perhaps we'll even have a chicken tonight!" She cupped Amelia's chin in her hand. "I don't know what to think. It frightens me to death, every minute you're gone— but the extra coins are a big help." She looked Amelia up and down. "What do you think, Estelle—have we raised a young woman of business?"

"I'd say so." Estelle smiled at Amelia. "What do you call yourself now?"

"Emile. Emile Duprey. I'm your little brother, in case anyone asks."

"Ah," Estelle said. *"Alors, tu est Français, comme moi."*

"Oui," Amelia said, "we're both French."

"And no relation to me." Mother looked hurt.

"It's only a disguise," Amelia said. "We're all in the same family." For some reason, that word—*family*—made her eyes fill.

Mother wiped Amelia's cheeks with her apron hem. "Don't cry." She turned to Estelle. "Can you imagine what Gran would say about Amelia wandering through a strange city with a group of wild boys?"

"I'm not 'wandering,'" Amelia said. "I know where I'm going. And we're not wild. Julius is in charge."

"Who's Julius?" Mother asked.

"He's the boss of the newsboys. He organizes every-thing." Amelia was about to add that he was an orphan, when she remembered his fear about being sent to the Or-phan's Asylum.

"Does Julius know you're a girl?" Mother asked.

Amelia nodded. "He loaned me his cap." She pointed at the pile of canvas on the deck, eager to change the subject. "Why are you cutting up the sails?"

"Your mother is quite the businesswoman too," Estelle said. "She sold three shirts before they were even made. We'll use this old sailcloth to stitch men's trousers, if we can find a needle strong enough to pierce the fabric. We have plenty to do now."

Amelia's stomach growled so loudly that they all laughed. "I bought some bread." She presented Mother with the warm loaf.

Mother sniffed it and smiled. "A little mouse has tasted this already."

"I couldn't help it," Amelia said. "I was starving."

After feasting on warm bread and goat's milk, Amelia's cheeks grew warm and her eyes felt heavy. She was about to doze off when she felt Mother's hand cup her own. "I worry about what you're doing," Mother said.

Amelia sat up, suddenly awake, as Mother went on. "Es-telle and Rosanna persuaded me that you're safer dressed as a boy, especially if you go out on your own."

"Does that mean I can keep on selling newspapers?" Amelia asked.

"For now," Mother said. "But our business is already under way. When we get on our feet, this charade will end and you'll be my daughter again."

"I'm always your daughter." Amelia hugged Mother. But would she have to stop working? Though she'd been in two fights, lost some of her money, and worn herself out, Amelia had to admit: she loved the sound of coins clinking in her pocket.

* * *

March 28, 1851
Dearest Gran,

It has been raining hard and the dusty streets have turned to mud. When Mother and Estelle send me to do their errands my boots sink to my ankles. But my legs are strong from running up and down the steep hills. Sometimes I visit newspaper offices. I like to see how they make the papers. If they don't have enough paper to print on they might use bucher paper. Or paper they find in the streets.

I am glad you are living with Uncle Paul so you dont feel lonesome. Do you have any special visitors at the farm?

Write a letter soon to your granddaughter,

Amelia

P.S. We named our ship the Beatrice, after you!

CHAPTER

✴ 29 ✴

The Whole Wide World

ON THE last day of March, Amelia found Patrick out on the Long Wharf, watching a ship unload barrels of molasses. She pulled the balloon poster from her pocket and smoothed it out on her knee. "The balloon launch is tomorrow at dawn," she said. "Where is North Point?"

"Just past Telegraph Hill," Patrick said.

"Then we'll have to be up early."

Patrick wrinkled his nose. *"We?"*

"Of course. Don't you want to see the balloon take off?" Before he could answer, Amelia said, "Come sleep on the *Beatrice.* You're so good about waking early." Patrick hesitated but Amelia cupped his elbow and pulled him toward the ship. "You haven't seen the goats in days. They're lonesome for you."

After supper, Mother offered him a pallet inside, but Patrick shook his head. "I'm used to sleeping outdoors." He took a blanket and curled up on the deck with Smoky, their new cat. Patrick reminded Amelia of Uncle Paul's cow dog, who refused to come into the house, even in the winter.

In the days since they'd met, Amelia had tried to discover where Patrick and Henry lived, but he always pursed his mouth when she asked. Perhaps he thought she would give him away, report to someone that he was an orphan—but of course, she never would.

Mother assumed they were meeting the mail boat the next morning, and Amelia didn't correct her. The steamer *was* due any day, and if her plan didn't work, no one would ever know.

Amelia tossed and turned all night and sat up fast when Patrick rapped on the door. "Hsst!" he whispered. "It's four o'clock."

Had she even slept? Amelia dressed quietly and patted her pockets. She carried her spyglass in one, two pieces of folded paper and her Thoreau pencil in the other. She poked her head out the door. The brightest stars still glittered overhead, and a planet hung low on the horizon. No fog—at least, not yet. Was this what the balloonist meant by "Weather permitting"?

Patrick waited near the ladder, his watch cradled in his hand. The goats muttered as Amelia crossed the deck. "Shhh," she scolded, and slid down the rungs to the street. How had she ever managed in a skirt?

She stood at the bottom of the ladder, waiting for her eyes to adjust to the dark. The street was deserted. Ships creaked against their anchor lines at the wharf and a solitary mule clopped past. Amelia clucked to the mule, and its ears flattened in warning. Although it had no rider, the mule seemed to know where it was going.

Patrick nudged her. "What are you waiting for?"

"Nothing." They set off down the street.

"This better be good." Patrick's teeth were chattering. "What if the steamer comes and we're not there?"

"Then we're out of luck. You can skip this, if you want." But Patrick tagged right along beside her. As dawn turned the sky to silver, the air seemed to grow colder. Amelia tucked her hands under her cloak. They rounded Telegraph Hill and hurried to the next point, where Amelia stopped so quickly that Patrick bumped into her. "Hey—" he began, but Amelia hushed him.

They stood still, staring. Someone had cleared a wide circle in the grass on the hillside and enclosed it with a temporary fence. Six or seven dark figures moved about inside the enclosure, hurrying back and forth between two wooden boxes on wheels. Long tubes ran from each box, each one attached to an enormous piece of cloth. Barrels and kegs, some cut in half, surrounded the boxes, and an eerie hissing sound came from beneath the cloth, which writhed and billowed in the dim light, lifting and swelling as if an enormous animal were trapped inside. A wicker basket, big enough to hold a few men, lay tipped on its side near the contraption.

Patrick peered over her shoulder. "What are they doing?" he whispered.

"I don't know. Let's get closer." They dropped to their hands and knees and crept through the tall grass to the fence, where someone had tacked up a line of posters. Amelia squinted to make out the words in the dim light.

A BRAVE ASCENT AT SUNRISE! YOUR CHANCE TO SEE THE BAY FROM THE AIR! one sign said. Another, printed in an unsteady hand, warned, DO NOT ENTER. PROPERTY OF G. BEALE.

Amelia and Patrick ducked as a small man dressed in a long coat and a top hat bustled past. "No open flames, no smoking anywhere!" he called out to the men, gesturing at the tubes snaking across the ground. "The gas flowing into the balloon is highly flammable! No matches or pipes please!" Amelia held her breath. Was the gas making that hissing noise? She wanted to ask, but was afraid the man would send her away.

"Mr. Beale, shall we add more iron filings?" a man called from his post beside one of the barrels. The man in the top hat hurried over to him. So that was the aeronaut. He looked more like a Boston solicitor than a balloonist. But Amelia had never seen an aeronaut—*or* a balloon—in her life.

The sky lightened as the balloon grew. At first, it looked like a hoopskirt fit for a giantess. Then, as the bottom half began to fill, it became a globe. Two men draped an enormous piece of netting over the top of the balloon to hold its shape, while others shifted the basket so that it stood upright beneath the globe. As the sun rose, the cloth took on the color of the cardinal that sang outside Gran's kitchen window. Should she write that down? Amelia was about to pull paper from her pocket when Mr. Beale waved his arms at the crowd of men forming outside the fence.

"I need four strong volunteers to hold the tether lines," he called. "View the launch for free! Otherwise, my boys will be around to collect your dollar. And for fifty dollars—only fifty dollars!—some lucky man can join me for a magnificent view of the city and the bay from the air."

"You didn't tell me we had to pay to watch," Patrick whispered.

"I didn't know." Amelia poked her head above the grass. And she should have guessed: Mr. Beale's "boys" were Julius and Nico. They stood outside the fence, collecting money. How did they manage to be everywhere? She nudged Patrick. "If Julius is here, then we haven't missed the mail boat," she said.

Patrick pointed to the crest of the next hill. "We could climb up there and watch for nothing," he said.

But Amelia wasn't listening. When only three men volunteered to help Mr. Beale, she scrambled to her feet, pulling Patrick with her, and leaned against the fence, waving. "Sir!" Amelia called in her deepest voice. "We can help you. Give us a line."

Mr. Beale peered at her and laughed. "Two *boys*? Sorry. *Four* lads your size couldn't keep hold of the *Star of the West* when she's filled with gas." He turned his back and cajoled the crowd until a fourth man volunteered. But his line was snarled and he struggled to untie it, his feet tangling in the rope. Mr. Beal joined him and the two men fussed at the line, cussing.

Now was her chance. Amelia slipped through the fence and rushed over. "Let me try." She worked at the rope and loosened the knots. Mr. Beale started to protest, then nodded his approval. "Hold her tight now!" he called to the other men, while Amelia retied the line to the balloon and handed the rope to the fourth man. Mr. Beale yanked on her knots to make sure they were tight and shot her an approving glance. "Clever boy." The men held the tether lines as the balloon tugged and stretched skyward, as if it couldn't wait to fly. The men who had been busy with the boxes and hoses hurried to the balloon. They were fiddling with a long length of cloth that dangled from the bottom of the sphere.

"What keeps the balloon in the air?" Amelia asked.

"The gas in the balloon is lighter than the air we breathe." Mr. Beale pointed to the boxes on wheels. "We made the gas in those boxes. It flows through the tubes and into the balloon. When she's ready, the gas will lift her up above the city."

Patrick came up beside them. His blue eyes were round and full of light. "Just imagine. You could see the whole world from up there. The whole wide world. Maybe all the way to Ireland."

"Not the *whole* world," Amelia said. But how much *could* you see? What if she flew to Concord and waved to Gran and Uncle Paul? Amelia was about to pull out her paper and write down what Mr. Beale had told her when he beckoned to them. "Come here, lads."

Amelia and Patrick glanced at each other. Were they in trouble? Mr. Beale's black eyes were so piercing, Amelia wondered if he could see through her disguise. But then he smiled and rubbed his hands, his mustache quivering with excitement. "Just the right size for a more important job." He turned his palm up and gestured at the basket, like a queen's servant showing his majesty to a throne. "Climb right in."

The balloon's basket bounced as if it might take off any minute and the swelling crowd began to buzz. "Hold those lines!" Mr. Beale cried.

Patrick backed away. "We only wanted to look, sir. We don't want to fly."

"Of course you don't," Mr. Beale said. "*I'm* the aeronaut. Just one lucky customer will ride with me across the bay this morning. But you boys can be my ballast, keep the car steady while we load the sandbags. Come on, lads. You can tell your parents you came close to having a balloon ride."

Amelia guessed it was the mention of "parents" that made Patrick scowl. As they were about to climb over the side, the basket took a slight hop to the side. A gasp rose from the crowd. "No need to panic!" Mr. Beale cried. He hoisted a sack full of sand and lowered it into the basket. The balloon steadied. "In you go, lads."

For one awful moment Amelia thought everyone would see her pantalettes—but then she remembered that she was Emile, who wore trousers. Amelia nodded at Patrick and they clambered in together. The aeronaut pointed at a long rope that dangled from inside the neck of the balloon. "Don't touch that," he said. "This line opens the rip panel at the top of the balloon. If you release the gas in the envelope, I'll lose my fortune."

"Envelope?" Amelia nudged Patrick. "I've never seen a letter that big."

Mr. Beale left them and rushed about the site, gesturing and calling out to his helpers. The men lifted more sandbags over the side. With the sandbags at their feet, there was hardly room for them to stand. How would Mr. Beale fit, with his passenger?

Amelia tipped her head back and admired the balloon. The *Star of the West* was beautiful. Her red silk stretched up above them, higher than any building Amelia had ever seen. Golden stars and a few planets were sprinkled across the fabric, just like the stars that had pricked the night sky earlier this morning.

She pulled out her paper and pencil and scribbled some notes. "Star of the West. Iron filings help to make the gas . . ." (*But how?* she wondered.) "Enough silk for all the women in San Francisco . . ." But the editor had said, "Just the facts." Was that a fact, or a guess?

"Why are you *writing*?" Patrick asked. His eyes looked ready to pop from his head. Amelia studied the silk gores that made up the balloon, held together with thousands of tiny stitches. Even Mother and Estelle, who sewed fast, would take months to stitch something this big.

The silk shone in the sunlight. Was it coated with something greasy? Amelia wanted to touch it, but the envelope was too far above her head. A cold wind tugged at the fabric, and the basket shuddered. Patrick reached for the basket's rim. "Should we get out?" he asked.

A man tossed in another sandbag. "This ballast will hold you," he said. "Mr. Beale will throw some bags overboard when it's time to take flight. Wait until he tells you what to do." He set a small satchel at their feet. "Food for the voyage," he said. "No nibbling."

The balloonist seemed to have forgotten all about them. He climbed the fence and stood with his back to them, waving his arms and calling out to the crowd like a barker at the circus. "Just one dollar to watch the ascent!" he cried. "Fifty dollars gives a lucky man the chance of a lifetime—to see the bay from the air!"

"Or to drown in cold water," one man answered, and the crowd jeered.

Amelia felt sorry for Mr. Beale, but he bounced on his

toes as if he might lift off from the ground on his own.

"The *Star of the West* brings you the best entertainment in town," he said. "The first balloon ascent in this brand-new state of the union!"

A man with a mustache and spectacles stepped forward from the crowd. "How long will she stay aloft?" he asked. "And how do you get down?"

Amelia knew that voice. Her shoulders slumped in disappointment when she saw the editor of the *Alta* standing at the fence, notebook in hand. Of *course* he would be here to write the story. How dumb could she be?

"The *Star of the West* will carry you across the bay and then some," Mr. Beale was saying. "If we need to go higher, we toss out the ballast. When it's time to come down, we pull on the crown line to open the rip panel and release the gas. Perfectly simple. Care to join me?"

"I have a paper to bring out," the editor said. "But if you visit me after your ascent, I'll put your story in the *Alta*." He gestured to the crowd. "And I'll tell the story of the brave man who goes with him, as well."

Amelia turned her back on the editor. He would never read her story now.

"Last chance!" Mr. Beale opened his arms as if to give the whole crowd a hug. "You'll see the bay—and be famous all over town!"

"You'll get stuck in a tree!" a man called out from the crowd. "I saw an ascent like that back East."

Mr. Beale raised his hand to his brow and scanned the hillside, like a sailor on the lookout for a whale. "Not a tree in sight," he said. Now the crowd was laughing with him. "We'll sail over the bay, lift above the hills, and land softly in the plains beside the Sacramento River. And we'll celebrate our landing in style." Mr. Beale reached into a bag at his feet and hoisted a bottle of champagne above his head.

A heavy-set man, dressed in many layers of clothing, put up his hand. "I'll join you," he said.

Mr. Beale looked him up and down. "Sorry, sir—I'm not sure we have enough gas to get you aloft." The man stomped away as the crowd roared.

"Would your balloon carry me to the mines?" It was a boy's voice.

"Look, it's Nico," Patrick said.

Did Nico think he could find his father in the balloon? Amelia nearly laughed until Nico leaned over the fence, pointed at her, and cried, "Sir! What's that *girl* doing in your basket?"

CHAPTER

✴ 30 ✴

Higher Than the Birds

MR. BEALE turned to stare at her just as a gust of wind tore the piece of paper from Amelia's hand. She lunged for it, the basket jumped, and they almost tipped over. Patrick screamed and started to climb out. "Stay where you are, boys! Men, hold the tethers!" Mr. Beale shouted and scrambled over the fence. He tripped and fell over the tubing as a stronger gust of wind yanked a tether from one man's hands. A helper lunged for the rope but it whipped at his face and knocked him down.

The wind hummed in the ropes that held the basket to the netting. The basket leaped like a rabbit beneath Amelia's feet. She hoisted one leg to climb out but Mr. Beale screamed. "Don't jump! We'll lose the balloon! Hang tight, I'm coming to get you. Someone, throw in my duffel—she needs more ballast to hold her against the wind!"

One of the men holding a tether line tossed Mr. Beale's duffel at them, but it missed and the man lost his hold on the rope. Now two lines whipped in the wind. "Help!" Amelia screamed. The basket lurched again, and Patrick tumbled backward, his arms and legs flailing like an upside-down beetle's. Amelia lunged for Patrick and the basket righted itself. She grasped the rim with one hand, grabbed for Patrick with the other—

How did it happen? *How?* One minute, Amelia was gripping the basket's rim with all her might. In the next instant, her stomach sank and the basket bounced like a buggy pulled by a runaway mare. The crowd roared in horror—and the balloon took flight.

Amelia leaned out, straining to reach the men who dashed after them. "Catch us!" she screamed.

"Hold on!" Mr. Beale's face was purple. "Give me your hands—wait!"

The editor of the *Alta* raced below the basket. "Boys! Tell me your names! I'll put you in my story."

"Jump!" Patrick screamed.

Amelia peered over the edge. "It's too late!"

The balloon was already higher than the tallest ship's mast. They were headed straight for the harbor. The balloonist ran in circles now, screaming orders. "Pull on the crown line!" he screamed. "Let out the gas!"

Was he crazy? They were skimming the point, headed for the bay. If Amelia let out the gas, they would smash on the rocks, or drown. The *Star of the West* flew toward the water faster than any horse could gallop. Two boys—Julius and Nico?—broke away from the crowd and dashed after them. In another instant, Amelia and Patrick were already too high to pick out faces; too high to hear more than distant screams, fading like the shriek of gulls winging out to sea.

The blood rushed from Amelia's head, and she doubled over. "I don't want to die!" she moaned.

Patrick shook her. "Look!" he cried. "This is brilliant! We're flying!"

Amelia wedged her boots between two sandbags and grabbed the basket's rim. The city fell away beneath them: jumbled roofs, the zigzag network of streets pieced together like a crazy quilt, the semaphore on Telegraph Hill— everything grew smaller and smaller, as if the city were shrinking.

Amelia's stomach lurched and she clapped a hand over her mouth. The balloon sailed high above the bay, headed for the folded hills rising in the east. They floated toward clouds that loomed above the ridges and valleys. The only sound was the creak of the ropes holding the basket. The wind must be blowing—how else could they be moving?— but Amelia felt nothing, not even a whisper of a breeze. They seemed borne on a swift, silent current. A hawk soared beneath them. Blood rushed like water in Amelia's ears. "We're higher than the birds," she whispered.

"We're flying!" Patrick cried again. "We'll be famous!"

Amelia turned on him. "It's no good being famous if you're dead!"

Patrick's face crumpled. "This was *your* idea!"

He was right. Amelia took a deep breath, then another, until her hands stopped shaking. Her spyglass! How could she have forgotten? She pulled it out and opened it to its full length.

"What are you doing?" Patrick asked.

"Finding a place to land." She cupped the lens to her eye and focused on the far side of the bay. "Where did Mr. Beale say he would come down?"

Patrick's brow furrowed. "He said he'd go over the hills and land near some river. But how do we get past those mountains?"

Amelia followed his pointing hand. The hills rose just beyond the bay. Would they smash into them? Would it hurt to die, or would she be in heaven with Granddad? Poor Mother and Estelle. They might faint, or die of the apoplexy, when they heard the news. What if she never saw them again?

Amelia swallowed hard. "We've got to land."

Patrick pointed down. "Not now."

She peered over the edge. The bay was dark and ominous, dotted with small islands.

"Mr. Beale tosses out the sandbags to go higher," Patrick said.

Amelia squeezed his hand. "I'm glad you were listening." She tried to see over the hills with her spyglass, but the balloon was moving so fast she couldn't hold the glass still, and it made her seasick. It seemed as if the mountains rushed toward them while the city dropped away in the other direction. She shoved the spyglass back into her pocket. "We're too low to get over the mountains. We need to go higher. Help me dump some sand."

They crouched beside a sandbag and wrestled it to their knees, then to the basket's rim. The sandbag was as heavy as one of Uncle Paul's ram lambs, and just as awkward to lift. "One . . . two . . . three!" Amelia cried. They pushed the bag over the side. It plummeted toward the bay, end over end. The basket swung crazily and Amelia fell to her knees, nearly knocking Patrick down. The basket and the balloon lifted—but only a little. "Another one!" They each took an end of a bag, hoisted it, and peered over the edge as the bag twisted and tumbled toward the water. It made Amelia sick to watch. Would their bodies plummet to the earth in the same way if the balloon collapsed? She kept her eyes on the hills as the balloon rose, just skimming the top of the ridge.

"It's freezing up here." Patrick's teeth chattered and he shivered all over. Amelia took off her cloak and wrapped it around his shoulders, but she immediately regretted it. The air was colder than Boston in January.

A wide marshy plain opened up ahead and a brown river twisted through the marshland like a ribbon. Low hills rose beyond the meadows. The tall mountain with its snowy peak—the one she'd seen from Telegraph Hill—stood out against the blue sky in the distance. Amelia shivered. "We've got to land on a flat place. But now we're up too high."

"Mr. Beale said he pulled on a crown line, or something, when he wants to come down," Patrick reminded her.

"That's right, he talked about opening a rip panel." Amelia looked up and her heart seemed to stop. The rip panel rope was tangled in the balloon's netting, high above her head. She stood on tiptoe, but she couldn't reach it. She blinked back tears. Patrick looked so young and innocent, his small hands gripping the edge of the basket, his eyes wide as he watched the land rush away beneath them. How could she tell him they might die?

The balloon had finished its long glide over an arm of the bay. Now it followed a river. For one crazy moment, Amelia tried to memorize what she saw. No matter what the *Alta* editor wrote in his story, he could never describe this view. If she survived, she would write how the world looked from the sky; how the river cut through green marshes; how clipper ships bobbed in the bay behind them like toys; how layers of hills loomed in the distance. She shuddered. If they were smashed to bits, she'd never write another word.

They'd missed their chance to land on the grassy plain. Now another range of hills drew closer. Amelia focused her spyglass on spiked trees that climbed up and down the hills, trees that could shred the balloon's silk and crumple its wicker basket. Her heart skipped when she saw what lay beyond: another line of hills, higher than the first, and beyond that second line, craggy mountains, as high and impassable as a castle wall. Patrick clutched her hand.

"I'm scared," he whispered.

Scared? Amelia was *terrified*, but she didn't speak. She held Patrick tight. The balloon sailed on.

CHAPTER
* 31 *

Don't Look Down

"PULL ON the rope!" Patrick cried. "We're going higher."

"The rope is tangled in the netting."

Patrick's eyes brimmed with tears. "Will we die?"

"I hope not."

He squared his shoulders and swiped his cheeks with his sleeve. "That's all right," he said. "I'll see me ma and da again."

"Don't say that!" Amelia shouldn't be angry with Patrick; he was too young. She studied the landscape through her spyglass again. The balloon had shifted course and they followed another river as it twisted through a narrow valley. Here the land looked welcoming. The rolling hills were covered with pale green grass and only a few trees. She steadied the spyglass. Could those black dots in the distance be people? "I think I see some men. They could help us if we land," Amelia said.

"Lift me up," Patrick said. "I'll try to reach the rope."

"Good idea." Amelia put her arms around Patrick and

hoisted him as high as she could, but the line dangled just above his fingertips.

Amelia let him down with a thump. "I'll have to climb up. I'm taller."

"What if you fall?"

Amelia didn't answer. She thought of Four-Fingered Jim, how he scampered into the ship's rigging high above the sea, never losing his balance even when the ship pitched and rolled. When she asked how he did it, Jim had said, "Don't ever look down. That's my secret. Fix your gaze on the horizon." And hadn't she climbed partway up the mast on the *Beatrice*, to cut sailcloth for Mother and Estelle? Thank goodness for her trousers.

Amelia pocketed the spyglass and grabbed two of the ropes that fixed the balloon to the basket. "Stand on that last sandbag. Give me a leg up and hang on to my feet. Hurry. We're running out of time."

Patrick balanced on the sandbag and wove his hands together while Amelia grasped the taut ropes. She set one foot into his hands, then hitched herself onto the basket's rim and crouched there a moment, hanging tight. She tried to pretend she was on Uncle Paul's tree swing. *Don't look down, don't look down.*

"Hold tight to my britches!" she cried. Patrick's nails dug into her legs through her pants. The valve rope dangled overhead, just out of reach. Carefully, carefully—so frightened she thought she would faint—Amelia stood on tiptoe, one arm wrapped tight around the rigging while her fingertips groped for the valve line. She caught it, but the line was knotted. She heard Jim's raspy voice saying, "For a girl, you've got a way with knots."

She could *tie* knots just fine—but could she loosen one this high above the ground? The basket wobbled, and for a split second, she looked down. Her head spun. She closed her eyes until the dizziness passed. When she opened them, the mountains had inched closer. "Hurry!" Patrick cried.

Finally she pried the line loose. The rope slapped her face, caught her cheek, and fell behind her shoulder. Amelia jumped backward into the basket and dropped to her knees. Her hands smarted, but the valve line swung free above them.

"Get *up*," Patrick said. "The mountains are too close."

She scrambled to her feet. Patrick was right; the hills were closing in. "I hope we don't land in the river. Here we go." She yanked on the line. Nothing happened. She gave it a stronger tug. The balloon tipped, and the floor sank beneath their feet. "We're going down!" Patrick cried. Amelia pulled on the rope again. The balloon dropped, steadily at first, then faster. The wind whistled, a hawk veered out of their path, and the earth rose to meet them. The river widened. Trees stood apart from each other. A dark speck became a man, another turned into a mule. Patrick screamed. "We're going to crash!"

Amelia dropped the rope and reached for the last sand-bag. "Throw it overboard!" They wrestled the sack to the railing and pushed it over. The basket swung wildly, then steadied. Their pace seemed to slow.

"More!" Amelia screamed. As fast as they could, they tossed everything out: A box of nails, two coiled shanks of rope, the food bag. The balloon slowed but still they sank, plunging toward the river. The basket swayed, the ropes twisted above them, and the balloon deflated, faster and faster. Julius's cap flew from Amelia's head, her ears popped, and Patrick screamed. They fell to their knees and Amelia pulled Patrick close.

A second later, they hit the ground, bounced, hit again. The basket galloped like a carriage dragged by a bolting horse, tossing them from side to side. Amelia thrashed and lunged for something steady to hold on to. Her forehead smacked the floor and she saw stars. She couldn't breathe. An enormous, writhing weight bound her arms and legs. She was smothered in cloth. The earth spun on its axis. A giant wave rose above her, gathered her up, and spit her out the other side.

The world went black.

CHAPTER

✳ 32 ✳

Une Jeune Fille

"SOMEONE'S IN there. I saw them leaning over the edge. They looked like children. I swear."

"You're daft."

"Give you the rights to my claim if I'm wrong. Be careful with that knife. Watch you don't cut them."

"Cuidado!"

Voices. From far, far away. Who was speaking Spanish? Amelia opened her eyes. She couldn't see anything. Did it hurt this much when you died? She tried to move but she was bound like a swaddled baby. Something warm trickled down her cheek. A sharp pain pushed against her thigh.

She moaned. Was she back on the *Unicorn*, in a windstorm? No. She was having a nightmare. The kind where something chases you, but your feet and legs are frozen. She fought against the cloth bindings. "Help me!"

"I told you! There's a child in there. Careful now. Where are you?"

"Here!" Amelia punched the cloth. "Get me out!" It

wasn't a dream. Everything rushed back: the balloon deflating. The basket hitting the ground and bouncing along. Her head cracking. . . . She thrashed and gasped for breath. The fabric pulled tight. She was drowning in cloth. "Help me."

"Steady now." A man's voice was close. "Keep talking. We won't hurt you."

"Where's Patrick?" Why couldn't she hear him? "Find us," she pleaded. "Please."

"Hang on, lad," a deep voice said.

Lad. Even wrapped tight in balloon silk, they assumed she was a boy. She heard the rip of fabric, felt hands that poked and prodded. The cloth lifted from her face. Sunshine flooded over her. Two pairs of dark eyes floated above two noses and a double mustache. The words that came from his twin mouths made no sense.

"*Sea fuerte.*"

"He's right, lad: be strong." That same deep voice washed over her. "You've got a nasty gash. Hold still while we wipe the blood."

A cloth mopped her face. Someone sobbed.

"No need to carry on. It looks worse than it is. Head cuts bleed like the dickens."

Was she the one crying?

"Leave him be." Another voice. How many men were peering at her now? "I'll look after this one. Lucky we're near that doctor in Sonora. Keep searching. Must be someone else. The boys I saw were too small to sail this thing on their own. Maybe the aeronaut had the apoplexy, or fell out during the crash."

"No," Amelia said. "No one else..." Her voice sounded hollow, her words jumbled. Had she even spoken? The ground kept spinning, whether her eyes were open or closed.

Far away, so far it might have been underground, she heard mewling. Smoky the cat? The sound came again. She held still, opened her eyes. The double-faced man now had one mustache, one nose. "That's Patrick. A little boy. We flew the balloon alone."

After that, she remembered nothing.

THE NEXT time she woke she was swaying above the ground, suspended in some sort of hammock. She tried to sit up, but she was wrapped too snug to move. Bright patches of sky flashed between the tree branches overhead, and she jounced along, held up by two men. A stocky man stumbled at her feet, his fist holding up one end of her litter, but she couldn't see the man behind her. Thick cloth, wound tight around her forehead, blocked her view. "Wait!" she cried.

"He's coming to." The men lowered the hammock to the ground. Sharp stones pressed against her spine and a bearded man with kind eyes loomed over her. "Awake, are you?"

Amelia found her voice. "Where's Patrick? Is he all right?"

"Right as rain. Sitting up on Señor Hernandez's mule like a little prince."

"Please, let me see him."

Moments later, Patrick peered at her, his face covered with scratches, his hair matted on one side. He gave her a twisted smile. "They found me inside the basket. My knees and elbows are all scraped up." He pointed to his torn trousers, looking proud.

"Never mind," said the bearded man. "You can show off your wounds later. Your friend needs a doctor." He hoisted Patrick back up onto the mule. "Ready, Señor Hernandez?"

"*Sí, sí. Uno . . . dos . . . tres . . .* " On the count of three, Amelia felt her hammock rise again. The steady swing of their makeshift litter made her seasick. She gripped the fabric with both hands and recognized the balloon's red silk. The balloonist was so proud of the *Star of the West*. Would he blame them for losing it? She groaned.

"Feeling a little green?" the bearded man called over his shoulder. "You weren't making much sense when we loaded you up. Calling for your mother. And someone named Stella, perhaps?"

"Estelle. Our friend."

"*Dónde está el hombre*—the man who flies the balloon?" asked the man they called Señor.

How could she explain? Her head was full of cotton wool. "He's in San Francisco. It was an accident."

Someone laughed. "Lucky you didn't kill us, tossing things overboard."

"Sorry." Amelia's vision blurred again. Her head was higher than her feet as the men slid down a steep hill. Thick pointed firs blocked the sunlight. She closed her eyes and woke later to the sound of rushing water. "Where are we?"

"Knight's Ferry," the man in front called over his shoulder. "Don't worry, we'll get you across." They lifted her into a ferry made of two canoes lashed together. The bearded man held her steady as they poled across the swollen river. They carried her up the bank on the other side, where a family of Indians with jet-black hair sat in a circle. The men lowered Amelia gently into the tall grass, as if she were made of the finest porcelain. Someone offered her a cup of goat's milk, but the smell made her nauseated. She thought of the goats on the *Beatrice*, of Mother and Estelle. Would she ever see them again? As the ferry took on new passengers and turned around, Amelia tugged at the hem of Señor's serape. "Where are those men going?"

"To San Francisco."

Amelia felt desperate. "Then I'm going the wrong way!"

"Be still, *niño*. You need to see the doctor in Sonora."

Amelia called out to the strangers boarding the ferry. "Find my mother in San Francisco. Tell her we're alive!" But the river rushed and boiled over her words.

Señor and the bearded man loaded her onto a nest of hay in a wagon and rolled the balloon silk into a pillow beneath her head. The world spun above her as they jolted along. Sometimes the men were in the wagon, sometimes out. "Lean right!" they called, or, "Take her to the left!" The wheels strained and creaked uphill. The silver buttons running down Señor's trousers jingled and jangled as he hurried alongside. Where was Sonora? Would she ever see Mother and Estelle again?

A WOMAN'S low voice woke her. French words. Estelle? She blinked, tried to open her eyes. "Don't move." A man's voice this time.

Amelia lay still. Smelled smoke. And a smell that reminded her of the *Alta*. The voices were low and steady. *"Keep your eyes closed. Won't take long. Two stitches to hold it."*

A prick above her eye. Pain, searing pain. Another prick, piercing. A tugging. Someone screaming. A hand, gripping her own. *"Reste tranquille, mon cher."* And a throbbing; a hammer inside her head.

Fingers at her collar, a hand on her pocket: *"Something's in here—must have bruised him badly. Undo those buttons."*

"No. Don't!"

" . . . *Mais regardez, Monsieur—l'enfant n'est pas un garçon— c'est une jeune fille. A young girl."*

CHAPTER

✴ 33 ✴

Sonora

THE NEXT time Amelia opened her eyes, she found herself on a low platform, curled up under a heavy blanket. The wall in front of her was made of rough-hewn logs covered with bark. She smelled wood smoke, seared meat, and fresh pine. Rain drummed on the roof. Was she dreaming? Amelia rolled over and peered around a room dimly lit by one small window. Across the dirt floor, a man crouched on the hearth with his back to her, tending a fire. Amelia's head throbbed and she needed a privy. She threw off the blanket, swung her feet to the side, and clutched the edge of the platform as the floor tipped toward her. "Help!" Amelia closed her eyes, but the room kept whirling.

The door swung open and footsteps hurried toward her. *"Attends!"* Strong hands steadied her.

Amelia waited for her head to stop spinning, then looked up at a pair of miners dressed in identical clothes: red flannel shirts, dark trousers, and wide hats. Was she still seeing double?

The tall miner touched the brim of his hat and went back

to his place at the fire. *"Bonjour, ma petite,"* said the shorter miner in a high-pitched voice. A slim hand with long fingers reached up to remove a floppy hat, revealing a crown of hair and beautiful dark eyes with long lashes.

"Bonjour—Madame?" Amelia stammered.

"Oui," the woman said. *"Je suis Madame Arnaud."* She sat beside Amelia on the bench. *"Tu es Française?"*

"No. I mean, *non, madame."* Amelia wanted to explain, but the French words wouldn't come. Had she forgotten everything Estelle had taught her? She looked around the room. "Where's Patrick? Is he all right?"

"Mais oui. Il dorme—he sleeps." The woman pointed to a huddled form on a pallet near the fire. A tuft of Patrick's hair poked out from beneath a blanket.

"Where are we?" Amelia asked.

"Sonora," the woman answered. "In the diggings." She pronounced it "dee-gings." The woman wrapped Amelia in a shawl and led her down a slick path to a privy tucked in a pine grove. Rain sluiced over their shoulders and dripped from the boughs. The bruise on Amelia's thigh throbbed with every step. She hesitated inside the privy when Madame reached to help her with her trousers; she'd never been undressed by a stranger. But Madame soothed her. "I know—you are girl," she said. *"Une jeune fille."* Amelia held onto Madame's arm, grateful for her help, and sucked in her breath when she saw the long bruise on her leg. It was the color of a turnip top: purple streaked with yellow. She must have fallen on her spyglass. Where was it now? Was the glass broken? She didn't know those words in French.

Madame chattered as Amelia stumbled back to the cabin. The woman pointed to her own pants, then at Amelia's. "Oh," Amelia said, understanding. "We are women—*femmes*—who dress like men?"

"*Oui!*" The woman laughed. "*Comme les hommes.*"

Back inside, Madame washed Amelia's face and tended to her wound. Tears ran down Amelia's cheeks and into her mouth. The woman tried to comfort her, but it wasn't the cut that made her weep, but the gentle touch of Madame's hands, so like Mother's, as she wiped Amelia's brow, rubbed salve over her bruises, and helped her into a clean blouse. Then Madame brought her bread and fresh water, and—best of all—a tin of preserved peaches. The sweet fruit melted in Amelia's mouth. "*Merci, madame,*" Amelia said. "*Merci beaucoup.*" She gripped the woman's hand. "I want to go home. To San Francisco. I need my mother—*ma mère,*" she said. "And Estelle, our friend. *Notre . . . amie?*" She struggled to find the words.

"*Pas encore,*" the woman said. "Not yet. You must rest. The journey is long, more than sixty miles. And it rains—*il pleut. Les chemins sont comme l'huile.*"

The roads were like *oil*? Did Madame mean they were slippery? And she was sixty miles from home? Were they in the mountains she had seen from the balloon? Amelia curled up under the blanket and watched the fire. Her brain sloshed around like bilge water in the *Unicorn*. She couldn't think straight, but she knew she was in trouble: sick and bruised in a strange town with no money and no way to earn it. Mother and Estelle didn't know where she was—or if she was alive. Had Julius, or even Nico, told them about the balloon?

ALL DAY, Madame Arnaud cared for Amelia with tenderness, feeding her soup and fresh bread and holding her steady when she tried to walk. At first, the room spun whenever Amelia stood up, and objects doubled, so that the cabin sometimes had two chimneys and two doors. The hammering in Amelia's head mimicked the rain pounding on the roof. When she left the cabin to use the privy, gripping Madame's arm, she glimpsed tents scattered among oaks and pines, and a line of rooftops in the street below their cabin.

That first night, Mr. Walker—the bearded man who had rescued them from the crash—appeared at the door. "I've come to check on the adventurers. And I brought a few treats from my store." He set a clutch of fresh eggs on the stump that Madame Arnaud used for a table, then held up a piece of chocolate. "Anyone interested?"

"I am!" Patrick jumped up, but Amelia stayed on the platform, the blanket wrapped around her like a cloak.

Mr. Walker glanced at Madame. "Everyone's curious about the boys who fell from the sky," he said. "Let us know when you're ready for visitors."

Madame glanced at Amelia, who shook her head. "Not yet," Amelia said.

"I'll talk to them!" Patrick said, between bites of chocolate.

Madame smiled. "Later," she said.

Amelia was relieved. She didn't want company. And Mr. Walker had said "boys." Was Madame keeping her secret? After Mr. Walker left, Amelia reached for Madame's hand. "When can I go home?"

"*Pas maintenant. Tu es trop fragile.*"

Not now. Then when? And perhaps she *was* too fragile. Amelia felt as delicate as a robin's egg. Patrick, on the other hand, hardly seemed bruised, and sauntered off with Madame's husband after breakfast the next morning. "Monsieur's going to show me where he pans for gold," he called from the door. "I'll help him when the rain stops. We'll find a nugget as big as my fist."

"Better get rich quick so we can get home," Amelia said.

Patrick left without a backward glance and came home wet, muddy—and happy. "The French word for red is *rouge*," he announced that night. "So I'm calling them Monsieur and Madame Rouge." Patrick helped the Arnauds haul water and firewood, and even stirred the cornmeal mush for Madame, chattering away while they answered in a mix of

French and English. After dinner, Patrick settled on Madame's lap by the fire, his legs dangling. "Sing me a song," he said.

Madame sang a haunting French tune and Amelia turned to the wall to hide her tears. All her life, she had dreamed of a family that looked like this: a mother, a father, and a child sitting by a cozy fire. She felt alone and distant, as if she were still in the balloon, soaring above the mountains.

On the third night, Madame Arnaud opened the door to Mr. Walker and a small crowd of miners who stood behind him, peering into the cabin. "May we pay our respects to the children who fell from the sky?" Mr. Walker asked.

Madame let them in. Ducking their heads as they came through the door, the miners doffed their hats and bowed to Amelia and Patrick. Their hair was slicked down and their faces scrubbed, as if they were visiting the president. Amelia felt like a butterfly that someone had captured and pinned for display, but the men were kind and polite. Some brought small gifts: a smooth green stone; a tin of sardines; a hawk's feather. "Pardon our excitement," Mr. Walker said. "We don't see many children in the diggings. We miss the ones we left at home."

Amelia sat still while Patrick told their story, his chest puffed out, his hands waving and swooping as he described their flight and the crash. He referred to her as "Emile," and she didn't correct him. It was easier being a boy. "We were like ducks shot from the sky," Patrick said, and glanced at Amelia, as if he needed her approval. She nodded and smiled.

The rain stopped the next day, and Amelia could finally walk on her own. She stepped outside in the late afternoon and sat on the front stoop overlooking the valley. The Arnauds' cabin was perched on a ridge above the town's main street, where men on horseback trotted past miners who bustled along on foot, laden with picks and shovels. Campfires already flickered on the opposite hillside in front of the rows of tents, shooting sparks into the branches of oaks and pines. A donkey clomped along the road, laden with firewood. Sounds of men laughing drifted from a cabin above, and Amelia even heard someone plunking out a gentle tune on a piano. Mother would like that.

Suddenly, Patrick appeared on the brow of the hill. He rushed toward her carrying a flat wooden pan and wiggled in beside her on the stoop. "Look!" He dropped the pan and set a tiny pebble in her hand, smaller than a kernel of corn. "My own nugget! It's grand!" He snatched it back before Amelia could even study it. "When you're better, you can pan for gold to pay your way home."

"*My* way home? What about yours?"

Patrick didn't answer. Instead, he picked up the pan and circled it in the air in front of her. "A Mexican gave me this wooden gold pan. It's called a *batea*. He taught me to fill it with stones and water and shake it—like this." He circled the pan in the air and shook it sideways. "He said I was lucky to find gold, after so much rain. We'll find much more in the summer when the rivers run dry."

"The *summer*? We won't be here that long."

Patrick shrugged and ran to meet Monsieur Arnaud, who was trudging up the hill carrying a pick and shovel.

Amelia stood up slowly and held on to the doorframe. For the first time, the ground stayed firm. Enough resting. Time to do something that would help her get home.

CHAPTER

✳ 34 ✳

Young Balloonists Survive!

AMELIA SAT on a stump with a flat board on her lap the next morning, writing a letter to Mother and Estelle. Madame had left for the river, carrying a shovel just like Monsieur. Tomorrow—*"demain"*—she would show Amelia how to pan for gold. Now Patrick and the Arnauds were working among the groups of miners who bustled on the distant riverbank like ants on an anthill. The smash of hammers on stone bounced from one hillside to the other. How did the miners stand the din?

Dearest Mother and Estelle,

We are safe in Sonora, in the diggings. Patrick and I went up in a balloon—and we servived!

I want to come home but the road is closed and we are far away. Madame and Monsieur Arnaud are taking care of us. Madame says we must ride a Dearborn wagon out of the mountains. Then we take a stagecoach to Stockton and a steamer to San Francisco. Madame cant afford our

tickets but she will help me pan for gold to earn my fare.
Madame is very strong. She digs for gold like a man.

I'm sorry about the balloon. We didn't mean to take
off. The hills looked like green pillows and the rivers were
like ribbons. The wind carried us a long way. I felt like a
bird without wings.

I wish you could come and get me. Please try.

With love from your daughter Amelia. An aeronaut
by mistake.

Amelia frowned as she read over her letter. She made
the balloon flight sound like fun. She could never find the
right words to describe her terror. Besides, how would she
pay to post her letter? Monsieur had told her that the mail
left town with the express man—but how could a wagon
get here with the road closed? She threw her Thoreau pencil to the ground in disgust.

"Troubles?" Mr. Walker stood beside her, his thumbs
hooked through his braces.

"I wrote my mother to tell her I'm safe, but I don't have
money for postage. And who can fix my spelling?"

"Can't help you there." He stroked his beard. "So you
know how to write."

"Yes," Amelia said. "I've been to school."

Mr. Walker reached into his pocket and pulled out
four two-bit coins. "I wasn't so lucky," he said. "I'll pay you

a dollar to write a letter to my wife and sons."

She could earn a dollar so easily? Amelia couldn't believe it. "I'm out of paper."

"I'll take care of that." Mr. Walker pointed to a large tent at the end of the street. "I carry a bit of everything in my store. We're the assay office, too, where the miners exchange their gold dust for coins." He peered at her. "You took your bandage off."

She nodded. "Madame wants the doctor to look at it. Where does he live?"

"Dr. Gunn? At the newspaper office."

Amelia stood up so fast that her head spun and she caught his arm for balance. "Sonora has a newspaper?"

"Why, of course. The *Sonora Herald*. First paper in the southern mines. Go down the path to the main street. Look for the two-story building with the sign out front." He frowned. "The hill is steep. Shall I help you?"

"No, thank you. I'm better now." Amelia took a deep breath. Her legs suddenly felt strong. A newspaper! There might be a way out of this town after all.

She slipped the letter into her pocket, put on her cloak, and started down the trail. The path was steep, but she managed to reach the street without falling. Sonora had prettier houses than San Francisco. Some were blue, others a pale tan, with fancy decorations on their porches. The stores had signs in Spanish, French, and German, and she heard those languages—and many more—as she hurried along the main street. She passed a hotel and a French restaurant. Estelle would like that! Men strolled by wearing colorful clothes although it was early morning. One had a flower in his hat, another wore a bright crimson scarf, another strode past with a fancy cane. Many men smiled and addressed her in different languages as they passed. Had everyone in town heard about the crash?

Amelia headed for the only two-story house on the street. Clothes dried in the sun, draped over half of the upstairs porch railing. A large sign took up the left side of the balcony, announcing in bold letters: **SONORA HERALD AND JOB PRINTING OFFICE**.

The front door was wide open. Amelia hesitated on the stoop, peering in. Two men stood with their backs to her, bent over a big wooden machine with a crank that reminded her of Uncle Paul's cider press. Amelia breathed deep. The room smelled of ink and something musty. She cleared her throat. The men turned to look at her. The older man was tall, with dark hair and a trim beard that grew from his ears around the bottom of his chin. He glanced at her, then wiped his hands on his apron and hurried over.

"Our young balloonist! Welcome. I'm Dr. Gunn. I doctored you after the crash, but perhaps you don't remember. May I look at your wound?" When Amelia nodded, he gently pushed back her hair. "Healing nicely," he said. "It won't show much under the hairline. How are you feeling?"

"Better." Amelia was distracted by the tray full of letters

that sat on a table near Dr. Gunn, and by the chest with open drawers holding even more letters. "Just like the *Alta*," she said.

Dr. Gunn squinted at her. "Do you mean the *Alta California*? Are you from San Francisco?"

Where *was* she from, anyway? "We got into the balloon in San Francisco. By mistake," she added.

The younger man, who had been staring at her, cleared his throat. "Dr. Gunn, weren't you saying we should put a story in the paper—about the balloon crash and the boys who survived?"

"I was." Dr. Gunn smiled. "Would you tell us about your adventure, so we could print it for you?"

"I wrote some of it myself." Amelia reached into her pocket. "It's a letter to my mother and her friend about the flight." She handed her paper to Dr. Gunn and screwed up her last bit of courage. "I didn't tell them how I climbed into the rigging and how we threw out the sandbags before the crash—but I could add that for you."

The room was quiet while Dr. Gunn read. She wondered if he might laugh at her, as the *Alta* editor had, but he nodded as he read, as if he agreed with what she'd written. Amelia was almost afraid to breathe. "'An aeronaut by mistake.' I like that," he said at last. "And your descriptions are nice—'a bird without wings.'" He pointed to her signature. "I'd love to hear the whole story, Miss Amelia."

The other man gaped at her. "You mean—"

"Yes," Dr. Gunn said. "Quite an adventure for a young girl."

Amelia studied the scuffed toes of her boots. "No one else knows I'm a girl—except for Madame and Monsieur. And Patrick."

"I learned you were a girl when I doctored you," Doctor Gunn said. "If you want to keep this a secret, we will— won't we, Garrett?" He gave the other man a sharp look and the man nodded.

"I'd like to publish your story," Dr. Gunn said. "I could say it's from an anonymous source, but readers would be more excited to know who you are. As a writer, wouldn't you prefer to have your own name attached to your story?"

As a writer. Is that what she was? "Yes, sir," she said at last. "Thank you. My full name is Amelia Forrester. I can tell you more. But will you fix my spellings?" When Dr. Gunn nodded, she cleared her throat: this was the hard part. "I need money to get home."

"We'll pay you, of course," Dr. Gunn said. "And we'll give you some newspapers to sell on the way."

Her name in print? Papers to sell? Amelia couldn't stop smiling.

Dr. Gunn disappeared into the next room and returned with a small cloth sack that jingled when he set it in her hand. "This should help to pay for your ticket. We'll make some additions and corrections and then Garrett, my printer's devil, will set it in time for tomorrow's edition. We'll return your letter when we're done. Your mother must long to hear from you."

Mother. How could she have forgotten? "She doesn't even know that I'm alive." Amelia struggled to keep her voice steady.

"So you hope to go soon," Dr. Gunn said.

"Yes," Amelia said, even though she didn't want to leave this wondrous room. She pointed to an oval looking glass on the far wall. "Could I look in your mirror?"

"Be my guest. My wife sent it from the East."

Amelia stood on tiptoe to see her reflection. Her face was blotchy, her matted curls were twisted every which way, and her eyes seemed dark and hollow beneath the scar, which cut a raw gash below her hairline. It pulsed a purplish red against her pale skin. She turned away, feeling a bit sick.

The doctor patted her shoulder. "Don't worry, the scar will fade." He smiled. "You're taking after Madame Johnson, the first American woman to make a balloon ascent. I wish you could stay until my wife and daughters arrive. They would be proud to meet you."

Amelia glanced at a page of newsprint drying on a rack near the press. "That *R* is backward," she said.

The man called Garrett slapped his forehead and Dr. Gunn laughed. "Be careful, Garrett, or you'll be out of a job." He waved Amelia to a chair. "Have a seat, young lady." He handed her a sheet of paper, a pen, and a bottle of ink. "Put down everything else you remember about your flight. I'll ask you questions, to prod your memory."

So Amelia sat and wrote. When she stumbled over her words, Dr. Gunn helped her. She described the aeronaut and his special gas. She wrote about climbing into the basket with Patrick; how the balloon took off, and what they'd seen from the air. "I climbed into the rigging to untangle the crown line," she told Dr. Gunn, dipping the pen into the bottle.

"Write that down," he said. "What courage!"

Amelia's dirty fingers left smudges on the page and her hand began to cramp. "Will you finish, if I tell you the words?"

"Of course." Dr. Gunn took up the pen.

"Please say that the men who rescued me were Mr. Walker and Señor Hernandez," Amelia told him. "Write that you treated my wounds—and that Madame and Monsieur Arnaud took care of us." She thought for a moment. "One more thing. Please write: *Patrick was very brave. He helped us land safely.*"

FOR THE rest of the day, Amelia watched as Dr. Gunn corrected her story, and as his printer's devil set her words in type, cranked the heavy press, and drew out the paper. Dr. Gunn showed her how to sort the used type and return each letter to its proper place in the little square boxes, and he didn't seem to mind her questions. Amelia learned that there were more *E*s in the box than *Q*s, because *E* is a more common letter, that the small pieces of wood that separated one word from the next were called "furniture," and that the frame that held the letters in place was called the "chase."

Soon her fingers were smudged with ink, but she didn't mind. When the second page came off the press, Amelia found her very own words set in wet black ink. Magic! Now *her* story was news. A sentence in bold type sat atop the first column: **AN AERONAUT BY MISTAKE! INTREPID YOUNG BALLOONISTS SURVIVE CRASH IN THE MOUNTAINS!** And underneath, in a fancy script, Dr. Gunn had added: *"The following true story comes to us from Amelia Forrester, the young balloonist."*

"What does 'intrepid' mean?" Amelia asked.

"Fearless," Dr. Gunn said.

Amelia didn't tell him she'd been scared to death. Instead, she said, "Wait until Patrick sees this! And Mother— and Estelle!" She grabbed Dr. Gunn's hand and shook it, hard. "Thank you, sir!"

He laughed. "Garrett, I believe my young patient is cured."

To prove it was true, Amelia ran up the steep hill without stopping once to catch her breath.

CHAPTER

* 35 *

A Real Family

BY EVENING, many miners had heard that Amelia could read and write. She took down Mr. Walker's letter to his sons first, sitting in his tent store. "They're about your age, and Patrick's," he said. "It's hard to be so far from home." Amelia agreed. She concentrated on her spelling, but when he told her to write, at the end, "with love and affection from your father," her eyes felt hot and she pressed too hard on her pencil, breaking the lead.

"I don't know how to spell 'affection,'" she said, as Mr. Walker sharpened the pencil with his knife.

"Do the best you can." He squeezed her shoulder. "You must miss *your* mother and father."

She missed Mother and Estelle so much that her heart ached. But how could you miss a father you never knew? She took dictation from three other miners, though it was strange to hear their private thoughts. She had to guess with some words, such as *prospecting*, and she stumbled when one man wanted her to sign his letter "from your faithful husband." How many Ls in *faithful*?

While she took down their words, men came into the store with sacks of gold dust and tiny nuggets. Mr. Walker weighed the gold on a scale and exchanged it for coins while a man with a gun stood guard beside him. When a husky blond miner set down a chunk as big as his thumbnail, the tent went silent and Amelia lost her place on the page. The miner kissed the bills that Mr. Walker counted out, shouting something in a language Amelia had never heard.

"The Swede is happy," said the man at her elbow. "Most days we toil from sunup to sundown for a few grains of that dust." Amelia was startled; she'd forgotten what she was doing. But the man didn't seem to care; when she finished his letter, he paid her with a tiny nugget the color of dark butter. She held it up to the lamplight. "My first piece of gold," she said. "This will help to pay my way home—if the Dearborn wagon ever comes."

"It won't be long, now that the rain has stopped," Mr. Walker said. "Take our letters with you and mail them in Stockton."

After the men left, Amelia scooped her pile of coins off the crate she had used as a table. She had six dollars, plus the nugget—and the money from Dr. Gunn. Some coins were for postage and the rest paid for her writing. Estelle would laugh, if she knew men had *paid* Amelia to use a pen. But no one could tell her exactly how much her passage would cost. Rosanna had paid eight dollars for a steamer ticket, but had she sailed to Sacramento or Stockton? Amelia didn't know.

Dr. Gunn had told her she must also pay for the stage out of Sonora. Was there a fee for the ferry? And what about Patrick? Had he found enough gold dust, mining with the Arnauds, to pay his own way?

Too many questions. Amelia stood outside the tent store, watching campfires flicker on the hillside across the river. She looked up. The brightest stars she'd ever seen pricked the black bowl of the sky. She opened her spyglass to bring them closer. The crash had scarred the mahogany, but somehow the lens had stayed intact. Did Mother and Estelle watch the same stars at night? Were they frantic with worry? Her palms sweated with guilt in spite of the cold. She stowed her spyglass and hurried down the road in the starlight.

Patrick sat on a stump by the fire, his head bent forward while Monsieur cut his hair. Madame sat beside him, blacking his old shoes. Amelia caught her breath. Once again, they looked like a family: mother, father, and son. *"Bon soir,"* she said softly.

"Good evening to you," Monsieur said. His scissors clipped and snipped in a steady rhythm. Amelia stood by the fire, warming her hands. "I earned some money for my ticket. Now we have to find enough for Patrick."

Monsieur and Madame glanced at each other and spoke in a quick French that Amelia didn't understand. Patrick kept his head down, avoiding her eyes.

Madame reached for Amelia's hand and held it tight. *"Ma*

petite . . ." She stopped and sent her husband another worried look.

Monsieur set down the scissors. "We ask—" He struggled for the words.

Patrick jumped in. "They want me to stay here," he said. "They'd be my ma and da." His eyes shone. *"Ma père et ma mère?"* he asked, looking at Monsieur.

"Mon père," Monsieur said, correcting him with a smile.

Amelia felt as if she'd swallowed a stone. "What about Henry?" she asked. *And what about me?* she wondered.

Patrick shrugged. "Henry won't mind. He didn't like moving all the time to keep us from the Orphan's Asylum. He took care of me as a favor to me da. It's better to have a *real* family, with a ma and a da, you know?"

So *her* family—Mother and Estelle, Gran and Uncle Paul—wasn't real? Amelia bit her lip. She mustn't cry, not when Patrick looked so happy. And he was an orphan; of course he needed parents. Besides, the Arnauds were kind. Amelia sank down onto the platform and pulled the blanket around her. How could she travel alone?

As if she'd read Amelia's thoughts, Madame sat beside her and pulled her close. "You must not go alone—*pas toute seule.*" She stroked Amelia's hand. "We fix it."

Amelia tried to smile. Madame meant well. But how *could* she get home? For one crazy moment, Amelia almost wished for another balloon.

The fire crackled and steam rose from the iron kettle.

Monsieur ruffled Patrick's hair and set his scissors on the shelf. The cabin was cozy, but Amelia felt as lonesome as the stars she had seen through her spyglass.

"Will you be a boy or a girl when you go back?" Patrick asked suddenly.

"I don't know," Amelia said. When her story was published, her secret would be out. But did it matter what she wore?

As if she'd read her mind, Madame gestured at her own shirt and trousers. *"Reste comme un garçon, maintenant,"* she said. *"C'est le meilleur*—is best. *Non?"* She winked at Amelia.

In spite of her confusion, Amelia smiled. Madame was right. Dressing like a boy *was* best. For now.

CHAPTER

✸ 36 ✸

Stockton Mañana!

AFTER A quick breakfast the next morning, Madame handed Amelia an old pair of gloves. "We try to find more gold. For your tee-ket," she said. *"Allons-y."*

"All right, let's go," Amelia said. Patrick skipped along ahead of them, asking Monsieur questions, while Amelia and Madame followed behind, hoisting a heavy shovel. Although Amelia carried nothing but a tin gold pan, she felt weighted down. She scuffed her boots as they passed the *Herald* offices, which were still closed. If only she could sit on the front stoop and wait for the paper—with *her* story—to appear.

It was still early, but the sun baked her skin through her shirt and the din from the river was deafening. Amelia slid down the riverbank, skirting piles of rocks stacked into towers as she followed Madame upstream to their claim. She passed men shoveling rocks, and men standing waist deep in the river, sifting and shaking the pebbles they gathered in their shallow pans. Two Mexican miners pulled a serape tight and bounced it like a bedsheet, shaking bits of gravel up and down on the woolen cloak.

"What are they doing?" she yelled over the hubbub. Madame didn't hear her, but Patrick stood on tiptoe to yell into her ear.

"They're separating the dry gravel from the gold dust." He pointed to three men shoveling stones into a long box beside the river. "That's a Long Tom. Come on, I'll show you our cradle!" He ran to catch up to Monsieur. Amelia jumped aside as a man stumbled out of the river and heaved his shovel at the bank. He cursed the high water, his bad luck, and California itself in a string of oaths that made Amelia cringe. She almost tripped on a man who lay half buried in the sand, his feet and legs covered all the way to his waist. "Excuse me," Amelia said.

"That's all right, lad." The man's teeth chattered. "Got a touch of the chilblains. They tell me the warm sand will cure it."

Was the gold worth all this trouble? She caught up to Patrick and the Arnauds upstream. They were setting up their tools next to a wooden box with a handle on the side and a wide-open mouth beneath it. Patrick waved her over. His freckles were ruddy in the sun. "I'm going to rock the cradle! But there's no baby inside."

Amelia watched while Madame and Monsieur shoveled a slush of gravel and muddy water onto the screen stretched across the top of the box. Madame rolled up her sleeves. Her arms were muscled like a man's, and her shovel was as full as Monsieur's each time she lifted it. Amelia felt useless when Patrick grabbed the handle and rocked the cradle back and forth, back and forth. "The gold is heavier than the stones!" he called. "It will come out at the bottom." But Amelia didn't see gold anywhere.

While Patrick rocked the cradle, Madame set down her shovel and showed Amelia how to pan for gold. She waded into the river and Amelia followed, wincing when the icy water seeped into her boots. First Madame scooped a mix of stones and sand into the pan, then held the pan underwater as she pushed out the bigger stones. Then she stirred the gravel with her fingers, getting rid of the pebbles. Finally, she swirled the pan around and around, letting in fresh water, sifting, stirring, and shaking, spilling gravel over the rim. Amelia watched carefully, but she still didn't see so much as a speck of gold dust in the bottom of the pan.

Madame handed her the pan. The sun inched toward noon as Amelia scooped and poured, circled the pan and shook it, over and over. Her arms ached, her back was sore, her feet were numb with cold. Tears of frustration pricked her eyes. Once, a golden flake emerged from the slurry, but Monsieur shook his head when she showed it to him. "Fool's gold," he said.

Amelia dropped the pan and sat in the sun, stretching her legs out in front of her to dry her boots and trousers.

Madame nodded her approval. *"Très bien,"* she said.

But Amelia knew she hadn't done a good job. She looked up and down the length of the river. Nothing but men in trousers; not a single skirt. If Madame could work in the mines with all these men, then surely she, Amelia, could travel alone to San Francisco. Besides, she was a newsgirl, not a miner. What was she waiting for?

Amelia brushed herself off and waved good-bye to Patrick before she scrambled up the riverbank to the main street. Her boots squelched with every step as she climbed the *Herald's* front stoop. She hesitated before knocking, but Dr. Gunn threw open the door. "Come in!" he said, smiling. "We were wondering where you were."

Amelia pointed to her wet boots and trousers. "I was panning for gold," she said. "But no luck. It's too hard."

"I agree." He disappeared and came back with a stack of papers. "Can you manage?"

"Of course." Amelia hugged the papers to her chest. The bundle felt like an old friend. She was already figuring: One for Patrick, one for Mother and Estelle, one for Gran and Uncle Paul—and the rest to help with her passage home, if she could sell them. "Thank you, Dr. Gunn. Thank you for everything."

She plopped down under an oak tree, skimmed the front page—with its poem, a story, and some jokes—and turned to the inside. The words that she had written and dictated to Dr. Gunn shimmered in black and white for everyone to read. And Dr. Gunn made her sound like a heroine! Amelia couldn't help smiling. Then she glanced at the back page, where a boxed ad jumped out at her.

"For Stockton and San Francisco: The new and splendid steamer Sophie . . . *Returning, leave Stockton every Monday Wednesday and Friday."* A steamer with Mother's name? And what day of the week was it now? How many days would it take her to reach Stockton? Doctor Gunn would know.

She was about to climb the *Herald*'s steps again when she heard the steady clop-clop of hooves, the clank of a bell, the jingle of metal. Was it the Dearborn at last? She stood on tiptoe and peered down the street. A man strode toward her, leading a string of mules. Rows of jingling silver buttons winked in the sun on each side of his leather chaps, and a big sombrero half covered his face—but she knew that man: it was her rescuer, Señor Hernandez!

"Señor!" she cried. She dropped her paper and ran to meet him.

He swept his sombrero off his head and beamed, his smile wide beneath his dark mustache. *"Hola!"* he said. "My young *amigo*. You are well?"

"Sí!" Amelia clapped her hands. Señor Hernandez looked ready for a parade. He wore a fringed sash around his waist, and a thick blanket draped over one shoulder. "Where are you going?" she asked.

"To Stockton. I leave *mañana*." He pointed to his mules, laden with saddlebags and boxes. "I'm the *arriero*, the mule driver. I take packages to the steamships and bring supplies back to the mines. I go into all the little camps where the stage cannot go." He squinted at her, his dark eyebrows pulled into a straight line. "Something is wrong? You are hurting?"

Amelia laughed. "No. Not anymore," she said. "Take me with you to Stockton *mañana. Por favor.*"

FROM THAT moment, things happened very fast. The *Herald* story had revealed Amelia's secret, but the miners who knew her just gave her wider smiles and tipped their hats. Amelia was too busy to care. Although Señor and his mule train would follow a slow and winding route to Stockton, the Arnauds and Mr. Walker agreed that she would be safe traveling with him. So that afternoon, Amelia packed her few possessions into a shoulder bag cast off by one of the miners. The bag held her spyglass, her stack of newspapers, the letters from the miners, and a few sheets of paper from Mr. Walker's store—"in case you need to write things down," he said. That night, Patrick asked to hear the newspaper story twice before he tucked his copy of the *Herald* under his pallet.

Amelia was waiting in the gray dawn light when Señor's string of mules arrived, the lead mule's bell clanging and swinging. A small crowd gathered outside the log cabin: Mr. Walker, Madame and Monsieur, Dr. Gunn and his assistant—and Patrick, who kept his back to her. He traced a circle in the dirt with the toe of his boot. "Patrick, say good-bye," she begged.

He shook his head. She spun him around and pulled him close to hide her tears. He pushed her away. "Boys don't cry," he said, but the rims of his eyes were red.

"I'll never forget you," Amelia said.

"You better not." Everyone laughed, and Patrick swiped his nose with the back of his hand. "Tell Henry it's grand up here. He should move."

"I will."

Dr. Gunn shook her hand. "If you decide to fly again, write me another letter. Your story was good for my paper—we sold many copies yesterday."

"I'm glad." Amelia beamed. Wait until the *Alta* editor heard about this.

Madame had been standing apart, her hands behind her back. Now she stepped close and gave Amelia a red flannel shirt—just like her own, but smaller. "So you look like us," she said. *"Bon voyage. Ne m'oublies pas."*

"How could I forget you?" Amelia held up the shirt in front of her. "It's beautiful. *C'est beau.*" She closed her eyes, searching for the right words. *"L'amie de ma mère*—the friend of my mother—is Estelle. She is French too. *Aussi française.* Please come see us," she said, giving up on the French.

But Madame understood. *"Bien sûr,"* she said. They hugged each other tight.

Mr. Walker swept his broad-brimmed hat off his head

and plunked it over Amelia's curls. It smelled of animal grease and wood smoke. "Now you have your own California slouch. Roll it up at night for a pillow." He cleared his throat. "Send us a line when you reach San Francisco, will you?"

Amelia nodded. She would miss them all, especially Patrick, but she couldn't wait to leave. She opened her arms to the little crowd. "Thank you, everyone," she said. "*Merci beaucoup. Gracias.* You saved my life."

"*Vamos,*" said Señor Hernandez. "How do you feel about riding a mule?"

"Fine," Amelia said. "I had a pony at home."

Señor laughed. "A mule's gait is not so smooth. But El Jefe will take you where we need to go. He's the boss." Amelia stepped into the basket he made with his hands and let him hoist her onto the mule's withers. She wriggled into the tiny space in front of the load of boxes, saddlebags, and crates. Señor Hernandez clucked up the mule and it jolted forward. Amelia twined her fingers through its mane, gave everyone a final wave, and turned toward the west. Her tears dried quickly in the sunshine. She was headed home.

Home. Such a beautiful word, with its warm *mmmm* sound, the sound she made after one bite of Gran's peach cobbler. But where *was* home? Until this winter, home meant waking in the snug room she shared with Gran, hearing the scrape of the stove grates, breathing in the smell of hot biscuits. And home meant summer days at Uncle Paul's, driving his Belgian mare into the woodlot where they had cut the trees for their little house—the house they had shipped to San Francisco. The *Beatrice*, half ship, half house, was only a temporary home. Would their new house be waiting for her when she came back?

The mule missed a step and Amelia clutched its mane to keep from sliding over its withers. Señor Hernandez glanced over his shoulder. "Ready for *l'aventura*?" he asked.

Another adventure sounded fine. Amelia sat up tall and gripped El Jefe with her legs. The low hills, sprinkled with oak and pine, rolled out before the mule train. She was headed west at last. *"Sí, Señor,"* she said. "I'm ready. *Listo.*"

CHAPTER

Niña o Niño?

THE ROAD out of Sonora followed the river. Though Amelia
had traveled this route before in the Dearborn wagon, she'd
been lying flat on her back. Now she took in the changing
views, wanting to remember everything so she could write
it down later: the blush of spring green under the oaks and
pines; bright flowers that looked like Gran's summer pop-
pies bending before the wind; the wide-open sky, as blue as
Estelle's eyes; the rounded hills with rocky tops looming
above them.

About an hour downriver, Amelia called out, "Señor?"

He turned around. "You are *fría*—cold?" He started to
unwrap his serape.

"No, *gracias*. I want to walk." Before she could wiggle out
from her seat, Señor lifted her down as if she weighed nothing. Her legs were sore, though she hadn't been riding for
long. As he set her down, Amelia said, "You know that I'm
a girl, Señor?"

"*Sí!*" His mustache lifted above his smile. "In Murphy's

and in Columbia, they talk about *la niña*, the girl who dropped from the sky."

"But how do they know?" Amelia asked.

He looked sheepish. "I tell them," he said. "How the red balloon comes down, down, down, slow at first, then faster. How we saw your heads—and then, when you crashed, how we thought you must be dead. *Dios mío*." He crossed himself.

"But how did *you* know I was a girl?"

His cheeks grew red. "Señorita, when we found you, I see you have the voice and the shape of *una niña*. Your disguise will not work for long."

Now it was Amelia's turn to blush. She thought of something. "Have they heard about me on the way to Stockton?"

"Not yet. So, as we travel, will you be *niño* or *niña*?"

"*Niño*," she said. "It's safer. And I have no dress to wear. So I am Emile."

"*Muy bien*." Señor gave her the lead mule's rope. "Then people will not ask questions about us. You lead El Jefe; that is the boy's job. I keep the mules in line."

FOR THE next few days, they traveled up and down steep hills into mining towns and camps. Amelia learned to climb on and off El Jefe's back on her own so that she could ride when she was tired. When the mule balked, she talked to it softly, stroking its neck until it started walking again.

They climbed in and out of Jamestown, then Tuttletown, and crossed the river at Parrot's Ferry. At each camp, their bells announced their arrival. Men gathered to order shovels and gold pans; seeds and boots; skeins of yarn; paper and darning needles. They also paid Señor Hernandez to carry packages to the steamers.

"You want to send a package, you speak to me," Señor told the miners. "For letters, you ask Emile. He will post them for you." Men rushed to tents and cabins and returned with letters. Some were headed to towns Amelia knew: Derry, New Hampshire; Brimfield, Massachusetts. Others were addressed to places on the far side of the world: Paris, France; Santiago, Chile.

On one very rocky road outside of Angel's Camp, they passed a hand-painted sign for Jackass Hill. The name rang a bell and Amelia pulled up the mule. "Señor!" she cried. "Can we go up there?"

He waved her on from the back of the mule train. "The track is too steep. Why, you know someone?"

"Not really." Amelia thought of Nico, boasting that his father was getting rich in Jackass Hill. She felt a little guilty not looking for Mr. Liazos. But what would she say if she found him? What if he was like *her* father—and didn't even think about his child? She kicked up El Jefe and they plodded on.

In each camp, miners paid her fifty cents, even a dollar, to carry one letter—plus money for the postage. In some towns, men bought the *Herald*, although Amelia and Señor were careful not to give away her secret. Coins jingled in her pockets and her shoulder bag bulged with letters. But would they ever get to Stockton? Every time they headed west, Señor turned off the main road to visit another camp hidden in a steep ravine.

At night, when they built their fire under the pines, Amelia thought her legs would never take another step; that she couldn't climb on El Jefe's back again. But the next morning, she woke up feeling stronger, and when her toes pushed against the insides of her boots, she didn't complain. If boys didn't whine or cry, perhaps "intrepid" girls didn't either.

Señor Hernandez showed her how to start a fire, using the spark from his flint to ignite dry twigs and pinecones. She liked feeding the flames while he staked the mules and covered his goods with canvas. As he cooked tortillas and beans, she wrote down everything she'd seen on scraps of paper. Her only trouble came when she needed a privy, but Señor Hernandez found private spots behind the wide trunks of yellow pines. He stood guard and never once turned to look.

Once they left the mountains, the journey across the open, rolling country seemed to go on forever. The mules trudged under their loads as they wound through rocky ravines, their hooves sliding on coal-black cinders. A stagecoach passed, pulled by four teams of spirited horses, and

Amelia wished she could climb on board—but she couldn't leave Señor behind, and she had to hold on to her money.

As they walked into the setting sun one afternoon, rooftops and chimneys finally shimmered on the horizon like a mirage. "Stockton—*al fin*," Señor said. "We stay outside town tonight, for safety."

"Is it Wednesday or Thursday?" Amelia asked. If only she'd kept better track of the days.

"Is Thursday, perhaps," Señor said.

"What if I miss the *Sophie*? She sails on Friday."

"There are many ships," Señor said. "Why do you search for this one?"

"Sophie is my mother's name," Amelia admitted. "Maybe it's good luck."

Señor nodded as if he understood. "We will be there *mañana*. I promise."

Amelia twisted and turned on the hard ground. She woke hours later to find that Señor had covered her with his serape. He slept sitting straight up against his bundles, a long knife balanced on his knees. Its curved blade winked in the firelight. When Amelia stirred, Señor Hernandez startled awake, holding the knife high.

"It's only me," Amelia said. "What is that for?"

"*Mi cuchillo? Para bandidos.*" He pointed to the boxes and saddlebags behind him and drew his index finger across his neck.

Amelia shuddered. She hadn't thought about bandits.

Would she be safe when Señor said good-bye?

They rode into town early the next morning. Stockton was built on the flatlands beside the San Joaquin River, and it was bigger than Sonora, with warehouses, stores, and houses set along wide, dusty streets. There were no sidewalks, and the wooden houses had yards, though nothing but dirt grew inside their fences.

Amelia had put on her red shirt, in honor of Madame, and stowed her cloak in her shoulder bag. After traveling so many miles with gentle sounds—the jingle of El Jefe's bell, the steady thump of hoofbeats on stone, the wind tossing in the pines—it was a shock to come into the bustle of a real town. Men rushed up and down the wide streets, oxen leaned into their yokes as they hauled drays piled high with crates and barrels, and a mangy dog chased a chicken across the road in front of their caravan. Their mules were laden with boxes and crates that needed shipping, and Señor was suddenly as busy and nervous as the town itself. Amelia slid off El Jefe's back and gave the mule a farewell pat. "*Gracias*, Jefe," she said. "You carried me a long way."

Señor pulled up under a solitary tree. He pointed to a low building at the end of the street. "You can mail your letters there. I must deliver my goods." He glanced at the sun. "Buy your steamboat ticket and meet me by this tree at noon. I take you to the dock."

"I can go myself," Amelia said, but she was relieved when Señor shook his head.

"I promise Madame to see you to the boat." He touched his sombrero and led his line of mules away.

As she approached the post office Amelia realized that without Patrick's watch, she didn't know the time—and how would she find the ticket office? First things first. She hoisted her shoulder bag. She could mail her letters, sell a few more papers, and be that much closer to going home.

CHAPTER

38

Friday!

THE POST office was open, but Amelia hesitated on the front stoop. Not a single skirt in sight, and the small crowd of men in line looked rough and tired. Greasy hair tangled at their necks, their clothes were torn and unwashed, and the air reeked of wood smoke and stale sweat. But the miners had sent her off with their homesick messages as if she were a carrier pigeon. She couldn't let them down. Amelia took a deep breath and forced herself inside.

When she reached the front of the line, the clerk grumbled over all the different addresses. "How can one lad have this many relatives?" he asked. Amelia started to explain, but the clerk was more interested in making sure she paid what she owed.

Outside, the sun was higher in the sky, and her sack of coins had grown smaller. Did she have enough for her ticket home? Amelia didn't dare count her money here on the street. Maybe she should change her gold nugget into coins—but Madame had sewn it into a secret pocket for safety. She remembered, from the *Herald* ad, that the Sophie sailed on Monday, Wednesday, and Friday. What day was it today?

As she stood in the dusty street, feeling lost, the first woman she'd seen all morning passed by. She wore a skirt chopped off above the ankles and carried a basket full of bread. The sweet, heady smell tickled Amelia's nose. She hurried after the woman and plucked her sleeve. "Excuse me, ma'am. What day is it?"

The woman nearly tripped; she steadied her basket and scowled. "Friday," the woman said. "Where have you been, young man?"

So it *was* Friday! Amelia smiled and her stomach began to growl. She held up her paper. "I have the *Sonora Herald*—"

"And *I* have a basket of bread to deliver." The woman waved her away and started down the street, but Amelia trotted alongside, folding the paper open to the second page. "Read about the children who fell from the sky—and lived!"

The woman finally stopped. "The ones in the balloon? I heard that story. It's true?"

"Very true." Amelia took off her hat and pushed back her hair, showing her scar. "I was one of the children."

"Go on," the woman said, but she took the paper from Amelia. "How much?"

Amelia's mouth was watering. "I'll trade you for a loaf of bread."

"Done." The woman tucked the newspaper under her arm. "But don't tell stories, son. It will get you nowhere." She bustled off.

Son. Amelia sucked in her breath. She'd nearly made a foolish mistake. If the woman *had* believed her—then everyone would learn she was a girl. She wasn't ready to spill that secret here, especially in a strange town without Madame or Señor beside her. She tore pieces from the warm loaf, gobbling it down. After a few weeks in the diggings, she was eating like a miner. What would Mother say?

She ate half the loaf and stowed the rest in her shoulder bag before counting her papers. Only three copies left: one for Mother and Estelle, one to show the *Alta* editor, and one for Gran and Uncle Paul—she needed them all. The sun was higher in the sky—Señor would worry if she didn't show up. But what if the *Sophie* sailed soon or had already left? She should check at the levee first.

The wharves on the San Joaquin were like a miniature version of San Francisco's harbor. Stores and warehouses lined the riverbanks. Barrels lay on their sides beside pyramids of grain sacks. Amelia checked the boats at every slip and finally found the *Sophie*, bobbing at anchor. Men and boys trudged up the steep gangplank lugging crates and parcels, while a line of men waited to board. Their clothing was worn, their hands swollen, and one man's hair was as tangled as a blackberry thicket. But the man at the end of the line was better dressed; he wore a waistcoat and a brushed top hat. His boots, freshly blackened, gleamed in the sun. Since Dr. Gunn had said she was brave, she stepped up to the well-dressed man. "Excuse me, sir—where do you buy a ticket?"

He looked down his nose at her—as if she had a bad smell. "Buying a ticket for yourself?" he asked. When she nodded, he pointed at the levee. "Ticket office is over there. Better hurry; we sail within the hour. Young to be traveling alone, aren't you?"

A sailor staggered past carrying a bulging burlap sack. "An orphan?" he asked. "The *Sophie* needs a cabin boy."

"I'm not an orphan." Suddenly everyone was looking at her. Amelia spoke through clenched teeth. "My mother is waiting for me in San Francisco."

"Likely story!" another sailor called out. "They all say that. Here lad, give me a hand with this bale. We could use your help."

Amelia turned and dodged in and out of the crowd. She should have said she was buying tickets for her mother. She passed black faces, white faces, faces the color of walnut, as she searched for the ticket office. If only Señor were here! She came out into the open and bent over to catch her breath. When she stood up, she heard shouts and the drumming of hooves.

"Runaway mule! Watchit!" A short, stocky man trundled after a mule.

Amelia jumped out of the way as the mule galloped past.

"Jefe!" She joined the chase. What did Señor say to make him stop? "Jefe! *Para!*"

The mule slowed to a trot, then a walk. Did he recognize her voice? Amelia rushed over and grabbed the mule's halter rope. "There, there, Jefe, it's all right," she said. The mule's ears flattened and it tossed its head, snorting. The man who had been chasing El Jefe swore an oath that made her ears ring. "I'll take him," Amelia said. "He belongs to Señor Hernandez, the *arriero.*"

The man slapped El Jefe's haunch and the mule lashed out with his hind leg, just missing him. "Ugly brute. Tell your Señor that his mule is a menace. He kicked my dog; might have broken his ribs." The man trudged off. Amelia rubbed the hard nub between El Jefe's ears until he settled down. She led him to a fence, set her bag on the ground, and tied his rope to the railing with two half hitches. "Stay here, Jefe." A boat's whistle sounded from the river. She'd better buy her ticket.

"So you're good with knots. Lucky for you, lucky for us."

She whirled around and found herself hemmed in by the two sailors who had been loading the *Sophie.* One sailor was swarthy, with a dark beard; the other was small and wiry. She ducked under the taller man's arm, but the short sailor grabbed her and twisted her arm up behind her back. "Let me go!" Amelia cried.

"Quiet." Something clicked near her ear. A knife's sharp blade flashed in front of her face and its cold tip grazed her neck. "You're going to walk to the levee between us. We're all friends, understand? No calling out. We don't want no accidents—like a boy who gets his neck cut by mistake. Do we?"

Amelia shook so hard she was afraid she might soil her britches.

"Do we?" the small sailor growled.

"No sir," she whispered. She looked away. The sailor's right eye was half-closed, but the left one bored into her.

"Good lad. This knife will stay open but hidden. You just walk between us, natural-like, as if we work together. We're going to the ship now. Keep quiet and you'll be safe and sound." He held her elbow tight while the other sailor gripped her shoulder.

"That hurts! Where am I going?" Amelia asked.

"Ha!" The sailor's laugh was harsh. "On board the *Sophie*, and you won't have to pay. Isn't that what you wanted? And then, if you're lucky, maybe on a nice long journey overseas."

She was being shanghaied! Amelia remembered Patrick's story: how they tied boys up, drugged them, and sent them on boats to China. She tried to twist out of his grip, but the sailor's nails pinched through her shirt. "I meant what I said. We could accuse you of all sorts of things—stealing a mule, for instance."

"But I didn't! It belongs to—"

"That's enough. You want a gag on your mouth? That's how we usually handle boys like you."

Amelia couldn't help it; wetness trickled down the leg of her britches. She twisted her neck as they walked her away, giving El Jefe one last look. Her shoulder bag lay on the ground. Her papers! Now no one would ever see her story. And she couldn't leave Uncle Paul's spyglass behind. Tears coursed down her cheeks. Her coin sack was in her pocket, but she didn't dare touch it. Would they steal that, too?

The men pushed her through the crowd, down the dock, and onto the *Sophie*'s deck, chatting over her head as if they were all old friends. Amelia craned her neck, hoping to see Señor, but she was surrounded by strangers.

The men bustled her into a cabin, and shoved her onto a bench. The swarthy sailor took her scarf from her neck and used it to cinch her hands behind her back. "See if your skill with knots can help you now," he said with a nasty laugh. "You can have a nice little rest here until we shove off. Then you'll go to the engine room to shovel coal." He poked the other sailor. "Told you I'd find a way out of that job."

The smaller sailor squinted at her. "If you know what's good for you, you'll stay quiet," he said. "Otherwise we might find passage for you on a clipper out of San Francisco."

They turned to go. Desperate, Amelia played her last card. "I can't be your cabin boy," she cried. "I'm a *girl*!"

Both men burst out laughing. "That's a new one!" the heavier man said. The key turned in the lock. And then, silence.

CHAPTER
✳ 39 ✳

Old Peabody, Peabody

TEARS STREAMED down Amelia's face and into her mouth but she had no way to wipe her face. *Stop*, she told herself in a whisper. She stood up and circled the little cabin, stepping carefully to keep her balance. The cabin was some sort of officer's mess, like the one Julius lived in, but not as fancy. Benches were pulled up to a square table with a lip around the edge, and a porthole on the starboard side gave her a narrow view of the levee. The *Sophie* sat low in the water, while the levee rose at an angle high above the waterline. She peered up at the porthole. From this angle, she saw a parade of boots shuffling past atop the levee. Were those the passengers, waiting to get on?

The porthole was latched with a hook just above her head. Amelia turned around and tried to move her wrists up higher on her back, but she couldn't even reach her shoulder blades. "Help!" she cried, but the feet kept on moving. No one could hear her, with the porthole closed.

She screamed again, louder this time. Footsteps clomped

outside the door and a gruff voice called out, "Quiet in there—didn't I warn you?"

"Yes, sir." Amelia forced herself to wait. She took one breath. And another. When the footsteps went on, she inched over to a bench and pushed it with her knees to get it closer to the porthole, but it tumbled over with a crash. She held her breath. The ship shuddered with thumps and creaks as the boat was loaded, covering the sound. She pushed a second bench gently with the side of her boot, nudging it bit by bit until it was wedged up against the wall, then leaned over and hitched herself up awkwardly, knees first.

She stood on the bench and turned around slowly until her back faced the porthole, then stretched her hands toward her shoulder blades as far as they would go, groping until she found the latch. Her fingers slipped off once, then twice. Finally, she caught hold of the hook with her thumb and forefinger. She pushed and prodded, twisted her body to press harder—and the latch lifted. She nearly fell, but her kerchief caught a bolt on the wall, steadying her. Finally, she shoved the porthole open with her forehead.

"Help!" she screamed.

A pair of men's heavy boots slowed, but only for a moment. Five or six more people passed. If she screamed again, would the sailors come back and gag her? But if she didn't yell, who would ever find her?

She screwed up her face, filled her lungs, and was about

to scream when a trim pair of boots passed by; *women's* black boots, laced to the ankle, one heel worn lower than the other. And above the boots, two hems, in yellow silk—

Estelle's Turkish trousers? But how could that be? The boots shuffled forward and the yellow fabric fluttered in the breeze. Was it Estelle? Only one way to find out. Amelia took a deep breath, stood on tiptoe, and whistled, high and clear, the song of the white-throated sparrow: *Old Peabody, Peabody, Peabody!*

A man's rough clogs passed between Amelia and the woman's boots. Amelia whistled the song again—and again—and listened. No response, no sound but the clomp of shoes on the wooden planking, the thud of something heavy hitting the *Sophie's* deck. She licked her tears, willing them to stop. She couldn't whistle if she was crying. One more try. *Old Peabody, Peabody, Peabody . . .*

And then, pure and sweet as the bird calling from the deep woods in springtime, came the reply: *Old Peabody, Peabody, Peabody.* And a scream: "Amelia! Where are you?"

"Over here!" So what if the sailors heard her now? "Look down at the porthole! Help me!"

She saw the boots first, then the flowing hems of the pantaloons, then Estelle's gloved hands, gripping the edge of the dock as she knelt—and finally her beautiful face, framed by butter-yellow curls.

"Amelia? Wave to me!"

"I can't!" Amelia cried. "I'm tied up. Kidnapped!"

Estelle disappeared. Within moments, pandemonium erupted: screams, yelling, footsteps in the hall, oaths piled on oaths. Estelle's voice grew louder and closer while Amelia slid from the bench and kicked at the door, not caring that her boots scuffed the wood.

And then the key turned, the door flew open, and Estelle was there; Estelle with her cheeks burnished red, her eyes narrowed to icy blue points. She pushed the small sailor into the room ahead of her and he cowered, as if in front of a lioness. "How dare you kidnap my daughter!" Before he could answer, Estelle lunged for the sailor and slapped him hard, across the face. He nearly fell over in shock. Amelia's jaw dropped. Gentle Estelle, hitting someone!

"Untie her, you fiend." Estelle held Amelia tight while the sailor loosened her bindings. Amelia sobbed against Estelle's shoulder, breathing in her smell of violets and wood smoke. "*Ma petite*, my little one, *ma chérie*. Are you all right?"

Amelia nodded and stepped away, pushing her hair back as she wiped her eyes.

Estelle gasped. "Look at your face! Did he do that to you?"

The sailor started for the door, but Estelle blocked his way. "Stay right there," she said. "I'm going to speak to your captain."

"*Niño!*" Heavy steps sounded on the deck outside, accented by a familiar jingling sound. "Emile? *Donde está mi niño?*"

"In here, Señor!" Amelia called.

Señor Hernandez burst into the tiny room, brandishing Amelia's hat and shoulder bag. "These were with El Jefe— but you were lost, *perdido*. Then I remembered the ship, with the name of your mother . . ." His dark eyes flickered from Amelia to the sailor and back again, and his face darkened. He dropped Amelia's bag and yanked his knife from its scabbard. The heels of his boots clicked on the floorboards and his silver buttons jingled as he stalked toward the sailor. "Did he hurt you, *niño*? Tell me the truth."

"He tried to—to shanghai me," Amelia stammered. The sailor opened his mouth as he backed up against the wall, but he didn't make a sound.

Estelle pointed at Señor. "Amelia, who is *this* man?"

Amelia didn't know where to begin. "Señor . . . is my friend. He rescued me twice. Señor, Estelle is my—" She hesitated. "My mother," she said, because how else could she explain? Estelle squeezed Amelia's hand and blinked back tears.

Señor shook the knife at the sailor. "I should kill you!"

The sailor screamed, his voice still as high-pitched as a girl's. "I didn't know—"

"Excuse me!"

They all turned around. A short, wide man wearing a captain's cap and jacket stood in the doorway, his hands on his hips. "What in the devil's name is going on here?" he roared.

Amelia clapped a hand over her mouth. Too late: Estelle's eyes were dancing, too. While the men in the room shouted, interrupted each other, and shook their fists, Amelia and Estelle collapsed onto a bench and laughed until they cried. Estelle wrapped Amelia in a tight embrace and the din in the room disappeared. "It's a miracle," Estelle whispered in her ear. "A blessed miracle."

Amelia trembled from head to foot, much too happy to speak.

CHAPTER

✳ 40 ✳

Hasta Luego

WHEN IT was all over—after the captain heard Amelia's story; after a constable came to hustle the two sailors from the ship; and after the captain apologized to Estelle, insisting that she and Amelia travel to San Francisco as his honored guests—Amelia and Estelle followed Señor to the gangplank.

"*Muchas gracias,* Señor," Amelia said.

He bowed deep and kissed her hand as if she were a lady. "*Adiós,* niña," he said, with the accent on the final *a.*

Amelia blushed. "I will always be your *niño.* Will I see you again?" she asked.

He smiled. "In California, all paths cross—and cross again," he said. "Like the web of a spider. *Hasta luego.*"

"*Sí,*" Amelia said. "See you later. Say *adiós* to El Jefe for me." She waved to Señor until he disappeared in the crowd on the dock, and then hooked her arm through Estelle's. They leaned against the railing as sailors untied the ship's lines from the dock and jumped onboard. The ship's whistle sounded and the engine rumbled as the paddle wheel began to turn. Black smoke spewed from the *Sophie's* smokestack. Estelle looked a little green. "You said you would never step foot on a ship again," Amelia said.

"I changed my mind."

Shouts rang out along the deck as the *Sophie* inched away from the levee into the channel. They slipped past a long warehouse that loomed over the dock, past small sailboats with their sails furled, past barrels stacked on their sides. Amelia clutched Estelle's hand. "How did you know I was here?" Amelia asked.

"It's a long story," Estelle said. "Let's talk inside."

Amelia followed her along the deck to the sumptuous stateroom that the captain had set aside for them. The other passengers gawked and whispered as they passed, and Amelia was glad when they shut the door behind them and sank onto a leather settee. "Tell me everything," she said.

Estelle pulled Amelia close. "The newspaper boy, Julius, found us after the balloon took off. He told us what happened. He was shaken to the core."

Julius, afraid? Amelia couldn't believe it.

Estelle went on, her voice trembling. "Of course we imagined the worst. Your mother fainted dead away at the news. I thought she would never recover."

Amelia shuddered. "Is she all right?"

"Sophie's had a hard time of it, but she *will* be fine when I bring you home."

"I'm sorry. I knew you would be frightened. We didn't mean to fly."

"Of course not. We tried to find the balloonist, to see if he could help, but he had skipped town. He was afraid we'd charge him with murder. Your mother was ready to throw him off a cliff." Estelle wiped Amelia's face with the hem of her cloak. "Dear child. Have I told you enough?"

"Not yet. How did you know to come to Stockton?"

"Because of the *Alta*. Julius said that the editor had witnessed the ascent. The *Alta* published a story about you the next day. We visited the editor, who promised to let us know if he heard anything. I think he felt guilty that they let the balloon escape. He seemed to know you?"

"I guess." Amelia was too tired to explain. "Go on."

Estelle sighed and dabbed her eyes with her sleeve. "Many horrible long days went by, when your mother assumed you had died. I refused to believe it. Then the *Alta*'s editor came to the ship. He told us that a man had come in from a place called Knight's Ferry. This traveler had seen two boys who survived a balloon crash. He said the younger one was only bruised, but the older boy, who was carried away in a litter, begged someone to take a message to his mother in San Francisco. When the editor told us this story, we were frantic. Were you the injured child? How could we find you?"

Amelia imagined Mother and Estelle, stuck on the

Beatrice, worrying and talking into the night. It made her heart ache. "I guess I yelled at someone at the ferry crossing, but I don't really remember. I was so dizzy."

Estelle stroked her hair. "Still, that traveler gave us hope. We wanted to search for you together, but we have so many orders at the shop. Rosanna hasn't returned, I don't know how to milk the goats, and your mother is the better seamstress. It made more sense for me to come. When I heard that a steamer with your mother's name was leaving the next day, I had to take that ship, in spite of my seasickness."

"I thought the *Sophie* was a lucky boat too." Amelia snuggled against Estelle as if she were five years old again. "Why were you on the levee just now?"

"I had a bite to eat at a little restaurant, and I was on my way to the ticket office down the way, to find out about the next stage to Knight's Ferry." Estelle shivered. "If you hadn't whistled, I might have left without knowing you were here."

"Those sailors wanted to ship me out to China as a cabin boy," Amelia said. "You saved my life. You and Señor."

Estelle cupped Amelia's chin in her hand. "You saved your own life—and mine," she said. "I couldn't live without you."

Was that true? Amelia's throat was too full to speak. She unbuckled her shoulder bag and opened the *Herald* to her story. "Look."

Estelle read the headline out loud. "'An Aeronaut by Mistake: Intrepid Young Balloonists Survive Crash in the

Mountains—'" She laughed. "Amelia, that's you?"

"Yes, and I wrote the story. It was a letter to you and Mother, but the editor helped me make it longer. He fixed my spelling, too."

"Our young author. So the knock on your head didn't change your spelling habits." Estelle smiled and handed the paper back. "Read it aloud, will you?"

Even though Amelia had read the story many times, it was still strange and wonderful to find her own words on the page. When she was done, Estelle pulled her close. "I can't believe you're here." She rubbed her forehead. "I am a bit green. Let's go outside again for some air."

THEY STOOD at the bow and Estelle gripped Amelia's hand, as if she might lose her to the river. The *Sophie* was moving fast now, with smoke spewing from her smokestack. Red-wing blackbirds flew up out of the reeds at the river's edge, the bars on their wings flashing like tiny red flags. Flocks of ducks wheeled in clumsy circles, quacking and calling, as the *Sophie* followed the San Joaquin's twists and turns through flat marshland. The reeds on the riverbanks were so tall, Amelia felt as if they traveled through a green tunnel. She closed her eyes and took off her hat, letting the spring sunshine warm her face. The *Sophie's* engine hummed.

Estelle combed her fingers through Amelia's hair. "When your curls grow out, we can fix your hair so it covers your scar."

"That's what Dr. Gunn said."

"His name is *Gun*?"

"Yes, with an extra *N*. He's the newspaper editor and the doctor. He was very kind." In fact, Amelia thought, except for the two sailors, all the men on her journey had treated her with the kindness of a father. "You look so serious," Estelle said. "Did anyone hurt you?"

"No one. Everyone was good to me." Before she lost her nerve, Amelia asked, "Why won't Mother speak to me about my father?"

Estelle was quiet for so long, her eyes fixed on the dark current slipping away beneath them, that Amelia thought she hadn't heard her, or that she was seasick again. Finally, Estelle said, "I can't tell you."

"But you're like a mother to me. You even said so."

"*C'est vrai*. It's true." Estelle's smile was sad. "But this is between you and Sophie. I don't know her reasons for keeping silent."

"You could ask her. She listens to you."

"I'll try." A chill wind blew across the bow and they both shivered. "Let's get warm," Estelle said. Amelia nodded and followed her back to the stateroom. She stretched out on the settee, her head in Estelle's lap, and cuddled under her cloak. The steady chug of the engine carried her into the soundest sleep she'd had in weeks.

CHAPTER

✳ 41 ✳

You're Alive!

DARKNESS HAD settled over the city when the *Sophie* finally docked, and Amelia was quiet as they picked their way home. The rain had turned the streets to mud; twice Amelia sank to her ankles. She was grateful when the saloon doors opened, spilling light to illuminate the ruts.

"You first," Estelle said when they reached the foot of the ladder.

Amelia couldn't move. Why was she so afraid? "Go on." Estelle pressed Amelia's back. "She'll probably faint from happiness this time."

Amelia hoisted her shoulder bag and climbed slowly from one rung to the next until she reached the deck of the *Beatrice*. A candle gleamed in the window of the house. The goats muttered, then scrabbled to their feet, bleating and pleading. "Hush, girls!" Amelia whispered. Smoky mewed and twined between her ankles, purring like a small engine.

"Everyone is glad to see you," Estelle said.

The door to the little house opened a crack. "Who's there?" Mother called.

Amelia couldn't answer. She dropped her bag and stumbled into her mother's arms. Mother staggered, fell to her
knees, and gripped Amelia around her waist. She wailed, a
long, mournful sound that made Amelia shake, and pulled
her to the floor into her lap. "You're alive! Amelia, my Amelia." She stroked her hair, ran a finger over her scar. Amelia
had never felt such a gentle touch. "My dearest, only daughter," Mother whispered.

They held each other tight. No one spoke for a long, long
time.

MOTHER AND Estelle sat with Amelia on her pallet and
talked into the night. Amelia answered so many questions
she felt as if she were in a schoolroom. *Why hadn't she written? What had happened to Patrick? Why did they climb into the
balloon in the first place?* Even after Mother read the newspaper story, she still had questions. Finally, Amelia opened her
shoulder bag, took out the coin sack, and set it in Mother's
hands. "For the little house," Amelia said.

Mother's eyes opened wide as she dumped out the mix
of coins. "So much money." American dollars and two-bit
coins gleamed on the blanket, among English shillings,
French francs, Dutch and German florins.

"Look," Estelle said, picking up a silver coin. "A rupee, all
the way from India."

"How did you earn this?" Mother asked.

"Selling papers, writing letters. Men even paid me to carry their letters to a post office."

"You should keep this for yourself," Mother said. "We have nearly enough to buy land in Happy Valley."

"It's for the house," Amelia insisted. She touched the waistband of her pants. "I have a gold nugget in here, stitched into a secret pocket. Maybe you can clip it out in the morning." She yawned.

Estelle laughed. "Don't tell me you were panning for gold, too!"

"I tried, but I didn't find anything. My nugget is from a miner who paid me to write a letter to his family. I saved it for you, Estelle, to thank you for bringing me home." That miner was a father who knew his children and missed them, Amelia remembered. A sense of dread seeped into her bones. She rolled Mr. Walker's hat into a pillow as she had every night on the trail with Señor, and pulled the blanket up over her head. She felt like a ship that had run low on coal: completely out of steam.

AMELIA WOKE to the *snip-snip* of Mother's scissors. Sunlight warmed the chair where Mother sat, clipping the stitches from the secret pocket that Madame had sewn into her trousers. Amelia sat up. She was dressed in her night shift. "Did you undress me last night?"

"Yes. You never moved." Mother wriggled her finger

into the waist of the pants and pulled out the tiny nugget, holding it up to the light. "Real gold. So this is what all the fuss is about. We'll have to save it, to remind us of our early days here."

Amelia shivered. "Are you cold?" Mother asked. "I have water warming for a bath."

Amelia wasn't cold; only afraid of what lay ahead. "Where's Estelle?" she asked.

"At the wharf." Mother lifted the heavy pot from the stove. "A clipper came in yesterday—I think our little house might be onboard. Our luck has changed for the better now that you're home. Come, help me fill the tub."

They mixed hot water from the stove with a bucket of cool water from the well and Amelia climbed in, ashamed of her grimy feet, the smudges on her face, the ring of dirt at her neck. Mother turned Amelia's hands over and stroked her palms, lifted her hair above the scar, ran a hand over her calf. "Look at your muscles, like a farm boy's."

"Mother, don't." Amelia twisted away, then wrinkled her nose as she slid deeper into the water. "I smell terrible."

Mother handed her a clean rag and a rough chunk of soap. "Forgive me. I need to check you over to make sure everything is there, as I did when you were born."

Amelia drew up her knees. The heat soothed the stiffness in her back and shoulders. She looked up into Mother's hazel eyes. "When I was born, where was my father?"

Mother winced, but for once, she answered. "Far away."

She touched her lips with her forefinger before Amelia could ask the next question. "Estelle warned that you would be asking. Bath first, and breakfast. Then we'll talk. I promise."

Amelia couldn't believe it. She thanked Estelle silently and scrubbed herself with the soap. When Mother brought Amelia her old gingham dress, her petticoat and apron, she groaned. "Mother—"

"You won't pass as a boy much longer," Mother said.

Amelia looked down at herself and blushed. She draped the rag over her chest as Mother washed her back and poured clean water over her hair. When she had dried off and stepped into her underclothes, they discovered that her dress was too tight across the bodice and under the arms. Mother sat back on her heels. "I've been stitching a green calico for Rosanna. You'll have to wear it—at least, for now."

Amelia's spirits slumped as Mother drew the new dress over her head. It *was* pretty, but the skirt caught at her knees and the collar felt like a noose at her throat. Mother took off the dress to hem it while Amelia sat wrapped in a blanket, eating her breakfast of biscuits and warm goat's milk. She waited, but Mother didn't speak of her father—or anything else. Finally, Amelia said, "Madame Arnaud, the woman who cared for us in Sonora, dresses in britches and a red flannel shirt. She made me the one I wore yesterday. She and her husband look just alike and no one minds."

"That's fine," Mother said. "I know Estelle was more

comfortable traveling in her pantaloons. Once your trousers are clean again—if that's possible!—you can put them on. But please, let me have my daughter today, the little girl who makes my heart dance."

Amelia bit her lip to hold back tears. Mother had never spoken of her this way. Amelia put on the dress and stood patiently while Mother buttoned it up the back. "My prayers were answered at last." Mother kissed the crown of Amelia's head and combed out her hair. "Your curls are growing. You'll be a young woman soon."

Did she *want* to be a woman? Perhaps, if she could be like Madame. But she wouldn't say that to Mother, especially not today. Amelia went to the looking glass and studied her reflection. The scar was still angry above her eyebrow, but her curls were almost long enough to hide it. She turned around. "I read Uncle Paul's letter," she said.

Mother's face paled. "When?"

"The day the pigs came through our tent. Uncle Paul said someone called 'Mr. Y' had visited the farm." She took a deep breath. She couldn't lose her nerve. "Is he my father?"

"Yes." Mother put on her shawl and handed Amelia her cloak and bonnet. "It's chilly. And you need to shade your face."

Amelia tied the hated ribbons under her chin. For a moment, she almost wished she were back in Sonora. "Where are we going?"

"To the place where I waited for you to come home."

CHAPTER

✳ 42 ✳

She's Gone Mad!

MOTHER LED Amelia down the ladder, along the street, and through the chaparral to Telegraph Hill. Wildflowers bent before the wind and gulls shrieked above the harbor. Partway to the tower, Mother veered off on a smaller path and led Amelia to a big boulder facing east. She scrambled onto the rock's smooth top like a girl, and Amelia followed, tripping on the hem of her skirt. "See why I'd rather wear trousers?"

Mother didn't answer. They sat quietly, watching boats with full sails scud before the wind. "I came here every day," Mother said at last. "Mr. Abbott had seen the balloon take off and sail across the bay, so he was very kind to me— and astonished to learn you were the aeronaut. I knew you couldn't come back this way, but it gave me comfort to watch for you." Mother's voice shook. "Your father's name was—is—Mr. Yeomans. Douglas Yeomans."

Amelia waited for a bell to sound, for a weight to lift, but nothing happened. "Why didn't you tell me?"

"I was ashamed," Mother said, "and afraid. He didn't

know about you. I thought—if he found out—that he might steal you from me." She turned Amelia's hand over, tracing the lines in her palm as if she could read her fortune. "I didn't want to hurt you," she said at last. "Perhaps it was wrong, to keep it a secret."

"How was he my father?" Amelia asked.

"In the usual way." Mother ducked her chin, her eyes hidden by the sides of her bonnet. "Douglas came to Concord for a month, to help a friend build a barn. He was charming, with a sweet smile like yours, and soft chestnut curls. I was flattered when he courted me, but Gran didn't trust him. I was so young, only five years older than you are now." She turned to face Amelia. "When you cut your hair, I couldn't believe how you resembled him."

Amelia had waited for this news all her life—yet now it made her feel small. "Perhaps you'd like me better if I didn't look like him."

Mother gripped Amelia's shoulders and looked her in the eye. "Never. You are my beautiful girl."

"Even with my scar?"

"Even then." Mother took a deep breath. "Let me finish my story." She gazed out across the bay, as if she could see all the way back to Concord. "It was a beautiful summer day. I was walking near the river. Douglas came bounding through the tall grass like a frisky colt. I had promised Gran that I wouldn't see him alone, but how was I to know he would find me?"

Mother wiped her eyes with her apron. "He kissed me, and I liked it for a while. Then—it turned into something else. We should have stopped, but we didn't. Afterward, we were both so ashamed."

Amelia was too embarrassed—and shocked—to speak. Of course, she knew how babies were made, and she had watched sheep give birth to baby lambs on Uncle Paul's farm. But since she didn't have a father, it was easy to pretend that Mother had never done anything like that.

"He came to see me the next day, and apologized. He asked me to marry him." Mother glanced at Amelia. Her chin trembled. "I said no."

Amelia stared. "Why?"

"We were so young. Gran didn't approve. You know how she can be, if she doesn't like someone. I didn't suspect . . . that we had started a child." She picked at a loose thread in her skirt. "He was leaving soon to go back to his home, in New York State, and then on to Ohio, with his Concord friend, to start a farm. They talked about the rich soil out west and how they would earn their fortunes. I didn't want to leave Gran. And I think . . ." She dabbed her eyes with her apron and faced Amelia. "Even though it caused a scandal, I didn't love him enough to be his wife."

Amelia couldn't speak. A whirlwind tossed and turned inside her, stronger than the wind blowing in from the sea.

"He came back before he left town," Mother said. "Took

off his cap on the porch, was polite to Gran. Gave me his address and asked me to write if I changed my mind. I never did." Mother took Amelia's hand. "I always knew this day would come, and I wondered if you could ever forgive me."

Amelia dug her nails into her palms. She wouldn't cry.

"Your father knew nothing about you," Mother went on. "Gran took me to Boston. I met dear Estelle, whom I *do* love, and the three of us welcomed you into the world."

Amelia thought of Patrick and the Arnauds; of how often she'd dreamed of a family like his new one. She made herself ask the next question, though she couldn't look Mother in the eye. "So when people asked why I had no father, you lied?"

Mother sighed. "Yes. I said that we were engaged, that your father jilted me and ran away. I lived with the shame of it. But Estelle taught me to hold my head high. As you do, too."

"But I don't!" Amelia clenched her fists. "You told me to think of him as dead. If he knows nothing about me, then why did he come to see Uncle Paul?"

"He was passing through," Mother said. "Paul says he was seeking news of me. He wondered if I had married. Whether I had children."

So he *was* looking for her, just as she'd imagined. "I didn't see that part of the letter." Amelia couldn't help her icy tone. "What did Uncle Paul tell him?"

"That I had moved to California with a friend. Uncle Paul didn't mention you, so you're safe."

"Is my father dangerous, then?"

Mother winced and reached for her, but Amelia scrambled off the rock. "Amelia, please understand," Mother begged. "I was afraid of losing you forever. We women have so few rights. If your father wanted, he could come and claim you, take you away from me."

"And I have no right to know my father?" When Mother didn't answer, Amelia asked, "Is this why we never lived in Concord?"

"No. I wanted more than life on a farm." Mother gazed off into the distance. "'A house is no home unless it contain food and fire for the mind as well as for the body.' Margaret Fuller wrote that. You remember, when we were in Boston, I attended meetings where women discussed the issues of our time. I met women who had traveled to Seneca Falls, to vote on the Declaration Affirming the Rights of Women. We talked of women's desire to vote, to own property, to keep their children if they divorce." Mother's face was drawn. She suddenly looked old. "When Estelle and I heard that women had new freedoms in California, that we could own land and start a business, that I could keep my child without fear, we decided to leave." She sighed. "Little did I know the harms you would face here."

Amelia glared at her mother. "Why *didn't* you marry him?

I was always ashamed!" she cried. "In school, the boys all teased me. They called me a ba—" She gulped. She couldn't say the word. "A bad name. They called *you* bad names!" Mother wept, but Amelia couldn't stop. "Why didn't you make up a *better* lie? Pretend you'd been married? Change your name? And Uncle Paul was like a father. He loved me. But you took us away from him, too!"

"Amelia—"

"You're a liar! I hate you!"

Mother held out her arms but Amelia darted away. The storm inside rattled her bones, made her dizzy again. She stumbled down the twisting path through the chaparral. Mother called out to her, but she only ran faster. Tears blinded her and she fell, scraping her palms on stones. She scrambled to her feet and thorns caught the hem of her new dress, which ripped when she tugged it free. Mother's entreaties—"Stop! Wait!"—grew faint behind her. If only she'd stayed with Patrick and the Arnauds in Sonora!

She stopped cold at the bottom of the hill. Gran had known. So had Uncle Paul. Even Estelle. They all knew the truth—and no one had told her.

She picked up a stone and hurled it at the side of a warehouse. It hit with a satisfying whack. She snatched up another stone: *Thump!* And a third: *Ping!* A stout woman rounded the corner, shook her fist, and cried out, "Stop that!"

Mrs. Liazos. Amelia gasped, picked up her skirts, and dashed for the *Beatrice*. Mrs. Liazos's voice rose to a high-pitched whine behind her. "It's Amelia! The one who flew away. The girl's gone mad!"

Amelia raced past as if she hadn't heard. The woman was right. She *was* mad. Mad enough to do something foolish— or smart—or both.

CHAPTER

43

A Girl After My Own Heart

ESTELLE WAS leaning over the railing when Amelia came back. Her bright smile faded when Amelia reached the deck. Amelia ducked under Estelle's outstretched arms and faced her down. "You *knew*," she said. "Why didn't you tell me?"

"I couldn't," Estelle said. "Don't be hard on your mother. She did what she thought was right."

"It wasn't right *at all*." Amelia went into the house and grabbed her shoulder bag, checking to make sure her papers and notes from the journey were still inside. As she slithered down the ladder, she caught the hem of her dress twice beneath the heel of her boots and swallowed a sailor's oath. Mother stood at the bottom, her eyes swollen from crying. "Amelia, don't spoil our reunion."

"*I* didn't spoil anything." Amelia set her jaw to keep it from wobbling. "There's something I need to do."

Mother gripped her elbow. "Not alone."

Amelia twisted away. "Mother, I've traveled hundreds of miles on my own, and I can't walk a few blocks by myself? I'm going to the *Alta*. You can't stop me."

She lifted her skirts and ran, half listening for Mother's protest, but she heard nothing but the usual city sounds: clopping hooves, men hollering, the rasp of a saw. She stopped at the top of the street, gasping for breath. The hills had turned green since she'd left, and the bay sparkled in the sunshine. Had she really flown across that water? Patrick's voice piped up inside her head, as if he stood beside her: *"We're flying!"*

She missed Patrick's excitement, the splash of freckles across his nose. For a few weeks, she'd nearly had a little brother. Now she had lost him—and gained a father. If this man called Yeomans knew about her, would he come to find her, at last? And what then?

She squared her shoulders. No time to think of that now. A man tipped his hat as she passed and Amelia looked him straight in the eye until he hurried away. She had learned the ways of a boy. Perhaps she would keep them.

Tip recognized her first. He ran around her in circles, barking, then planted his forepaws on her skirt as she opened the door. "Tip!" the editor scolded. "That's no way to treat a lady." He tipped his chair back on two legs and squinted at her over his glasses. "May I help you, miss?"

"You don't remember me?" Amelia pulled the Sonora *Herald* from her bag, opened it to her story, and set it on his desk.

He stared at the headline, then at her. The legs of his chair thudded against the floor. He opened his mouth, shut it again. Finally, his voice emerged in a croak. "You're—the child from the balloon? The one who kept after me to, to—"

"To publish my letter. Yes. You ran after us that day, when the balloon took off." She pushed back her hair to show her scar and pointed to the headline. "I'm Amelia Forrester. That's my story."

He coughed once, cleared his throat. "Your mother spoke to me, said her daughter had flown away in the balloon. I couldn't believe you were a girl."

"Why not?" She remembered something Dr. Gunn had told her. "Women in France have gone up in balloons. And women in the East, as well." She tapped the paper. "Read the story. Please," she added, trying to be polite.

The editor twisted one end of his mustache as he read to the bottom of the page, then looked up at her, shaking his head. "I'm afraid I reported your probable death, which caused your mother some distress."

"And you told me you only print the facts," Amelia said. "Remember?"

"Yes." He looked away. "You must admit, it seemed impossible that two children could fly away and survive. I corrected the story after a man appeared with the news that two *boys* had survived the crash. The other child is all right, then?" he asked.

"Patrick's fine. He stayed in Sonora with a French couple."

"The *Herald* editor makes it sound as if—as if you wrote the story yourself."

"I did. Dr. Gunn helped me with the spelling and set my words in type. He *paid* me, too." Amelia waited. When the editor didn't react, she said, "I have another story to tell, about traveling with an *arriero*—and the sailors who tried to shanghai me."

The editor shook his head. "Come now, miss. A balloon crash *and* a shanghai?"

"If you don't believe me, there are other editors in town," she said, and snatched the *Herald* away from him.

He stood up so quickly that Tip yapped and scurried toward the door. "Wait a minute. How do I know you really can write?"

"If you give me some paper and a pen, I'll show you."

He threw his head back and laughed. "Miss Forrester, I do believe you are the most dogged young lady I've ever met. Like Tip when he's after a rat." To Amelia's surprise, he pulled open a drawer, gave her a stack of blue-lined paper and a pen, and pointed her to a small table and chair in the next room. "Show me what you can do."

Amelia set out her paper scraps. Her handwriting was abysmal and nothing was in order. Where should she begin? She tugged at her hair, crossed and uncrossed her ankles, chewed on her thumbnail. Finally, she called, "Could I pretend I'm writing a letter?"

"Of course," the editor said.

And so she began. *Dear Gran and Uncle Paul . . .*

The words tumbled out. She told them about the crash, about Madame and Monsieur and their red shirts, about the miners from all over the world, about her trip out of the mountains and the sailors who tried to shanghai her—and about her rescue. When she was finished, the sun's angle had changed, casting a pool of sunlight over Tip, who was asleep on the floor. Her fingertips were stained with ink and she knew she had misspelled many words, but Gran and Uncle Paul would like her letter, although it would probably scare Gran to death.

The editor squinted, held the paper away from his face, then passed it back to her. "You think I can parse that scrawl? Read it out aloud." He followed along as she read. "You need more schooling," he said when she finished. "Your spelling and penmanship are wretched"—Amelia held her breath—"but it's an exciting story."

"Will you print it?"

"With corrections. And I'll add some notes about the balloon flight, taken from your other story."

Amelia's face went hot with pleasure and she nearly forgot to ask the important question. "How much will you pay me?"

He laughed. "Quite the businesswoman, aren't you? How about two dollars—and a stack of papers to sell when the story comes out."

"Fine." Amelia bent to give Tip a farewell pat and remembered to thank the editor.

"My pleasure," he said. "I lost another printer's devil since you left. Perhaps a girl would do a better job after all. You interested?"

Amelia thought about the moment when Dr. Gunn pulled her story off the press, the thrill of seeing her own words shining in wet ink. "I'd rather do what you do: run around the city looking for news; write a story someone wants to read."

"A girl after my own heart. I'll see you in the morning." He gave her a mock salute as she hurried away.

CHAPTER

✳ 44 ✳

No Matter What Happens

AMELIA COULD hear the tumult aboard the *Beatrice* when she reached the docks. She broke into a run. The goats were blatting and tugging at their ropes on the hillside and excited voices rose from the deck. Rosanna was leaning over the railing, her face ruddy inside her bonnet.

"You're home!" Amelia cried. She fought her skirt as she scrambled up the ladder. Rosanna leaned over to help her onto the deck.

"I was just hearing about your adventure—look at your face!—is it all true? And what are you doing in a *dress*, for heaven's sake? Come meet Otis; I've been telling him all about you."

Amelia threw her arms around her friend and shook Mr. Baker's hand. "Charmed," he said. "Delighted." He swept off his hat, revealing a bald forehead that gleamed in the sun. "Rosanna has been raving about you."

Really? Amelia couldn't stop smiling.

The Bakers' arrival provided a perfect distraction for the afternoon. Amelia avoided Mother's eyes as she shared her stories, showed off the article in the *Herald*, and told the Bakers about her time in Sonora. Mother and Estelle listened intently, as if they hadn't heard these tales already.

When Amelia finally stopped to catch her breath, Mother reached for Rosanna's hand. "Tell us about your brother," she said softly.

Amelia bit her lip. How could she have forgotten Rosanna's sad errand? Her friend's face crumpled. "We buried him at Murphy's," Rosanna said.

"Murphy's!" Amelia gasped. "That town was near me, in Sonora."

Rosanna stared at her, astonished. "If only I'd known. It was lonesome, burying him in that wilderness. All those big oak trees and rounded hills—he's so far from home. We are too." She glanced at her husband. "We've been wondering—if we should leave."

"Don't go," Amelia pleaded. But that was selfish. She couldn't keep Rosanna here. Their little group fell silent. A cold wind snapped Amelia's shirt and trousers, strung up on a halyard. Estelle glanced at Mother, who cleared her throat.

"Our house has arrived on the clipper," Mother said. "We must find someone to unload it and put it together. Thanks to Amelia's coins—and to all the orders that came in after our advertisements in the *Alta*—we have enough money to purchase our land."

Rosanna smiled at Amelia through her tears. "Don't tell

me you went on earning money after the accident? Amelia, you're a star."

"She *is*," Estelle said, and Mother nodded.

Amelia looked away, embarrassed. Gran would scold her for feeling proud, but Gran wasn't here. She sat up tall. "Thank you."

"Please stay with us until you're settled," Rosanna said. "The ship is big enough for everyone. Even the goats." As if they understood, Daisy and Charrie blatted from the hillside, and they all laughed.

"I could help you set up your house," Mr. Baker said. "After all, you watched over our ship and the animals while we were gone."

Estelle clapped her hands. "Would you?" As the grown-ups chattered and made plans, Amelia slipped across the planking to the hillside. She scratched Charrie behind the ears, then rubbed Daisy's flat nose. "Everything is so confusing," she said. "Perhaps it's better to be a goat. You only have to worry about eating and drinking. And getting milked. You don't know your father, either." Daisy muttered and gently butted Amelia's belly. "Silly goat," Amelia said. She buried her face in Daisy's warm neck. Finally, she was able to cry.

THE *BEATRICE* became as busy as a real ship. Mother and Estelle reorganized their fabrics, storing some in the shipping crate and Estelle's trunk while the Bakers settled in. Amelia was in charge of moving their pallets onto the deck—where Mother insisted they would sleep—and Mr. Baker rigged up the remaining canvas, making a slanted roof above their beds in case of rain.

When Amelia finally crawled under her blankets that night, even her bones felt tired. She sniffed Mr. Walker's hat before she rolled it into a pillow. Its smell of wood smoke brought back Señor's campfires, with sparks popping and drifting up under the pines and redwoods. Her journey seemed so far away now. At least she'd see it again in the paper tomorrow.

Mother bent over to kiss her good night and Amelia stiffened. "I hope you will understand someday," Mother said.

Amelia turned her face away. She inched closer to the railing and lay on her back. Clouds scudded across the stars. The goats pawed at their hay, making nests to sleep in. Amelia thought of Uncle Paul's barn, the sweet smell of hay in the loft, steam rising from the cows' backs when they filed in after a rain. Once, while Uncle Paul trod slowly along the side of the barn, tossing hay into the feedboxes, she had watched him from her perch on the grain bin and said, "I wish you were my father."

He had tickled her forehead with his beard. "Pumpkin"— that was his pet name for her—"I'm your uncle. Besides, what would I do without my favorite niece?"

"I'm your *only* niece," Amelia had said. Uncle Paul poked

her in the ribs then, and asked her to check on the new pig-
lets. He was just changing the subject, Amelia thought now.
So she would forget about it. But of course, she never had.

She pulled the blanket up over her face. Tears pooled in
her ears. What did Uncle Paul think of Douglas Yeomans?
What would he say if she wrote and asked him?

Mother and Estelle settled on their pallet nearby. "Good
night, Amelia," Estelle whispered. "We're so glad you're
home."

Amelia breathed steadily, pretending to be asleep. The
ship fell silent. Men's voices sounded from the saloon down
the street, and the new name pulsed inside her head: *Yeomans*. A strange-sounding word, like a farmer hallooing to
his cows. Yet it belonged to her now.

The wind was still blowing hard, although the sun had
set hours ago. She pulled her thin blankets up around her
shoulders. In the past, feeling this cold, she might have
snuggled under the covers next to Mother. Tonight, she was
alone.

She tossed and turned, trying to get comfortable, and
plumped up Mr. Walker's hat. Why was the smoky smell so
strong? A deep lonesome bell tolled in the distance. Amelia
clamped her hat over her head to shut out the noise. She was
drifting off when another bell rang out closer to the ship.
Amelia threw off her blankets, suddenly awake. She remembered those sounds from her very first day in the city: fire
bells! She scrambled to her feet and leaned out over the rail-

ing, peering up the hill. Flames shot from a building near the Plaza, high above the *Beatrice*, and she heard screams. A third bell clanged furiously out on Long Wharf.

Amelia gripped the railing, frozen with fear. She remembered Mrs. Liazos telling her, weeks ago, how fire could destroy the city in hours, how high winds fanned the flames, and how quickly canvas tents and wooden buildings burned. Amelia dropped to her knees and shook Mother and Estelle. "Fire!" she screamed. "Get up!"

The goats bleated and bawled. Amelia dashed to the little house and pounded on the door. "Fire!" she yelled. Mr. Baker shouted back. Amelia craned her neck and looked up. More buildings were on fire as flames jumped from one roof to the next. She yanked her shirt and breeches off the halyard, stepped into her boots, and jammed Mr. Walker's hat on her head. Her hands felt for her spyglass, which she shoved into her shoulder bag along with her newspapers.

Mr. Baker flung open the cabin door, took one look at the crest of the hill, and began yelling instructions, his thin hair sticking straight up on his head. "Stow everything in trunks and crates!" he cried. "Gather your blankets—I'll soak them in water to cover our goods. Hurry! A fire can torch the city in minutes! Rosanna, pile our goods under the beds. Shutter the house. Drench the outside walls with water!"

Mother and Estelle, who had slept in their clothes, rolled up their blankets and shoved them at Mr. Baker. He tossed them over the railing, slithered down the ladder, and disap-peared. Mother packed a small satchel and Amelia caught her elbow. "Don't forget your money."

"Got it." Mother patted her secret pocket.

While Mother and Estelle crammed loose bolts of fabric into the shipping crate, Amelia and Rosanna hoisted water buckets and dashed their contents against the wall of the little house. "Six buckets, just as the city requires, but we've barely soaked two walls!" Rosanna cried. She shut the door and Amelia helped her fasten the shutters.

Mr. Baker returned, dragging sodden blankets that reeked with a sharp odor. "What's that smell?" Estelle asked.

"Vinegar. The men on the wharf are dumping vinegar on a warehouse—they say it will stop the fire," Mr. Baker said. Mother and Estelle draped the wet blankets over Es-telle's trunk and the shipping crate.

The goats screamed, sounding like humans, and Amelia raced to untie them. Her eyes burned and she coughed as she tried to loosen her knots. Although it was the middle of the night, she could see clearly. Flames shot from roof-tops on the crest of the hill and the wind carried burning embers through the air. A hot coal landed on the deck near Amelia's feet. She stomped it out with the heel of her boot and freed the goats at last. They snorted and leaped away, their hooves scrabbling on the ship's decking. In seconds, they had crossed the plank and disappeared in the smoke.

"Charrie! Daisy! Come back!" Amelia cried.

Rosanna gasped. "We'll lose them!" She started for the pasture, but Mr. Baker grabbed her. "The wind's blowing this way and chaparral burns like whale oil. Come on!" He grabbed their camphene lantern and pushed them all toward the ladder. "Stay close to the bay," he yelled. "If the fire gets too close, we'll jump into the water."

Amelia danced from one foot to the other as the Bakers dropped bags and bundles from the deck and then slid down the ladder. It looked as though everything up near the Plaza was on fire. Would the Custom House burn, and the post office, too? What about the *Alta*? And Mrs. Liazos and Nico in their canvas tent? Would Julius be safe in his wooden captain's quarters? And surely a few wet blankets couldn't stop the flames from burning the *Beatrice* if the fire came down the hill.

"Hurry!" Mother shoved Amelia in the small of the back. Amelia slid down the ladder so fast that she stomped on Rosanna's fingers. "Sorry!" she cried. Mother came right behind her, followed by Estelle, swinging a basket. The cat mewled inside.

They reached the street and peered into the smoke. People streamed past in the dark, some dressed, others in their nightclothes. Men and women carried small children, baskets, and lumpy bundles. Drays pulled by maddened mules rumbled by, piled high with barrels and bags. Two men carrying a litter staggered beneath the weight of a woman and her baby. "This way!" The Bakers beckoned from the far side of the street. They rushed to join them as flames shot up toward the sky and dark smoke rolled over the bay.

"Stay near the water," Mr. Baker said. "And head for North Point—we'll be out of the wind."

"Where is that?" Estelle asked.

"Past Telegraph Hill. Where the balloon took off," Amelia said. Mr. Baker and Rosanna disappeared into the gloom.

Mother grabbed Amelia's hand. "Stay with me," she cried. "No matter what happens." Mother, Estelle, and Amelia stumbled along, trying to stick together while fleeing citizens jostled and bumped against them. Smoke stung Amelia's eyes and filled her lungs. Suddenly, a fire engine pulled by horses came clanging down the street. The team lunged and swerved, their eyes wide with panic. "Jump!" Mother cried.

Amelia leaped to the side of the road, her shoulder bag slamming against her ribs. Her hand slipped from Mother's grip as the engine thundered between them. Amelia fell to her knees and rolled to the side of the street. The horses galloped past, the engine bell clanging as the firemen dashed behind, trying to keep up. Amelia scrambled to her feet. "Mother, where are you?" She darted into the road, dodging through the crowds. "Mother! Estelle!"

She stood on tiptoe. Why didn't they answer? Instead, she heard the wild whinnying of a horse in trouble. Amelia groped forward through the smoke. A black form reared up in front of her, a horse pawing the air with its hooves. White stockings—was it the shoeshine pony? *"Dos reales!"* Amelia grabbed for the pony's bridle but he braced his legs wide and swung his neck from side to side, yanking on the reins, his ears flattened against his head. Was he trapped?

"Hold still!" Amelia tried to calm her voice in the midst of the tumult. She inched closer, keeping an eye on the pony's feet. "Hush, hush," she said. *"Dos reales. Dos reales."* The pony's withers and neck were lathered, but his ears pricked up and he shoved his nose against her pocket. "So you remember me? No apple today." Amelia groped for the bridle and finally rubbed the pony's nose. "Sh-h," she said. "It's all right."

She ran her hand along the reins until she found the spot where they were tangled in a fence, pulled them loose and clucked to the pony, but he wouldn't budge. "Mother! Estelle!" she cried. "I've caught a pony—we can carry your things on his back." Deafening explosions boomed from the hill above and the smoke thickened. Was the world ending? The pony whinnied and showed the whites of his eyes as he shook his head up and down. Amelia shouted for Mother over the din. Smoke enveloped her like fog and she pulled her kerchief over her face, coughing.

A man's voice bawled from behind her. "The wharf's on fire!"

Amelia spun around. The Apollo saloon burst into flames on the Long Wharf, and the fire raced down the dock, eating up bales and barrels. It licked along the planking and wound around the pilings toward the water. Only one warehouse stood intact, surrounded by flames. A strong smell of vinegar mixed with the smoke and made her sneeze. The pony whinnied and skittered sideways.

"Whoa!" Amelia yanked on the reins with all her strength and clamped her hat over the pony's eyes, as she'd seen Uncle Paul do with a frightened mare. The street was lit as if enormous gas lamps burned in the sky. Now the Niantic hotel was on fire too. The *Beatrice* was only two blocks from the hotel—would the flames consume everything they owned? Her face felt hot and the pony pranced sideways. Amelia couldn't breathe. Where could she go?

"Mother! Estelle!" she screamed, but it was useless. Did Mother and Estelle know how to find North Point? Had she lost them for good? No matter what, she had to get out of here. Above the horrible, crackling noise of flames devouring wood, of children wailing and men bawling, came the roar of the wind, drowning everything.

CHAPTER

Tongues of Fire

AMELIA SWALLOWED a sob, plunked her hat on her head, and dragged the pony to a crate where she scrambled onto his back. If only she had a saddle. She gripped the pony's belly with her legs. He pawed the ground and let out a shrill whinny but broke into a trot when she drummed her heels against his ribs. "Come on. We've got to find them."

Shouts went up behind her as they left the wharf. "The wind has changed! It's blowing toward the Plaza!"

Amelia glanced over her shoulder. Sure enough, the fire had spun on its heels like a racehorse at full gallop and sped back on itself, gobbling anything it had missed on its path to the wharf. Would their ship be spared, or was it too late? The smoke began to clear from the docks as the wind blew off the water.

Amelia felt trapped between two fires: the one on the wharf and the fire still burning above. Up near the Plaza, flames climbed the walls of both brick and wooden buildings and streamed from the rooftops like an ogre's hair combed out by the wind. A line of canvas tents burst into orange fireballs. The wooden planking on the street she had climbed so many times crackled and sent sparks flying. The pony jumped the ditch and she guided him along the side of the hill.

Telegraph Hill loomed like a dark cone in front of her, untouched by the flames, and North Point was just beyond. Had Mother and Estelle gone on ahead? Amelia looped the reins around her wrist and pulled her kerchief tight over her nose and mouth to shut out the smoke. The pony pranced and trembled all over as she urged him forward. "Easy boy, easy. We don't want to miss them."

As they headed north, Amelia felt the shock of this night sear itself into her memory. A man with his clothes in tatters stumbled past, his eyes wide with terror. Two men staggered under the weight of a third man with a burned face, his arms draped over their shoulders. Some men tore their hair, others sobbed. A woman hurried by, wearing a cloak over her torn petticoats. She stared at Amelia out of a blackened face. If Mother appeared, would Amelia even recognize her?

Death was all around them. The pony shied away from dead horses, dead rats, and a pair of burned oxen, their legs broken like twigs. Amelia held the reins tight when a mule galloped past, trailing the smell of singed hair. Her throat felt scorched. The pony tossed his head when they passed two burned bodies. Amelia clamped her kerchief over her mouth and forced herself to peer down at them. Their skin was blackened like charred paper but both corpses were men. She wiped her eyes on her sleeve and wished she could remember one of Gran's prayers. "Please," she whispered, as they turned away. "Please let Mother and Estelle be safe—and the Bakers, too."

The pony whinnied and Amelia kicked him into a canter to avoid an iron house, its glowing red sides collapsing inward like playing cards. Two firemen sprayed the building with a hose, but the water turned immediately to steam and a sickening odor came from inside. Amelia gagged. Were people trapped in there? Even with her kerchief on, she couldn't escape the suffocating smells swirling in the wind.

She pulled up below a street that seemed familiar. Was it Green Street? Charred signs littered the ground: one for a bakery, another for a shoe store. A sign for a shop that sold camphene oil for lamps dangled from a brick building with its insides burned out. She was about to urge the pony on when a tall boy emerged from the smoke, head down, fists clenched, his jacket in shreds. "Julius?" Amelia called. "Is that you?"

The boy stared at her out of bloodshot eyes. "It's Amelia," she told him. "Amelia Forrester." She slipped off the pony's back, holding tight to its reins.

It *was* Julius, though he hardly looked like himself. He

rubbed his eyes, as if she were a mirage. "We thought—" He gulped. "The paper said you were dead. Then they said you survived. Nico and I made money on those stories." He coughed and wiped his sooty face on his sleeve.

"I'm alive," Amelia said. "Barely." Julius's eyebrows and eyelashes were singed, giving him a strange look. "Are you all right? What about your captain's quarters?"

"Probably burned to a crisp. I didn't stay to watch." Julius gestured at his torn clothes. "This is all I own. I'm starting from scratch."

Amelia thought of the books on his shelves, the polished table, the little mirror where she'd first seen herself looking like a boy. "I'm sorry. I guess we are, too."

Explosions resounded from the hillside like cannon volleys. The pony reared up on his hind legs and the reins slipped from her hands. Julius grabbed for the pony's bridle and wrestled him down while Amelia clung to his mane. "What's that noise?" she cried.

"They blow up the houses with gunpowder to stop the fire," Julius said, "but it's no use. The fire roars through the hollows under the planked streets and comes up every-where. There's no stopping it."

Had the world gone mad? "Have you seen my mother and her friend?" Amelia's voice was hoarse from yelling. Julius shook his head. "What about Nico and Mrs. Liazos?" she asked.

"They went to North Point."

"That's where I'm going. We were all supposed to meet there." *Unless*—but she didn't dare finish her thought.

"Let's ride together. Could the pony carry us both?" Julius asked.

"We can try. His owner is a big man." Amelia used a barrel to climb onto the pony's back, and Julius clambered up behind her. The pony shied, but Amelia leaned forward and spoke softly into his ear. Julius grabbed her around the waist. Amelia's face felt hot, and not just from the fire. She'd never been so close to a boy before, but how else could Julius stay on? The pony skittered to the side and Julius nearly slid off.

"Whoa!" Amelia spoke to the pony in soothing tones, and when he calmed down, she loosened the reins to let him pick a safe path along the foot of Telegraph Hill. They zigzagged to the north and rode into the shadows. Burning rags and hot embers sailed by on the wind and the sky was lit with an eerie light somewhere between night and day. When the pony snuffled with fear, she stroked his neck and glanced back at Julius. "I wonder if anything is left from the balloon launch."

"I doubt it. They ran the aeronaut out of town. And your mother fainted dead away when I told her about the balloon," Julius said. "I hope she'll forgive me."

"Don't worry." Amelia blinked back tears. *She* needed

Mother's forgiveness too. She was grateful that Julius didn't ask questions about her flight. She didn't want to think about that now.

As they approached the point, the air was easier to breathe. "The city burned like this last May, too," Julius said.

"Yes, Nico's mother told me."

Julius sighed. "Can the phoenix ever rise from the ashes again?" His voice was thick with despair.

"It better. Otherwise, what will happen to us all?"

Julius didn't answer. The pony's steady hoofbeats were muffled as he picked his way in the dark. "Is Patrick all right, then?" Julius asked.

"He's fine. He stayed in the diggings, with a French couple."

"Smart," Julius said. "Maybe I'll join him there, when this is over. Can't imagine we'll have any papers to sell for a long time."

The *Alta*. How could she have forgotten? Would the editor survive? Would her story go up in flames? "I hope Tip is all right," she said.

"He'll come through. He's a tough little hound."

Like you, Amelia wanted to say—but she didn't.

A familiar field rose in front of them. Amelia shuddered. Even in the dim light, she remembered it all: the balloon filling, the way she and Patrick had slithered through the tall grass, her terror as the city fell away beneath them. Now shadowy figures rushed to and fro in the darkness, carrying shovels and bulging burlap sacks. The pony nearly bumped into two men who were digging holes while others mounded dirt over barrels and crates. "Are they burying their things?" Amelia whispered.

"I guess so," Julius said. One man stood with a foot on his suitcase and a rifle in his hand. They drew up in an empty spot and slid from the pony's back. Amelia peered through the haze. A lantern gleamed on the crown of the hill where the balloon had filled, casting a circle of light on a group of seated figures. Amelia picked out the dim outlines of four bonnets. Could it be? "Julius, take the reins." She ran.

"Mother! Estelle! Rosanna!" Amelia cried. Mother gave a small shriek and a stout woman—was it Mrs. Liazos?— stood up, hoisting the lantern. And there was Nico, who stared as Amelia threw herself into Mother's arms.

"We thought you were dead!" Nico said.

Amelia laughed. She was even glad to see Nico. "I'm alive," she said, her voice muffled against Mother's shoulder. They held each other tight. "I'm sorry," Amelia whispered.

Mother took off Amelia's hat and smoothed her hair. "I thought I'd lost you again." Her voice was so hoarse, Amelia could hardly understand her. "We called and called, and then the flames came too close. Mr. Baker led us here and insisted we wait. He's still looking for you."

"Oh, no." Amelia grabbed Rosanna's hand. "I didn't mean to get lost. The fire engine knocked me down."

"Otis will be all right," Rosanna said, but her face was drawn with worry.

"Who's holding that pony?" Estelle asked.

Amelia looked up. Julius stood apart, stroking the pony's nose. No one was searching for Julius. If he went missing, who would ever know? Amelia waved. "Julius, come over," she called.

He hesitated, but Nico called out, "Hurry up, Jules." Nico turned to Amelia. "How'd he get the shoeshine pony?"

"His reins were caught, and I freed him." Amelia was too tired to explain. Nico kept staring at her, as if she were a ghost, while Julius led the pony to the edge of their circle. He wrapped the reins around one wrist and squatted on his heels in the grass. Nico leaned against his mother; Amelia held on to Mother and Estelle.

Everyone was silent as flames poured into the night sky and bells clanged in the distance. After what seemed like hours, Mr. Baker returned with his lantern sputtering, the goats trotting after him like dogs. Rosanna let out a scream of relief and jumped up to throw her arms around his neck. "We're in luck," Mr. Baker told them. "The wind shifted just after the Niantic burned. Looks like our ship may have some damage—I didn't dare climb the ladder—but at least we still have a home. Many folks don't. They're saying a thousand homes are burning, even the brick houses. Iron houses were the worst—they melted and trapped people inside."

The women gasped and Amelia swallowed hard. A sour taste fouled the back of her throat. She leaned against Mother and glanced around their little circle. The Bakers sat a bit apart, holding hands. Julius and Nico soothed the pony in low voices while Mrs. Liazos whispered to Estelle. No one watched the fire. They all looked out on the bay and its shadowy islands, as if the dark water could bring them comfort. They'd seen enough destruction for one night.

CHAPTER

✳ 46 ✳

"Terrible Conflagration!"

THE SUN was a gray disc when it rose through the smoke. Amelia felt as if she'd filled her boots with stones as she followed their bedraggled group back to the *Beatrice*. Had she even slept? The city's center still smoldered, but the thump of hammers already echoed across the hills.

"Repairing, even rebuilding so soon," Mrs. Liazos said. "It's a bit spooky that the city burned on the same day last May."

Mr. Baker coughed. "There are rumors that this is not a coincidence."

Rosanna gasped. "You mean, someone started the fire on purpose?"

"Who would do that?" Amelia asked.

"There are crazy people everywhere," Mrs. Liazos said. "We'll check on our tent, see if there's anything left."

"If not, come to the ship," Rosanna said. "Do you know where it is?"

"*I* do," Nico said. He waved to Amelia before he trudged off. Amelia tried to remember why they'd once been sworn enemies. It seemed like years since they had sold newspapers on the streets. Someday, she'd tell him about passing the turn to Jackass Hill; he might like to know it was a real place.

"Julius, stay with us," Mother said as Nico disappeared. He hesitated, but Mr. Baker cupped his elbow. "I'll need some help, getting the place shipshape again," he said. "Pardon my feeble joke."

Julius gave him a weak smile, but he followed along, leading the pony. As they picked their way along the shoreline, Amelia lagged behind and imagined how she might describe their little group to Gran. *Mr. Baker's bald head showed through the hole in his hat*, she could write. *Mother and Estelle's skirts were heavy with mud. The goats were as sooty as chimney sweeps.* She wouldn't tell Gran that her granddaughter was dressed like a boy—or would she? And would she say, *Gran, I know about my father?* Not yet. Amelia watched her mother stride on ahead of her, her back straight, her head held high in spite of the bundles she carried under her arms. She would write, *Mother was kind to my friend Julius, who is an orphan.*

For Mother *was* kind. She was kind to Estelle, of course. And now to Rosanna and Mr. Baker. *Most of all, to me,* Amelia thought, *even though I scared her half to death and broke her heart.*

"Mother!" Amelia cried. "Wait."

"Child, what is it?" Mother set down her bundles. "Are you hurt?"

Amelia caught up to her mother and clutched her so tight that they both nearly fell over. "Amelia, what's wrong?"

Amelia couldn't speak. She wept against Mother's cloak while terrified people streamed past, many in tears themselves.

"It's all right," Mother said.

And it was.

MOTHER AND Amelia caught up to Rosanna and Estelle, who stood near the burned shell of the Niantic, holding hands. "I'm afraid to look," Rosanna said.

"I'll go." Amelia dashed ahead and crowed with delight. The hull of the *Beatrice* was blackened, her sails scorched, but Mr. Baker was right—the ship had survived. "Come on!" Amelia cried, beckoning to the women. She whirled around and nearly collided with a man dressed in a frayed tunic and a wide-brimmed hat, craning his neck at the foot of their ladder. "Mr. Wong!"

He let out a torrent of Chinese words and gripped the ladder, pointed at the sky, touched her scar. "Yes, I crashed in the balloon," she said.

Mr. Wong bowed once, twice, three times. Amelia did the same, until they knocked heads and staggered backward, laughing. But Amelia was glad she didn't speak Chinese. She couldn't bear to tell the story of her trip again.

The ship was a mess. A thin layer of ash and soot covered everything. Smoke had darkened the windows of the little house, a black scum floated on yesterday's milk, and the smell of death hung in the air. The blankets that covered their crate were stiff as boards, but when Mother and Estelle lifted the lid, they found that only the top layer was soiled.

"If we wipe them off, we might save the insides of the bolts of cloth," Estelle said.

"Thank goodness our little house is still on the clipper. But who knows how we will get it ashore, or where we will set it up." Mother's eyes looked sunken in her face.

Rosanna pointed to her skirt, torn at the hem. "Don't worry," she said. "You'll sell clothes as fast as you can make them. Your home is still here." She sighed. "Shabby as it is."

Amelia leaned out over the ship's railing. Nothing looked the same. And who was she now? Emile the newsboy had disappeared, though she still wore his clothes. Was she Amelia Forrester, or Miss Yeomans? *That* name certainly didn't fit. Everything was upside down.

The women started cleaning while Mr. Baker and Julius went in search of water. They returned with only two buckets, one for the goats and the pony—tethered at the base of the ladder—and the other to share on the deck. Amelia waited her turn for a drink, then wiped her face with a wet cloth. The rag came away the color of ash. The pony whickered and Amelia leaned over the railing. "Good boy," she called. The goats and the pony were hungry, but what could they eat? She'd have to find the pony's owner, if he was still alive. Mother spoke up as if she could read Amelia's mind. "You're not moving from this ship without me," she said.

Amelia was too tried to argue.

Mr. Baker and Julius went off to assess the damage. When they returned a few hours later, their faces were streaked with dirt, and Julius wouldn't look Amelia in the eye. He slipped away and sat with his back to them on the far side of the deck.

Rosanna started after him but Mr. Baker stopped her. "It was just as he feared," he said. "The poor boy lost everything. We should keep him with us for a while." He gestured at the hillside above them. "Total devastation. The city center is completely ruined, and there are looters everywhere. Three quarters of a mile, from north to south—gone. A third of a mile, east to west—gone. But imagine this." He held up a newspaper. "The *Alta* building survived the fire. They even put out a paper this morning. We have to save this for posterity."

Her story! Whoever "posterity" was, Amelia wanted to grab the *Alta*, but she waited, dancing from one foot to the other, while Mr. Baker spread the paper open on the table. "Listen to this: 'Terrible Conflagration! San Francisco Again in Ruins . . . Loss about Five Million Dollars.'"

Rosanna gasped. "Five *million*?"

Mr. Baker went on reading. "'San Francisco is again in ashes. The smoke and flames are ascending from several squares of our city as if the God of Destruction had seated himself in our midst and was gorging himself and all his ministers of devastation upon the ruin of our doomed city and its people'." Mr. Baker glanced up at them. "Phew! What a long sentence. Imagine, the editor composed this at five in the morning, with the city in flames all around him."

"Did you see the dog?" Amelia asked.

Mother raised her eyebrows. "What dog?"

"Tip, the ratter. He belongs to the *Alta*," Amelia said, bouncing on her toes. "May I read the paper?"

"Wait your turn," Mother said.

So Amelia paced while the grown-ups read the paper out loud, exclaiming over the figures. "Eighteen city blocks completely burned—how can that be?" Estelle asked. "And nearly two thousand homes." She looked around the ship. "We're lucky we have a place to sleep."

When Amelia finally had a chance to thumb through the pages herself, she couldn't find her story. Of course, the fire was more important. She thought of the editor turning up his nose at her letter about the shipwreck and saying, so many weeks ago, *"That's old news now."* Was her adventure castoff news too? It did seem like a dream that belonged to someone else.

It was hard to sleep that night. Julius and Mr. Baker retreated to the dank hold while Amelia and the women lined up on deck. Their pallets and blankets reeked of smoke, and

Amelia's belly pinched with hunger. The goats had given them only a few cups of milk, and their food stores were spoiled.

"Tomorrow will be a better day," Estelle said as she helped Amelia make a nest of her cloak and a bolt of flannel. "They say that farmers from the Mission road will set up their stands again." Amelia folded her hat into a pillow. When Estelle bent to kiss her forehead, Amelia wrapped her arms tight around her neck. "I'm so glad you're here," she whispered.

Estelle laughed softly. "Of course I'm here. Where else would I be?"

"Someplace . . ." Amelia couldn't explain. One thought had been nagging at her since she came home, nipping at her heels like a teething puppy. If Mother *had* married her father and moved away from Concord, she would never have known Estelle. And she couldn't live without dear Estelle. Neither could Mother. "Don't ever leave," Amelia said. She nestled against Estelle's chest, soaking in her warmth. *Please,* she begged silently. *Please, let this terrible day be over. Forever.*

CHAPTER

✳ 47 ✳

A True Newshound

WHEN AMELIA woke the next morning, her world had turned gray. The hulks of burned buildings, the fog lying at sea, the iron gray water of the bay, and the clouds above— everything was colorless and dreary. She helped the women scrub and clean until her hands were cracked and raw, but it seemed useless. The ash kept falling, drifting and blowing on the wind. It stuck to her hat brim and darkened the backs of her hands. Yet the city hummed and shook with the pounding of hammers, the rasp of saws. Drays rumbled past, loaded with lumber and bricks. "Phoenix City," Estelle said. "Rising from the ashes."

Mother shook her head. "It's hard to believe we'll ever recover. So many streets ruined, so many homes destroyed."

Amelia went about her jobs, dressed in her flannel shirt and trousers, though they reeked of smoke. She hauled water, wiped soot from the bolts of cloth, tended to the goats and the pony, but she was growing antsy. When could she go up the hill? Julius was gone all morning; when he returned at noon, he whistled from the bottom of the ladder.

Amelia leaned over the railing. Julius stood next to a man with a bruised face. "He's come for the pony," Julius called.

Amelia slid down the ladder. Julius held a small basket with a loaf of fresh bread, three apples, and a hunk of cheese. "Mrs. Liazos sent us a present. Her tent was spared," Julius said. Although Amelia's belly was pinched with hunger, she snatched the biggest apple and offered it to the pony.

"Wait, this is all we have for everyone," Julius said. Too late. The pony was already crunching the apple between his teeth, the juice dribbling from his lips. Amelia combed the pony's tangled mane while he ate, then gave him a final hug around the neck. "Thank you for saving my life," she whispered.

The man took the pony's bridle. "*Gracias.* Thank you, for find my horse," he said.

Amelia held back tears as the man led the pony away. Where would they go? Mr. Baker said most of the Plaza was ruined. Would the shoeshine boys find another place to work? What would the pony eat?

Her own belly gnawed with hunger and she followed Julius up the ladder.

"Julius, you're a genius!" Rosanna cried when she saw the food.

Julius's face reddened. "Mrs. Liazos had some food stored in a tin case," he said. "Her place is mobbed but she saved this for you." They sat on crates and boxes on the deck and parceled the food out onto tin plates. The bread was stale and the cheese dry, but no one complained. Julius glanced at Amelia. "Steamer day tomorrow. You still with us?"

"I don't know. Maybe." Amelia looked at Mother, whose eyebrows were raised. "There's something else I might need to do."

Julius shrugged. "Suit yourself."

She felt stung. Julius was welcoming her to his gang at last. She should be happy—but was that what she wanted? Would Mother even let her go?

"Wonder where they'll dock, now that the wharf is gone." Mr. Baker put on his cap and beckoned to Julius. "Everyone needs carpenters. Let's you and I see what we can do to earn some money." Julius's face broadened with a wide smile, and Amelia realized she'd never seen him look so happy. As they climbed down the ladder, she grabbed Mr. Walker's slouch and leaned over the railing.

"Julius!" she called. "Take this. I'm sorry I lost your cap." The slouch twirled twice as it floated down. Julius caught it, settled it over his rusty curls, and gave her a salute. He strode up the street. With the hat on, he was almost as tall as Mr. Baker.

Rosanna set her elbows on the railing beside Amelia. "Otis misses my brother as much as I do," she said. "Maybe Julius can ease the pain a bit. He's a nice boy."

Amelia nodded and squeezed Rosanna's hand, then headed for the little house. Mother and Estelle were too busy to notice her. They sat on the trunk, examining bolts of fabric, sorting them into piles. Amelia went inside and dipped a rag into the washbasin. She washed her face and hands and stood on tiptoe to look into the mirror. Her scar was losing its raw color, but her hair stuck up in every direction.

Rosanna came through the door and peered over Amelia's shoulder. "Goodness, I look a fright myself!" She found a comb and loosened Amelia's tangles, then her own. "Shall I cut your hair for you again?"

Amelia shook her head. "No. I'm letting it grow."

She went outside and stood in front of Mother, waiting for her to look up. "I need to go to the *Alta* newspaper office," she said.

Mother smoothed a bolt of flannel out on her knees and shook her head. "No more running off alone. It's not safe. Mr. Baker says there's looting and misery in the streets. Buildings are still smoldering. And who knows what people may do, when they've lost everything. Besides, it's time you dressed as a girl again."

Amelia didn't move. Mother finally met her gaze. "What is it you want?"

"Please come with me."

Mother sighed. "Amelia, you're going to wear me out."

Estelle's laughter made Amelia scowl. "What's so funny?" Amelia demanded.

Estelle tried to stop laughing, but her mouth kept turning up at the corners. "You two. You're so much alike. As hard to budge as burdock roots."

"How so?" Mother asked in a cold voice.

Estelle took Mother's hand. "Look what you've done. Raised a child with no father to help you. Left your own mother and a comfortable home to give your daughter freedoms we never had. Started a business . . ."

"It's *our* business. And we raised Amelia together," Mother said softly.

Estelle reached for Amelia's hand, pulling them into a tiny circle. "Now your daughter grows into a strong girl, behaves just like her bold, determined mother—and you're surprised?"

Mother laughed. "I give up." She set aside her fabric. "Fetch my bonnet and comb," she told Amelia. "Are you taking me someplace far away?"

"Not this time," Amelia said.

IT WAS hard to find the *Alta* office without the usual landmarks. The burned shells of buildings still smoked, and men dug through the rubble, searching for their possessions. On one corner, three men were already laying a course of bricks to form a new wall. As they climbed the hill, Mother and Amelia passed a bookstore with nothing left but its sign, and the remains of a bakery. The brick building was missing its roof but its walls were still standing. "Do you suppose they have bread?" Mother asked. Amelia peered in. The owner, dressed in trousers under a nightshirt, stared at his empty shelves. A cloying, charred smell replaced its usual sweet scent. "I'm sorry," Amelia whispered, and backed out quietly.

A few blocks from the Plaza, a line of men with guns stood guard in front of a pile of rubble that had once been the Custom House. "Let's keep going," Mother said, her kerchief over her mouth.

When they reached the newspaper's office, the brick building looked untouched, and the sign, with its bold lettering—**ALTA CALIFORNIA**—was still intact over the door. Amelia was about to knock when the terrier rushed up, yipping and whimpering.

"Tip!" Amelia bent to rub behind his ears. His fur smelled scorched. "This is Tip, their ratter," Amelia explained.

The door flew open and the editor peered out. He was rumpled everywhere, from his bushy eyebrows and mustache to his unbuttoned waistcoat. Like everyone else in town, his face was streaked with soot. "Morning, ma'am," he said to Mother. "Pardon Tip—he's been out all night— the rats are everywhere, since the fire. What can I do for you?"

Amelia waited for him to recognize them. Finally, Mother nudged her. "The gentleman is speaking to you," she said.

"I'm Amelia Forrester. Will you still print my story?" Amelia asked at last. Although Mother sucked in her breath beside her she stayed quiet.

"Mrs. Forrester!" The editor clapped his forehead and bowed to Mother. "Excuse me, ma'am. I'm so rattled, I didn't know you." He pointed to his ink-stained fingers. "Pardon me if I don't shake your hand." He peered at Amelia. "I can't keep up with you. One day, you're a girl, the next a boy. Who are you today?"

"I'm always Amelia." It felt fine to say that.

"Won't you come in?" They followed him into the front room. The editor picked up a sheaf of lined paper, and Amelia recognized her handwriting on the top page. "Your daughter's turned into quite the reporter."

Amelia was hot with pride. She remembered Jim, the day they arrived, saying she was "as nosy as a newspaper reporter." Was that so bad? After all, if she hadn't been so curious, she wouldn't know what the earth looked like from the sky. She wouldn't have met the Arnauds, or seen the mines, or learned how to fill her pockets with coins.

The editor tapped her story, now a mix of her scribbles and his own sloppy handwriting. "I was about to set your article in tomorrow's paper, but I'm short-handed, as you can see." He waved at the next room, which was empty. "Just Tip and me here. I sent my partner out to check on a few facts." He took off his cap and rubbed his hair, which only made it stand up even higher. "Someone told me a man saved his warehouse by dousing it with vinegar. Don't know if I believe that or not."

"That's right. I smelled vinegar when I passed the wharf," Amelia said. "I heard it was the Dewitt and Harrison Warehouse. Eighty thousand gallons of vinegar!"

"Who told you that?" Mother asked.

"Mr. Baker," Amelia said. "You can see the warehouse from our ship; it's still standing."

"What did I tell you! She's got a *nose* for a story—a true newshound." The editor laughed quietly at his own joke and then listed to the side. His face was ashen. He sank into the chair and wiped his face with a handkerchief. "Sorry, ma'am. I haven't slept in days. Could you loan me your daughter for a few hours? I need to set type for tomorrow's paper. My printer's devil got burned out; he promises to be back tomorrow. I could use someone to hand me the type, put it back where it belongs, nothing complicated. I'd pay her, of course. And walk her home, safe and sound," he added.

Mother glanced at Amelia. "Would you like to stay?"

Amelia grinned. "May I? That's the same job I did for the editor in Sonora."

"Very well," Mother said. "I'm sure you'll help this man and not get in his way. And I'll come back for her myself," Mother told the editor. "I'd like to see her story when you're done. I'm quite proud of my daughter, as you can imagine." She lifted her skirts, opened the door, and was gone.

The editor raised his eyebrows. "I see where you got your smarts."

Amelia was suddenly tongue-tied. "Thank you," she said at last.

CHAPTER

* 48 *

News!

AMELIA WAS up before dawn the next morning. She scrambled to her feet and tried to ignore her aching bones as she pulled her trousers and shirt from the rigging, where she'd hung them to dry last night. The water in Rosanna's washtub had been black after she'd washed out her things. And no matter how hard she'd scrubbed, she couldn't get the printer's ink off her hands.

The damp clothes made her shiver as she pulled them on, but Mother had agreed: as long as the city was a shambles, she could wear her trousers. "Soon you'll go to school," she had said, "and you'll wear a dress again."

Since the city was still in ruins, "soon" might be a long time from now. A sharp whistle sounded from the street. Amelia buttoned her shirt and peered over the railing. Three shadowy figures huddled together at the foot of the ladder. "Hurry up!" someone called in a scratchy voice. "It's steamer day."

She spotted Nico and Julius—who had spent the night

at the restaurant tent—and was that Henry? Amelia waved and stepped into her boots. Her toes were snug against the end. She was growing in every direction.

A hand touched her shoulder. Mother stood behind her, a blanket wrapped around her like Señor's *serape*, her hair loose on her shoulders. "Where are you going?"

"To pick up papers at the *Alta*," Amelia said. She kept her voice low; Estelle was still asleep. "I'll sell them nearby. Is that all right?"

Mother ran her fingers through Amelia's tangled curls. "As long as you save a copy for me," she said.

"Let's go!" one of the boys shouted.

Amelia started for the ladder, but Mother pulled her close. "No more surprises," she said. "Just come home safe."

"I promise." Amelia gave her a fierce hug in return.

"Took you long enough," Nico said when Amelia jumped to the ground.

She laughed. Nico would always be prickly as a porcu-pine, no matter what happened. "I've got something to do first," she said. "See you at the wharf."

"Wait." Henry blocked her way. "Where's Patrick?"

"In Sonora," Amelia said. "He's fine. He stayed there with a French couple who are panning for gold. He wants you to join him. I'll tell you more later." She wrapped her cloak tight against the fog and ran off before he could ask any more questions.

* * *

AN HOUR later, Amelia returned with a stack of papers tucked under her arm. The smell of fresh ink reminded her of Dr. Gunn and his printing press. As she hurried down the hill, Tip raced across the street ahead of her, his nose to the ground. "Tip, go home," Amelia said gently, but she couldn't scold him. Nothing bothered her today. Not only had the editor printed her story, but he'd also added a correction, apologizing for spreading rumors about her death.

The harbor was still a tangle of burned wharves and collapsed warehouses, and the docks rang out with the sounds of hammers and saws. Amelia glanced at the semaphore tower. An American flag flew from the top, and the semaphore's long arms had moved since yesterday. She smiled. Mr. Abbott must be all right.

Amelia passed the ruins of Long Wharf and headed for a crowd on one of the few docks that had survived the fire. Julius, Henry, and Nico were bundling papers as if it were a normal day, while the steamer's passengers huddled on the ship's deck, looking dazed and lost. Amelia tried to see the name of the ship, but the crowd on the wharf was in the way.

She hesitated a moment. Why would anyone buy papers now? But maybe the newcomers would want to know what happened. She had to try. Amelia stepped up onto a half-burned bale of cotton, pulled the top copy of the *Alta* from her stack, and waved it in the air. "News!" she cried. "Read about the fire! And the miracle return! 'Two Children Survive Crash of Balloon in the Mountains'! Read all about it!"

Heads swiveled. "That's her!" a boy cried. The whole gang circled around her. "Is it true, you fell from the sky?" a boy asked. "Where's Patrick?" another asked. "Looks like you cracked your head open," said a skinny boy, pointing to her scar. "*Tu es une* fille?" a French boy demanded, nearly spitting over the French word for *girl*.

Before she could answer anyone, Nico pushed the boys aside and glared up at her. "Where'd you get those papers?"

"From the *Alta*," she said. "I helped the editor write the story." She pointed to the headlines. Nico scowled and she remembered, too late, that he couldn't read. "That's my name. It says, 'We have received the following story from a survivor, young Amelia Forrester herself.'"

"So you're not with our gang now?" Julius asked. He looked disappointed.

"I never said that. Today I'm selling for the *Alta*," Amelia said. "I like fresh news. We could still work together—if you don't mind having a girl in your gang."

Julius shrugged. "As long as you do your job."

The boys returned to their sorting. The passengers began to file off the ship, and Amelia brandished the paper overhead as they stood in small groups, staring at the burned city in disbelief. "News!" she cried. "Read today's *Alta California*! Two children survive the balloon crash!"

No one moved. The passengers stood frozen on the

wharf, their necks craned toward the hilltop, where dust and ash swirled above crumpled buildings. How could she get their attention?

A tall man stepped from the crowd, a valise slung over his shoulder. He started toward her, then set down his bag and stared at the hill, shaking his head. When he drew the back of his hand across his eyes, Amelia gasped. She knew that hand! She jumped off her bale and ran to him, waving her paper.

"Hello, Jim! Fresh news! Read about the fire!"

"Not now." He brushed away the paper and scowled. "How'd you know my name?"

Amelia laughed. "Don't you recognize me? It's Amelia Forrester."

Jim's jaw dropped and he shook his head. "Miss Amelia. What on earth?" He pulled her into a quick hug, newspapers and all, then stepped back. His face was blotchy, as if he fought tears. He took off his cap and held it over his heart like a mourner at a grave. "What's happened here? We could see the light in the sky all the way from Monterey, a hundred miles off. I never dreamed we'd find the city in ashes."

"Not the *whole* city," Amelia said. "But thousands of houses. How did you get here? Where have you been?"

"I was on the *Unicorn* as usual. We've been down the coast and back since you landed." He shook his head. "Everything's changed in two months. Including you. You were a young lady then." He touched her forehead and frowned.

"You get burned in the fire? Is your mother all right?"

"Mother and Estelle are fine. And I fell from the sky." Amelia laughed and gave him a copy of the *Alta*. "Read my story. I went up in a balloon with a friend, by mistake. We crashed, and survived."

Jim raised his eyebrows. "Sounds like a tall tale to me. I'll buy a copy anyway." He reached into his pocket for coins.

Amelia waved his hand away. "For you, it's free. Your knots kept me *alive*," she said. "Come to our abandoned ship and I'll tell you all about it. Mother and Estelle will be so happy to see you. We're two blocks from where the Niantic used to be."

"The Niantic burned? I can't believe it." Jim shook his head.

"It's all in the paper. I'd better keep selling, or I'll miss the passengers." Amelia climbed back onto the bale and took a deep breath. "News!" she cried. "San Francisco burns! Read all about it!"

Jim stepped aside, muttering to himself as he examined the story. Two more dazed men bought papers and sat down on their baggage facing the bay, as if they might turn around and go home.

Amelia opened her mouth to shout out her news again, when a hand plucked at her cloak. She looked down.

"Excuse me." A girl about Amelia's age stood beside the cotton bale. Her eyes were a bright blue, and the line of freckles across her cheeks made Amelia suspect she didn't always wear the straw bonnet tied under her chin.

"We came on Jim's boat, and I heard what you told him," the girl said. "Was that really you, in that balloon? You flew up in the sky?"

"It's the truth," Amelia said, pointing to her scar. "I almost died, but some kind men rescued me."

"Come along, Lucinda." A man standing beside a pile of luggage beckoned to the girl.

"Papa, wait," she called. "Please, can we buy a paper?"

The man strode over and put his arm around the girl's shoulder. "Is that today's paper?" he asked.

Amelia nodded. "Hot off the press this morning."

"I can't believe anyone printed a paper under these conditions." The man held up a two-bit piece. "Better give me one." He glanced up the hill toward the ruined city and shook his head. "It's not what we expected."

"The *Alta* tells the whole story," Amelia said.

The man bought a paper and handed it to Lucinda, refusing Amelia's change. "Looks as if you need it more than we do, lad." His gray eyes were kind.

The man returned to his bags, but the girl lingered behind. She squinted at Amelia. "You're not a 'lad,' so why do you dress like a boy?"

Amelia laughed. "It's complicated. Come to our ship later and I'll explain." She described how to find the *Beatrice*. When Lucinda and her father struggled past with their valises, Amelia waved and Lucinda gave her a bright smile. As they disappeared into the crowd, Amelia realized that the girl and her father were alone.

No mother? How horrible. Amelia shivered, though the sun was warm. She was lucky. She had Mother *and* Estelle. She had no father—at least, not here. As Patrick had said, "Everyone has a da." But she had received kindness, protection, and lessons from many men: Uncle Paul, Four-Fingered Jim, Señor Hernandez, Dr. Gunn, Monsieur Arnaud, Mr. Wong. And another newspaper editor had printed her very own story in the paper.

"Conflagration!" she cried, using the *Alta's* word. "Read the local news!"

On the far side of the street, Nico cupped his hand around his mouth, trying to drown her out. "News! The *New York Herald*! Fresh off the boat!" he shouted, and waved his paper at the crowds streaming down the hill toward the burned docks.

"The news you need to read!" Julius bawled from higher up the hill. Papers flew from his hands.

Amelia laughed and turned toward the ship's passengers to call out her own headlines. "Today's news: *Miracle return!*" She brandished the paper with its story—*her* story— printed in black and white. Coins clinked and jingled into her open palm. No matter what Nico or Julius said, she had the best news of all: She was loved. And alive.

"News! Read all about it!"

A Note to Readers

✳

ON JANUARY 24, 1848, a group of men were deepening a millrace in the American River, on property owned by John Sutter. James Marshall, who was overseeing work at the new sawmill, later described what happened that day. "My eye was caught by something shining in the bottom of the ditch . . . it made my heart thump, for I was certain it was gold."[1]

Marshall *did* see gold, and news of the find soon spread to local residents, to the small hamlet of San Francisco, and eventually to the outside world. The discovery changed the American West forever. Within four years, 250,000 gold seekers had arrived in California from every corner of the globe. Most prospectors were men, but smaller numbers of women and children also joined the great migration.

At the same time, women in eastern states were agitating for equal rights. In July of 1848, the leaders of the women's rights movement held a convention in Seneca Falls, New York, where they voted on a "Declaration of Sentiments and Resolutions," affirming the rights of women. This convention was only the beginning, since most American women would wait another seventy-two years before they could vote. Still, California offered women opportunities that they didn't have in the East. Women could buy and sell property, start a business, get divorced, and work outside their homes. Black women who arrived in California as slaves could—and did—gain their freedom. The new state drew adventurous, enterprising women like a giant magnet.

The few women who traveled to California in the early days of the gold rush found that their skills were in great demand. Many became successful businesswomen. They ran hotels and boardinghouses, started laundries and restaurants, worked as seamstresses, taught school, and became stars on stage. Many took jobs unheard of for eastern women. They mined for gold, drove stagecoaches, sorted the mail. Some women published accounts of their adventures in newspapers and in books that became popular around the country.

In the early days of the gold rush, children worked hard to help their families survive. Boys and girls hauled water and cared for animals; they helped their parents run restaurants and shops, and some of the stronger children panned for gold. Boys and girls earned money dancing and singing for the miners in saloons and gambling halls. When the saloons closed for the night, young girls ran their hairpins between cracks in the floorboards to pick up spilled gold dust.

In San Francisco and in smaller towns, gangs of boys earned small fortunes selling newspapers on the streets. The most valuable papers came from the eastern United States. In an age where modern technology brings us the news almost as soon as it happens, it's hard to believe that an eight-week old newspaper could sell in the West for six times its original value, but it did. The newsboys ran a fierce, competitive business until the telegraph arrived, allowing news headlines to buzz through the wires from coast to coast.

I first learned about gold-rush children in the mid-1990s, when I was researching a nonfiction book called *The Gold Rush*. Two details from that research stayed with me. I was amazed to learn that newsboys could earn more money selling papers on the streets than their parents might make in a day's work running a store or panning for gold. And I discovered an account of an accidental balloon launch from that time period. According to a footnote in a scholarly thesis, a teenage boy who went up in a balloon by mistake was the first person to see parts of northern California from the air. I filed these stories away in my "Idea File," hoping that I could weave them into a novel someday.

I HAVE always loved newspapers. I learned to read by poring over *Little Lulu* comics in the newspaper's funny pages. I still prefer to find my news in a hard copy of the newspaper rather than online. Newspapers are in my blood: my great-grandfather wrote stories for western newspapers, and my novel *Orphan Journey Home* has appeared in serial form in newspapers around the country. I love to hear the thump of the morning paper when it hits the front door at dawn. During baseball season, I grab the sports section first, to catch up on my beloved Red Sox. Then I turn to the comics, then the opinion and letter page, and finally, the news itself. Like Amelia, I am something of a newshound.

While Amelia and her family and friends are fictional characters, the story's setting and many events are grounded in fact. San Francisco's frequent fires make it difficult to pinpoint the exact location of some buildings, but I have tried to base the city's layout—with its shops, wharves, and meeting places—on the maps, city directories, newspaper stories, and first-person accounts from that period. The stories that Amelia writes and sells to the paper are invented, but it was not unusual, in those times, for editors to print letters from travelers as if they were reporters' news accounts. The *Alta California* was a real—and successful—San Francisco paper. The *Sonora Herald,* edited by Dr. Gunn (a real person), was the first paper in the southern mines. The Boston headlines that Amelia and the newsboys call out are actual headlines from eastern papers in 1850 and 1851.

Within a few years of the gold discovery, thousands of travelers arrived in San Francisco, hoping to seek their fortunes. Many went to the mines—including the city's only teacher and some of his pupils—but thousands stepped off ships or covered wagons and decided to stay. The little settlement once known as Yerba Buena (because of the mint that grew wild on the hills) exploded into a bustling city. Its new residents lived in hastily built shacks, in tents, on abandoned ships, and in "iron houses." The city burned and was rebuilt so many times that residents named it "Phoenix City," after the mythical bird that rises from the ashes. The fire that Amelia survived took place on May 4, 1851, exactly one year to the day that a similar fire destroyed the city's core. While the *Alta California* was the only newspaper to escape the flames of the May 1851 fire, the *Alta* did succumb to a second disastrous fire in June of that year. But the city's residents wouldn't give up. First-person accounts of both fires describe the sounds of men hammering and sawing, rebuilding homes and businesses while the city still smoldered.

From the moment I started to write Amelia's story, I wanted to include a balloon ascent such as the one I'd read about. But was it true, or even possible? Luckily, a resourceful librarian at the Boston Public Library introduced me to Tom D. Crouch's wonderful book, *The Eagle Aloft: Two Centuries of the Balloon in America*. From this book, I learned that ballooning was an active sport in the nineteenth century. And I found a detailed account of the California teenager's accidental flight.

According to Crouch, in 1852 an Oakland aeronaut tried to launch a balloon filled with hydrogen, but the adults who hoped to be its first passengers were so heavy that the balloon couldn't take off. Joseph Gates, a sixteen-year-old boy selling oranges, volunteered to try it out. The balloon was tied to a flimsy board, rather than a basket, but Gates climbed on. Much to his surprise, the balloon lifted and sailed away. A newspaper reported that when the balloon's valve line became tangled in the netting, Gates "shinned up" and cut the line free with a knife. He landed in a flat area miles from the liftoff and returned to San Francisco by boat. Apparently, Gates never went near a balloon again.

[1] Quoted in J. S. Holliday. *The World Rushed In: The California Gold Rush Experience.* New York: Simon and Schuster, 1981. P. 33. Holliday's source: Bancroft.

Acknowledgments

✹

WHEN I write historical fiction, I feel like a "research detective," as I track down details to bring a story to life, illuminate a time period, or answer puzzling questions about the past. Research librarians are essential to my quest for information, and this book was no exception. I am profoundly grateful to Patricia Keats, Library Director of the Society of California Pioneers in San Francisco. As I sat at a long table surrounded by the library's collection, Pat brought me books, old maps, and nineteenth-century prints and photographs. In the months that followed, she continued to track down answers to the most obscure questions and sent me additional materials and resources. She has helped me bring the past to life.

Reference librarians at the Boston Athenaeum and the American Antiquarian Society in Worcester, Massachusetts, also offered invaluable help. Librarians at the Boston Public Library located newspapers from that period, and one reference librarian produced answers to questions about nineteenth-century ballooning within fifteen minutes of my phone call. Leslie Perrin Wilson, curator of Special Collections at the Concord Public Library in Concord,

Massachusetts, gave me access to some of Henry David Thoreau's original papers. When I traveled to Sonora, California, I received generous assistance from Sharon Marovich at the Sonora Museum, and from Jim Miller and Floyd P. Sydegaard at Columbia State Historic Park.

During a lovely talk on our front porch, my daughter-in-law, Vita Weinstein Murrow, offered insights into Amelia's emotional journey that allowed me to write the novel's most important scene. My son, Ethan Ketchum Murrow, an artist who has explored flight in his graphite drawings, assisted with technical aspects of ballooning and sent me to Werner Herzog's incredible documentary film, *The White Diamond*. I am grateful to them both.

Laura Kvasnosky, my friend and colleague—once a "printer's devil" herself—suggested that I visit the town of Sonora and its historical society. Laura shared details about the *Sonora Herald* and answered my questions about every aspect of the newspaper business. She also gave me the collection of her father's columns, *A Country Editor*, a book that provided additional insights into the area where Amelia lands after her balloon flight.

The following family members, friends, and colleagues provided moral support, answered specific questions, or gave me valuable feedback: Philip Algren, Janet Coleman, Eileen Christelow, Susan Goodman, Jane Harwell, Louise Hawes, Helen Hemphill, Karen Hesse, Marguerite Houle, Lisa Jahn-Clough, Becky Jackson, Joshua Keels, Anne Koedt, Ron Koertge, Ellen Levine, Ali Macalady, Frannie Moyer, Derek Ketchum Murrow, Carmen Richardson, Phyllis Root, Hollis Shore, Leslie Sills, Maura Stokes, Sarah Sullivan, Jane Resh Thomas, Katherine Turner, and Wendy Watson. Bob Mac-Lean passed away while this book was in process, but his friendship sustained me through every draft. Thanks to Kate DiCamillo for the perfect message at the right time, and to my dear colleagues at Hamline University for their inspiration and knowledge of craft. A salute to my talented students, past and present; they have taught me more than they know. I appreciate the encouragement of the Magnificent Eight, as well as the wit and intelligence of my Monday-night book group. And I thank my parents, Barbara and Richard Ketchum, for their courage and determination in the face of adversity.

Last, but not least, I am grateful to my husband, John Straus, for his careful readings of many drafts; to my insightful editor, Tracy Gates, for asking just the right questions; and to my agent, Ginger Knowlton, for her continued grace, humor, and wisdom.